FIRE SEASON

ALSO BY LEYNA KROW

I'm Fine, But You Appear to Be Sinking

FIRE SEASON

A Novel

LEYNA KROW

VIKING

VIKING
An imprint of Penguin Random House LLC
penguinrandomhouse.com

LIBRARY OF CONGRESS CATALOGING-IN-PUBLICATION DATA
Names: Krow, Leyna, author.
Title: Fire season : a novel / Leyna Krow.
Description: [New York City] : Viking, [2022]
Identifiers: LCCN 2022001398 (print) | LCCN 2022001399 (ebook) |
ISBN 9780593299609 (hardcover) | ISBN 9780593299616 (ebook)
Subjects: LCGFT: Novels.
Classification: LCC PS3611.R79 F57 2022 (print) |
LCC PS3611.R79 (ebook) | DDC 813/.6—dc23
LC record available at https://lccn.loc.gov/2022001398
LC ebook record available at https://lccn.loc.gov/2022001399

Printed in the United States of America
1st Printing

Book design by Daniel Lagin

For Scott

FIRE SEASON

Prologue

On a sultry summer evening in 1875, the naturalist, inventor, and statesman Winston Albert Chase gave a lecture at the Walnut Street Theatre in Philadelphia, Pennsylvania. His talk was titled "The American Criminal: A Study in Three Parts," wherein he put forth a theory that there are three types of people who engage in criminal acts. He presented, as evidence, a melding of ideas from Enlightenment-era French philosophy, modern psychiatry, and phrenology. There were also his own observations of human nature collected from his hometown of Washington, D.C., where, he joked, he had no shortage of criminals to observe. After the laughter from this remark died down, Chase told the audience of four hundred, all in formal attire, that he had brought with him for exhibition real-life criminals, one from each of the three classes he meant to expound upon. It was his intention to reveal them in turn and make an examination of their crimes and countenance. This would lead him to a conclusion not just about the three individual criminals present, but, in his own words, "about the nature of crime itself, its relation to greed, desire, our very way of living . . . and maybe even a little something about you yourselves, dear ladies and gentlemen."

This drew applause. Chase was a gifted orator. His audience expected, for the price of their tickets, to be entertained as well as educated. And on the night of his talk in Philadelphia, he did not disappoint.

Chase presented the first of his criminal specimens in a steel cage three feet in length on each side, wheeled onstage by two burly assistants. The criminal himself was a large man, exactly the sort the audience might be expecting. His dark hair was shaved almost to his white scalp. His eyebrows were close and thick. He had prominent scars on his chin and upper lip.

He was perched on a wooden chair inside his enclosure. At first, he just sat, looking out at the audience, who murmured among themselves, confirming all their own suspicions. Then, as Chase approached with his calipers and measuring tape, the large man leapt forward, seizing the cage bars with both hands. "Fuck you all, you rich bitches and cunts!" he shouted. The audience gasped and a few members even screamed, but Chase simply raised his hand. When he had silence again, he turned to the large man and gestured for him to take his seat, which he did. Chase then explained that this kind of criminal was moved almost as if by forces outside himself to commit sin. Murder, rape, vandalism, assault—none of these acts were beyond him. It was not that he had no understanding of right and wrong, but that, to him, right and wrong were irrelevant. They did not govern him. Only his basest impulses did.

"But he did not start out this way. He wasn't born full of evil. Though you would surely cross the street if you saw him tonight in your path, there was once a time when he would barely have caught your notice. This criminal starts small, with illicit acts that annoy rather than frighten, until he becomes seduced by the possibilities born of taking power into his own hands. He doesn't want to amass money and pleasure so much as he wants to see these commodities handed over. Unsettling? Yes. But wait until you meet the sorts for whom their criminality is inherent, etched into the very fiber of their being."

The large man was wheeled off and a second cage was brought forward, this one containing a youth in a school uniform. Once his cage was situated, the youngster stood, doffed his cap, and bowed. Again, the audience murmured, this time in surprise. What crimes could this dapper young man be capable of? Chase introduced the boy as "My nephew, recently graduated from Andover, with honors." Then there were chuckles as the men and women thought of their own Andover nephews and sons. Wouldn't they like to put those charming boys in a cage every once in a while?

"This little fellow," Chase explained, "is a liar and a thief. He fibs both when it is convenient to him, but also for the sake of the fib itself—the sheer fun of it. Using his wit and his smile, he deceives family, friends, teachers, and even young lovers for his own gain. He also takes money from any pocketbook or wallet handy, including that of his dear, generous uncle.

"This sort of criminal is acutely aware that what he does is wrong, but he is able to justify his ill deeds through the belief that the benefit to himself personally outweighs the deficit to his victims. There is a cunning to his ways, but also a cowardice, for he cannot rise above his own petty wants to think of his fellow man. His kind is quite loathsome, I think we will all agree. But of the three, he is the least dangerous to society at large."

Chase placed his index finger on his nephew's forehead and drew an imaginary line to the temple. "You can see the path of deceit here. Watch for it in other bright boys," he warned. "You will find they grow into men of success in many fields, finance in particular. Though I would advise you against engaging in business with him. His associates are likely to all end up in jail eventually, having taken the fall for his misdeeds."

Chase had saved his most shocking exhibit for last, of course. The third cage, wheeled onstage as the audience murmured in confusion, contained a woman, small and frail, seated in a rocking chair. The chair wobbled violently from the cage movers' efforts, and the old woman had to clutch its arms so as not to be pitched onto the floor. But once the moving was done and the rocking became more gentle, she picked up a ball of yarn and needles from her lap and began to knit, paying no attention to the audience whatsoever.

"Ladies and gentlemen, may I present to you the third criminal of the evening, my mother."

The gasps were resounding.

Chase went on to enumerate the woman's offenses. "My dearest mother is not the gentle matron she appears," he began. "She is, in fact, a person of great abilities, if you follow my meaning. In previous, more ignorant eras, she might have been labeled a witch. But we of the modern day know such beings do not exist. Instead, there is among us *a certain kind of woman* who can so subtly bend her cruelty as to seem almost magical. She can use her words to change the will of those around her so they do her bidding. This is a criminal who traffics in crimes of the psyche and the emotions."

He explained the many, many ways his mother had manipulated him and his siblings, ensnaring them to undertake acts they never would, in their right minds, have done on their own. Some such acts were benign (studying piano instead of violin), others bafflingly malicious (pushing a prep school rival down a flight of stairs).

"I did these things," Chase said. "But not because I wished them. She planted them in me. I must posit here that this sort of criminal is the most terrifying, not for the atrocities she commits, but for the mindset with which she undertakes them. This is a criminal who genuinely believes her deeds to be in the best interests of her victims. In this way, she can justify any act, great or small. There is no evil as ghastly as evil which calls itself good, and is peddled in public as such. Think of temptresses, of self-described soothsayers, of women who lure children from their homes for nefarious purposes. They are all of this kind."

As he spoke, his audience became more and more agitated. It was not clear if this agitation was in objection to Chase's claims (how could he speak so ill of his mother?) or in sympathy with them (as they considered their own mothers' abuses). The crowd grew in its loudness so that it became difficult for Chase to be heard over the din.

"Let the woman speak for herself!" cried a man from the front row.

Chase took the cue. He stood back and extended his arm to his mother, suggesting the floor was hers even though the cage confined her to just a few square feet of it. She chose to remain seated and rocking.

"Oh Winny boy, you know I ain't done none of those things to you," she said. "And certainly I ain't done none of them *for* you. Maybe that's what you mean by 'a certain kind of woman'? But tell me and the rest of these good people, would you, what criminal is the man of hubris? What criminal is the man who recasts himself in every scene as the hero or the victim?"

Chase smiled at this, and though he opened his mouth to reply, there was no room in the theater for his voice. Sound, in its entirety, had been eaten up by a thunderclap, immediately followed by the galloping of hail on the roof. The suddenness and violence of this noise sent a ripple of fear through the audience. But once the brief storm had subsided—it lasted twenty seconds at most—they laughed. They had been tricked into believing, for a moment, that an act of nature was something more sinister. Relieved of that notion, they found themselves very much amused by it. A timely little joke upon them all.

But then, the thunder returned. This time it did not stop. It did not arch and peal like real thunder. This was a different sound, and the crowd again grew restless, until the double doors at the front of the hall opened and a bull moose entered, its antlers as wide as a rowboat. The creature ran the length of the aisle to the stage, then turned and retreated, exiting the theater with surprising grace, its hooves tip-tapping on the carpet.

The audience followed.

Out in the streets, they were treated to further delights. Ostriches, flamingos, tapirs, spotted elk, and a black leopard with yellow eyes ran west along Walnut Street. These were the inhabitants of the brand-new Philadelphia Zoo, mysteriously escaped en masse.

After that, Chase made no effort to regain his audience. To those who did return to the theater, he simply bowed and bade a good evening. He said there was nothing more he could impart to them. He only hoped that they would take to heart what they had heard and seen that night.

In the coming days, the Philadelphia police, firemen, and postal workers, as well as hundreds of private citizens, mobilized to recapture the zoo animals. Though the search was exhaustive, very few of the nearly eight hundred escaped animals were ever located.

Meanwhile, Winston Albert Chase had extended his speaking tour with sold-out dates in a dozen cities along the Eastern Seaboard. Reports of the outlandish events that had accompanied his talk in Philadelphia spread, and audiences were eager to see if they might be repeated.

There was also considerable speculation about if and how Chase had engineered such a spectacle. Was the whole show an elaborate stunt, with rented circus animals playing the part of the zoo creatures, and a team of percussionists on the roof? There were some who accused Chase of chicanery. And there were others who lauded him as a great entertainer. Then there were those who took him at his word, and by extension cast blame on his mother. The woman was indeed a witch, they insisted. (And it was such a beautifully ironic twisting of his own sentiment that Chase could not have planned it better himself.) This theory was most popular among those who had been present at the Walnut Street Theatre.

Of course, Chase, his nephew, his mother, and even the large man—an ex-con and a failed actor whom Chase had hired as a favor to a friend—gave interviews asserting that the night's events were pure coincidence. And indeed, they were not repeated at subsequent shows.

But it should also be noted that the original cast did not reassemble for these later performances. Chase's mother was replaced with a retired ballerina, and his nephew with a second cousin. A new large man was commissioned in each city, typically found near the docks or rail yard. Anyone of sufficient size and seeking an easy night's work would do.

It was the loss of the nephew, who was headed to Harvard and did not have the time for additional shows with his uncle, that most pained Chase. He missed the youth's antics, the way he could pull anyone to him. Chase, lonesome in unfamiliar cities, thought fondly of the trouble they could have found together.

His mother he missed the least.

The woman was indeed a burden to her children, though not in the ways Chase had claimed. She was a person of great abilities, it was true. But as she insisted from her cage, she had never used these abilities to Chase's advantage or disadvantage. Instead, her love was for animals. She could speak to them, calling them out of dens and burrows. She fed them from her fingers and would go missing for days, following them through the woods near the family's remote home. She could not bear their mistreatment at the hands of humans, whom she thought to be a brutal, useless species. And on the rare occasion that she traveled into the city, she would unlatch the gates of yards containing beaten and starved dogs. She could do this with her mind, even from the confines of a buggy or train, a pack forming in her wake wherever she went.

PART I

BARTON

I

On August 4, 1889, Barton Heydale spent his lunch hour with a prostitute named Roslyn who lived and worked in a two-room apartment in Wolfe's Hotel on Railroad Avenue. The apartment was above a lunchroom, where Barton often stopped for something to eat after his visits with Roslyn. But on this day, he was consumed with the trouble of making a decision, and so he chose to forgo his meal in favor of sitting in Roslyn's tiny kitchen and smoking cigarettes.

The thing he was trying to decide: where, and when, to kill himself.

Barton had not set upon his path to suicide lightly. He'd assembled his justifications, which read as such: he was lonesome; he was generally disliked; and he was ugly. None of these conditions, he felt, had any hope of improving. They would only worsen as the months and years passed.

Barton was twenty-nine years old and the manager of the only bank in Spokane Falls. This position should have garnered him respect and power. It instead earned him nothing but ire from the local citizenry, who, it turned out, had little trust for institutions, financial or otherwise. As a result, Barton had not married, or even made a single friend, in his six years in Spokane Falls. The strain of this lonesomeness had taken a toll on him physically. He'd grown portly and unfit. He wheezed when he walked too quickly. And to top it off, he'd just the afternoon prior received a terrible haircut.

Strangely, though his hair would grow back, it was this final offense that convinced him he was beyond salvage. He could not continue to exist in his current form. So, today would be his last. His last breakfast, his last time washing his face, blowing his nose, tying his shoes. And here with Roslyn, his last fuck. The fucking had been the same quality as always; no great send-off. This observation depressed him even more.

After each cigarette he finished, he pitched the butt out the kitchen window and watched it spiral to the alley below, the last bits of ash and smoke forming a satisfying tail. Then he rolled and lit a new one. If Roslyn's apartment were on a higher floor, he reasoned, he would jump from the window. But Wolfe's was only two stories tall. In the other room, Roslyn snored, asleep in her bed. She was a drunk. The later in the day he called on her, the more likely he was to find her asleep or sick. On this particular day, she was already stewed by the time Barton arrived at noon, and barely able to finish performing her services before nodding off.

Even if Barton could not jump out of the window, he did think he'd like to jump from something. That seemed a good way. Dramatic and quick. He would do it someplace where everyone in town could see. Then they'd all feel bad for how they'd treated him. They'd be so sorry, they'd reexamine their whole lives and ways of being. Maybe some of them—those who'd known him most immediately—would kill themselves as well, unable to cope with their role in his death. It cheered him slightly to imagine. He would jump from the bridge into the river. That was his choice. He'd made his decision and that felt good too.

He kept an eye on his watch, and when it said five minutes to one, he stood up from the chair, ran a hand through his terrible hair to straighten it, left his money for Roslyn on the kitchen table, and headed back to work. He was very strict with his employees about taking only an hour for lunch, no more. He adhered to the same rule himself. So if he was not going to kill himself right then and there, he felt he must return to his desk, even though it was a Sunday and no one else would be at the bank to see if he came back on time—or at all, for that matter. Barton worked seven days a week. He had never been absent or late. And today, just because it was his last day, would be no exception.

When the end of his workday did come, Barton locked the bank and walked with courage and purpose to the Post Street Bridge as planned. When he got there, his pace slowed. He stopped in the middle and assessed the situation. He had wanted witnesses, a horrified and grieving public. But weren't there perhaps a few too many witnesses? The shores were taken over by families seeking solace from the late afternoon heat in the shade of pines, their feet in the water, children splashing nearby. Should children see such a thing? Barton had his ethics to consider. Also, the river was low. The summer's temperature had been unrelenting, and now, in August, only a foot or two of water passed below the bridge. It wasn't enough.

He couldn't swim and was counting on drowning in the mighty Spokane.

He backed away from the edge. He would have to do something else. He assured himself he would not dillydally. He would take his life in the privacy of his own house that very night. A public spectacle was not his style after all. Let the people of Spokane Falls learn of his demise later, through whispers and rumor, a haunting of sideways information. *Did he really . . . ?* they'd ask whenever they passed the bank. And the answer would be *Yes, he did.*

He'd hang himself in his parlor as soon as he got home. There was an oak crossbeam above his doorway that would be perfect for the purpose.

Barton lived just north of downtown. His house was on a hill and from his front windows he could see Spokane Falls spread out before him. First, there was the river and the sawmill. Then there was the rail yard for the Northern Pacific. Then Railroad Avenue, with its cramped tenements to the east, city hall to the west, and Roslyn and the lunchroom in the middle. His bank, the post office, and a crush of bars and hotels of varying repute lined the blocks beyond that.

Up on his hill, Barton's house stayed cool. He left his windows open in the evenings, and he generally found this to be his happiest time of day. Indeed, he felt his mood lift upon entering the house. He decided he would eat something. No need to kill himself on an empty stomach. But after that, he'd do it.

So, he enjoyed a large dinner and pretended, as he ate, to be a man in a fine, if not enviable, state. He accomplished this trick of the mind by taking stock of all the people he knew who were not having a nice meal in their nice homes on nice hills. There was the barber who had mutilated Barton's already receding hairline. In retrospect, Barton was certain he had looked more than a little syphilitic. This man was likely studying his own complexion in a mirror at this very moment, overtaken by the horror of his disease, and by the poor choices that had landed him in such a state. Then there were Jim and Del Dweller, Barton's rude and ungrateful employees at the bank—twin brothers who lived together in a stuffy house by the river and who were so cheap they probably only ever ate boiled potatoes. And lastly, there was Barton's father, that hateful man who Barton felt certain was miserable in a variety of ways, though he could not imagine any specifically. Barton ate and thought of these people and their unpleasant situations. It bolstered him so thoroughly, he thought he might not want to end his life that night after all. But once this notion entered his mind, he chided himself for it. *Coward*, he thought, *are you the sort who can't follow through on a plan?*

He was just finishing his meal when the bells began to sound. They were alarm bells from downtown. They startled him from the depths of his own mind. He went outside. It was still light out, so bright in comparison to Barton's dining room that he had to squint, and at first he could not see anything wrong at all.

"What is it?" Barton shouted to his neighbor, who was standing on his own porch with his wife and daughter.

"A fire," the man shouted back, pointing.

Now he could see. In the sharp light of the northern evening, a red-orange pocket emerged in the distance. The fire was so new, or so hot, or so something else—Barton did not know what—that it had not yet begun to produce smoke. Later, the smoke would come, and ash, which would rain down on the town. But at first, it was just the flames.

The fire was across the river and past the rail yard, in the heart of downtown. Barton looked. He allowed the fire to draw his eyes. In its brightness, he received a wonderful sight: a sparkling vision of brilliance and possibility. Barton was not a religious man, but he felt he was being gifted something from beyond himself.

Here now was a valid excuse to wait another day.

2

B arton had come to Spokane Falls in Washington Territory in 1883. He moved from Portland at the age of twenty-three to escape his domineering father and his depressive, overbearing mother. Barton's father was a lawyer. At the time, Barton was most of the way through his own training in law, his father having decreed that Barton would follow in his footsteps. The man was cold, calculating, and always after Barton about something, always berating him for any misstep. *Those papers are out of order. Those shoes are scuffed. Your brain is as small as your dick. Your mother swears you're mine but we never had any men as ugly on my side of the family.* Now, six years later, Barton could not recall the exact breaking point, only that one day he'd been at his job clerking for a Portland judge and the next he'd been on a train north, then a wagon coach east, bound for a place where silver had been discovered and any young man willing to work could make good for himself in the mines. This was what Barton wanted: to make good for himself. Himself and no one else.

His very first morning in Spokane Falls, he joined up with a group of other young men heading farther east to Coeur d'Alene. But once employed as a miner, Barton found the work did not suit him. It was an exhausting, dirty chore with no end. And so, after just two days, he quit and returned to Spokane Falls.

Back in town, it was his intention to go from business to business and inquire if any were hiring. It turned out he only needed to make one stop. The manager at the bank asked Barton if he could read and write and if he owned a second clean set of clothes. Barton said yes, and was told he could start as assistant manager right away. Six months later, this same manager skipped town to escape an improbably large gambling debt, leaving Barton in charge. Barton often thought back to this early turn of events. He wondered, had he gone into a different establishment first on his job hunt that day, might he now be living a completely different life—that of a hotelier, or a newspaperman, or even a dentist? Instead he'd ended up in a profession just as dreary as law. He'd borne his lot diligently these past six years, thinking surely the head of the only bank within a hundred miles was a position that, if taken seriously (as Barton took all things seriously), would make him a big man in the community. A respected man. Like his father in Portland, but less of an ass. This, however, had not turned out to be the case.

The big men of Spokane Falls weren't the men with two sets of clean clothes. They were prospectors in search of new claims. Loggers and sawmill workers covered in pitch, laughing loud in the bars. Cavalrymen telling stories of harrowing adventure and unceasing cruelty. They were men who held themselves up with their own bare, bleeding hands, who typified the wildness and ruggedness of a place that prided itself on being wild and rugged. The bank—holder of debts, giver of loans, reminder of reason and responsibility—was the opposite of all these things. And Barton himself, the personification of this oppositeness.

Spokane Falls had grown in the six years Barton had been there. At first, every building in town was made of wood, as if it were a prop in a play. The streets were dirt, which turned to mud in spring. Recently, though, Barton thought Spokane Falls had come to resemble a real city. There were three daily newspapers, an opera house, and a very fine bakery. And now, in 1889, Washington Territory was on the verge of being granted statehood. With that would come new money and new development. The flimsy clapboard buildings of the first half of the decade had mostly been replaced with more permanent structures. Many, like the bank, were made of brick or stone.

Barton wished he too could grow. He wished to be a city of a man. But Spokane Falls had not taken him along in this way. He felt the place picked on him just as his father had. If he had wanted to continue to be an abused rule follower, he would have stayed in Portland. For a long time, he had not known what to do about this problem.

Then he had decided to kill himself.

Then he saw the fire, and decided to do something else instead.

———

She thought about the city's changes too, sometimes. Though she felt no demands from it personally. And, conversely, she did not demand anything of it. A city was not a person. And even with people, she was not one to hold particular expectations.

She liked the bakery also, and the newspapers. The hotel where she lived got a single copy of each paper delivered in the mornings, and since most of the other residents weren't readers, she usually had her pick, even if she slept in. She had not been to the opera, but she appreciated the idea of it. For her, more than anything, the city was defined by sound. First it was the sawmill, all day and night, a din no one could escape. Then the trains came, pacing the day with their arrivals and departures. The rattle of horsecart wheels on the paved streets in the mornings. The shouting of men in the same streets after a certain time of night. Then, for a few hours again, only the sawmill.

She had never owned a clock. The place kept time for her. And even when it didn't, she was unconcerned.

———

3

It was the bank's stone exterior that saved it from the fire. Barton went there first thing Monday morning, earlier even than usual. He had never been so excited to start his workday.

He found his place of employment slightly singed, but otherwise unharmed both inside and out. It was one of only two buildings that remained on the block. A few nearby structures were still smoldering. Smoking debris—paper and small bits of wood—littered the road, swirling slightly each time a horse cart passed. The road itself was hot in places and Barton could feel the heat coming through his shoes. A team of men hauled buckets of water up from the river to a hardware store that continued to smoke.

Barton thought this was what cities in war must look like— blackened and hollowed. Families crouched on the sidewalks, protecting small piles of belongings. Carts full of furniture, food, and other merchandise rattled down the street as business owners salvaged their wares. People wandered the block, like Barton, assessing the damage. Some were distraught. One man was crying, not audibly, but Barton could see him shaking, his face in his hands.

Barton, however, felt fine. Better than fine; in fact, better than he had felt in days, if not weeks. It was like the night before when he'd thought of everyone he knew who he believed should be miserable. Here now were actual miserable people. No need to imagine. These people had lost their homes, their worldly possessions, their livelihoods. Barton had lost nothing. Barton, in fact, was poised to gain. The fire had shown him so.

The image he had seen the night before, it was like something shimmering. Wavy, starry speckles had filled his vision, the way a man might feel before he passes out. But Barton wasn't woozy. He felt strong. Because on the wave of this vision had come a plan, fully formed and brilliant.

He was going to steal money from the bank. And thanks to the fire, no one was ever going to know he was doing it.

Inside the First Bank of Spokane Falls, everything was quiet.

Much like Barton's home, the bank was cool and dark. In fact, aside from what came through the building's two front windows, there was no light at all; the power was out. Barton went around lighting oil lamps kept for this purpose. Electricity was still new to Spokane Falls, and even on days when there had been no disasters, its presence was not guaranteed. The oil lamps gave off a winter night's glow, incongruous with the heat and smoke outside. It made the bank seem a world apart from the rest of the city. And in many ways, Barton thought, it was—a lone bastion of civilization and order in an otherwise orderless place.

He opened his office and set about making his preparations. The bank remained quiet, with Barton working uninterrupted until just past ten, when the Dweller twins arrived.

Barton heard the door of the bank open, and then the sound of two sets of feet trying to lay themselves upon the floor as gently as possible, as if Barton would not hear them—and if he could not hear them, he could not scold them for being late. Though he had not missed the Dwellers, had in fact preferred their absence, he felt he should take a hard line out of principle.

"This tardiness is unacceptable," Barton yelled without getting up from his chair. "How do you men account for yourselves?"

The footsteps stopped and there was no further sound, but Barton knew, even without seeing them, that the brothers were conferring under their breath, arguing over who would be the one to speak for both. After a moment, footsteps resumed, this time a single set, and Jim's face popped through the doorway. He scowled at Barton.

"You got a haircut. It looks weird."

"Is that why you were late? Because of my hair? No? Then answer my question."

"We weren't sure if we were open," Jim said.

"Of course we're open," Barton said.

"We heard there were looters and a riot. It's martial law and the National Guard is coming to restore order."

This was from Del, who appeared at his brother's side. They were a strange vision taken in tandem; even after six years of working with them, Barton still thought so. The Dweller brothers were in their late thirties, a decade older than Barton, and yet they seemed to him childlike in many ways. Their moods swung from happy naivete to sullen insolence with little warning. They had identical boyish faces—too round, with eyes set too close together. Barton found them equally stupid and ugly.

"No looting here," Barton said, with a wave of his arm. "So, no excuse for tardiness."

He noticed both Dwellers had sandwiches in hand. Del's mouth was full of bread as he spoke.

"You were afraid of rioters, but not so afraid that you couldn't stop for a snack on the way?"

"We didn't stop," Del said. "We passed a man on the street who was giving them out. For anyone who was made destitute by the fire."

"You two have been made destitute?"

"No, but he wasn't asking for proof. And he had a lot of sandwiches. So we thought it was okay to take some."

Barton's anger flared, not for the Dwellers' dishonesty, but for their oversight. If they liked him at all, they would have pilfered a sandwich for him too.

"Stop dallying and start your work."

The Dwellers turned to leave, but then, as if in afterthought, Jim said, "There's a man waiting to speak to you. We found him out front when we came in."

A shimmering wave passed once more before Barton's eyes. He knew this was the start of it. His plan had been made, and now it was time to act.

"I'll fetch him straightaway," Barton said.

"He looks poor," Del said.

"You look poor."

With that, the Dwellers withdrew, ostensibly to do something work related, though Barton doubted how productive they would be. They were the sort who could make a holiday of anything out of the ordinary, even a fire.

4

The man Barton ushered into his office soon thereafter did look poor. His clothes were old and his face was gaunt. He was wearing a frayed hat he had not bothered to take off. Barton thought he would have liked the man even better if he'd been holding the hat, wringing it. Arriving literally hat in hand.

Barton asked what he could do for him.

"I need some money," the man said. He did not look at Barton when he spoke, only at his own shoes. "I was thinking, if you gave me some money today, I could pay it back later. I have a job. I'm good for it."

"You're asking for a loan," Barton said.

"Yes, a loan. Yes." He nodded gratefully, as if the word itself was all he'd come to Barton's office for.

"Of course. Of course you can have a loan," Barton said, kindly and helpfully, like the good banker he was.

He drew up the papers for a loan for five hundred dollars at 9 percent, the standard rate of interest for his institution.

"Do you read?" Barton asked.

The man shook his head no.

"Well, all this says is that you are being given this money and that you will return it to the bank with thirty percent interest within three years. You can make payments once a month, or once every two weeks, as you see fit for your schedule and budget."

"I can pay every two weeks," the man said, his eyes fixed on the slim stack of bills Barton had brought out from the safe. "I can pay every one week in fact, if you like."

Barton showed him where to make his mark on the document.

"Just bring the money back to me in this office," Barton said.

The men shook hands, the transaction completed.

Barton considered that perhaps his suicidal thoughts from the days prior had not been for a literal end of his life after all (and therefore it was perfectly reasonable that he had looked for excuses to stay his own hand at every opportunity). Instead, they were for a figurative death. He had wished only that particular version of himself dead and gone—the version who followed all the rules, just waiting for people to notice and declare him worthy of adoration. But why wait when there was power to be had that very day, and any day after, if only he was bold enough to take it? The fire had shown him this and he was eternally grateful for it.

What he'd done was so very simple. Washington Territory required interest rates be set at 10 percent or lower, but they could be amended if all parties involved were in understanding and agreement. The man he'd given the doctored loan to—his name was Sam Flint—did not know the rules. And so, by virtue of his ignorance, he had been both. Plus, it was unlikely Flint saw anything odd about 30 percent interest. Barton's was the only bank in Spokane

Falls, but it was not the only place a person could borrow money. Cardrooms and other less-than-reputable establishments were happy to provide that service to those in desperate circumstances, and their rates of return, Barton knew, were even higher. For a man who'd never dealt with a real bank before, 30 percent likely seemed reasonable. But of course the paperwork said 9. So, when Flint made his payments, Barton would have no choice but to take the excess money for himself so there would not be any irregularities in the bank's accounting. That was assuming Flint paid, which he might not. This was fine. The bank anticipated a certain percentage of defaults, and the owner, a cartoonishly large man named Zane Zeeb who lived in Walla Walla and controlled a dozen banks throughout Washington Territory, did not come down too harshly on Barton for these losses when they occurred. "It's all part of being in the business of business," Zeeb had a habit of saying whenever he stopped by the Spokane Falls branch for a visit.

Barton's plan was to give these same terms to every loan seeker. No one would be turned away and no one would be spared. This would be his way of finally getting what he deserved from the people of Spokane Falls. If he couldn't have their respect, he could at least have their money. He was finally going to make good for himself, be a big man in the big city.

The second person to apply for a 30 percent loan arrived at the bank hat in hand (as Barton preferred) but with a crude smile on his face. When Barton ushered him into his office, he leaned back in the chair offered to him, tipping it on two legs the way only children and the ostentatiously confident do. This man wanted to borrow money, yes, but not to repair any damage from the fire. He wanted to start a business with it. Barton gathered that he himself was not the only person in town to see the shimmering stars of opportunity. He congratulated the man on his entrepreneurial spirit and asked what sort of business it might be.

"Sir," the man asked in turn, "have you, as of late, had any difficulty breathing?"

"Can't say I have, no."

"What I mean is, have you noticed in yourself any ill effects from all the smoke in the air, and the ash?"

Barton said he felt fine.

"Well," the man said, "a lot of folks don't feel fine." As he said this, he ceased his rocking on the chair's legs and leaned forward so both his elbows rested against Barton's desk. "A lot of people feel sick as dogs from all the gunk in their lungs. But I've got something to help with that. I've got something to sell that will make everyone feel better in a flat second, as soon as they take it. I just need some money to get my shop up and going. Not even a shop, really, just one of those white tent deals, like how those fellows are selling paper goods and food near the bridges."

"You make medicine?" Barton asked.

"It's my own patented lung and chest medicine, yes," the man said.

"You have a patent?"

"Well, no, not specifically. It's brand-new, so I don't have a patent."

"So it's un-patented medicine, which you wish to sell from a tent by a bridge?"

This remark seemed to take the wind out of the man's sails.

"Well, I'm just trying to help people, is all. Provide a service in these hard times. The way those old buildings went up—what was in 'em? Now that's what we're all breathing. Take Wolfe's, for example. God only knows the materials that burned in there, if you catch my drift. And I figure if I can help people and help myself too, well what's the harm? No harm. It's practically community service."

"I'm sorry," Barton said. "Did you say Wolfe's? The hotel? The hotel burned?"

"Shit. Did Wolfe's burn? That's where the whole fire started. You know it? I've frequented on a few occasions myself. A man could have a fine time at Wolfe's."

"No," Barton said, pulling out his loan contract and folding it over so this man—more likely a reader than the last—could not see the true terms. "Never been."

———

She was also a person who lied easily. If pressed, she might have justified this behavior by saying, "Truth is a privilege and must be earned." But of course that was a sideways manner of putting it—a clever adage to smooth the way. What she really meant was some people's very survival depended on knowing when to tell the truth and when to lie. She had, many times already in her life, been such a person.

She'd lied to hide her drinking, hoping to save her first job, though it hadn't helped.

She'd lied about her past to every man she'd ever been romantically involved with, not wanting them to get too close to the person she really was, or the way she saw the world.

She had lied to Kate, every week for years, to get her money. Then she'd lied to herself and said nothing bad would come from it.

Perhaps the only person in her life she had never lied to was her father. He had never required such a thing from her, and this cemented her deep and abiding love for the man, despite his many, many faults.

———

5

Barton arrived at Wolfe's Hotel just after five o'clock. Or, rather, at what was left of Wolfe's Hotel, which wasn't much. Others were there already, a small crowd. Barton wondered if they'd been there all day. A vigil for the lost brothel? Or was it merely curiosity? People were eager to see where the fire had started, as if the site itself might hold some answers. They stood in twos and threes, whispering. Barton approached some of the blackened debris and toed it with his shoe. Had he visited just a couple of hours later the day before, he could have been present for the inferno.

"Someone died in there," Barton overheard a woman standing behind him say.

He wondered if it was Roslyn. Was it possible she had slept through the alarm bells, and also the sounds and smells of her apartment burning up around her? Barton thought it might be.

"Who died?" he asked, turning to the woman who'd spoken. "Do you know who it was?"

She shook her head. "But I heard a baby was born last night too. So it all evens out in the end, doesn't it?"

Barton said he supposed it did.

He stood among the crowd and listened to what others said. A man to his left was telling another that the fire had started in the lunchroom's kitchen—that it was an explosion of some sort, an act of deliberate malice, maybe even a bomb. The other man said he'd heard it was nothing so thrilling. Just a spark from a passing train that had landed in the wrong spot. No, a third said, the fire must have started on the top floor, fueled by fresh air from so many open windows. Perhaps a candle tipped over, or a cigarette was carelessly tossed.

Barton remembered his own cigarette-tossing from the day before—the moody satisfaction of dropping the butts out Roslyn's window.

All around him, people were gossiping, chattering, speculating wildly. Somewhere in the crowd, out of his sight, Barton picked out another conversation. "It's that fuckhead banker," a voice said. Then another voice said, "Where?" Then the first voice said, "Over there," and Barton felt himself being pointed at.

"Figures," the second voice said. "Vultures always come out at times like this."

A policeman in uniform appeared at the edge of the crowd. Barton watched as the officer struggled to part the sea of people gathered around the ruined hotel. He was gratified to see there was someone else in town who received as little respect as he did, if not less. When the policeman finally made it to the center of the crowd, he raised his hands and shouted for silence, which was not quickly granted.

"I know everyone is very upset about last night's fire, and about the loss of life at this particular location," the policeman said. "Let me assure you that myself, the fire department, and the water department are working to restore order and find out the cause of this great tragedy."

Barton wondered if he himself might be blamed for the fire, he and his damn cigarettes.

There was more murmuring in the crowd. They sounded angry to Barton, maybe even riotous. Was their anger for the police officer and his talk of law and order? Or for the loss of the hotel? He was certain he heard the word *banker* again. He wanted a cigarette to calm his nerves but didn't want to be seen holding a match.

The policeman resumed speaking, saying an investigation was under way to determine if the fire had been set deliberately or by accident, and that anyone who had lost their home could go to some address or another for help. "To prevent further looting and other improper behavior, we ask those without business in the downtown area to limit your activities there. And please obey the nighttime curfew," he continued. There was more, but Barton had stopped listening.

Barton knew he hadn't been the one to start the fire. He'd left the hotel in the early afternoon; the fire hadn't begun until hours later.

Still, the police would need to talk to anyone who had been at Wolfe's that day, wouldn't they? Police scrutiny, for any reason, was not something Barton wanted. He had imagined, the night before, that he was free to do what he liked at the bank precisely because in the chaos of disaster, no one would be looking at him. He warranted no attention, never had.

But oh, wouldn't the people of Spokane Falls like to see him charged with arson, maybe even murder? Not to mention fraud. A most satisfying conviction. *Good, hang the fuckhead banker,* people would say.

Just as quickly as he sank into his anxiety, he pulled himself out of it. This was only idle fear-making, he scolded himself. No one even knew he'd been to Wolfe's Hotel that day except Roslyn. And now here she was, likely dead.

Didn't he have better ways to occupy his mind? The answer was yes. He had his big plans, which were only half-laid.

6

On Tuesday, August 6, two days after the fire, men from the various national and territorial insurance organizations began to arrive in Spokane Falls, armed with the power to make good on policies for business owners and homeowners alike. They set up shop in the basement of downtown's largest remaining church, behind rickety wooden tables with banners displaying the names of each company. Barton was invited to visit this operation and speak with the insurance men, as many of their customers would be patronizing his bank in the coming days, looking to cash checks. He assured each that his bank was sound and had plenty of cash on hand. The insurance men were pleased. Barton too felt bolstered by these interactions. The insurance men had come from Seattle and Portland (more would arrive soon from Chicago, New York, elsewhere). They were professionals. They shook Barton's hand, looked him in the eye, and if they thought anything at all of his hair, they politely kept it to themselves. He felt he was among peers. He returned to the bank puffed up with the knowledge that there were in fact people in the world who saw and knew his worth.

The clients of the insurance men began arriving later that day, their checks in hand. Barton told Jim and Del to send all insurance check cashers directly to him. They didn't question this, happy to have their workload trimmed.

The first was a man so covered in pitch, Barton suspected he had literally been living inside a pine tree. What business or establishment such a person could have lost to the fire was beyond Barton's imagination. The man marched up to him, tossed his check down on the teller's desk, and said, simply, "Gimme."

No respect. From a person so dirty and sticky, he left prints on everything he touched. On a previous day, such treatment would have sent Barton roiling. He'd have been rude to the man. Then he would have taken his anger out on the Dwellers. Then he would have taken his anger out on himself. But not this day. On this day, he only smiled.

The man's check was for twenty-five dollars. Whatever he'd lost couldn't have been more than a shack. It didn't matter. Checks large and small would be treated the same. Barton took a narrow strip of blank paper from a drawer and in his most careful script wrote: "In lieu of $25. First Bank of Spokane Falls. August 6, 1889." He had a rubber stamp with his signature that he applied below this.

He explained to the pitch-stained man that the bank was out of paper currency, but that this note, which he held in his hand, was as good as cash, validated by the bank as it was.

The man looked at him with rightful suspicion. "I don't want that," he said. "I want money."

"This is money," Barton said. "It just looks different. Paper money stands for gold in a bank. That's all. This does too. It means the same."

The man's eyes narrowed and his body tensed. Barton stayed cool. He held his gaze and nodded slightly as if to say *Yes, you can do it, you can believe what I say*.

The pitch-covered man relented. "All right," he said. "As long as it's money."

"Trust me," Barton said, holding out the paper. "It's money."

And just like that, it was.

Barton took the twenty-five dollars. He pulled it from the till at the teller's desk and put it in his pants pocket. By the end of the day, he had $375.

7

The rumor the Dwellers had shared about the National Guard was true. Soldiers in uniform arrived the day after the insurance men and posted at the major entry points to downtown. Barton crossed the Post Street Bridge and at the end of it found himself waiting in a line with other men. When he got to the front, a corporal who looked about sixteen and dreadfully sweaty in his wool uniform asked him his purpose for entering the downtown area. Barton explained who he was. The boy soldier nodded and filled out a pass with Barton's name and occupation. He was instructed to show it from then on at any of the checkpoints and he'd be let through. Barton thanked him and didn't notice until he looked at the pass a few blocks later that all the information on it was misspelled. It read "Barron Hayhell. Barker."

At the bank, the Dwellers were already there, laughing and comparing their own pass cards. They'd come through a checkpoint on First Street, where the line was short—likely, Barton thought, because the guard was even more inept than the child he'd encountered at the bridge. Del's card identified him as Daniel. His occupation, vaguely, but not incorrectly: "Assistant." Jim's, however, was merely a scribble, a symbol of some sort that the brothers speculated about, but that Barton saw right away as a lopsided dollar sign. Jim then wondered if this was to indicate that he worked at the bank (obviously), or that he was a wealthy man who should be allowed to go where he pleased in the city. Normally, Barton would have put an end to such stupid talk, but on this morning he chuckled alongside them. He was energized by his new work, and it made him generous with his kindness and good feelings.

He worked again at the teller's desk cashing insurance checks. He grew confident, his explanation for the banknotes swift. He said it with a smile and most people smiled back because that's how smiles work. Though some seemed confused, no one complained.

Barton did wonder, though, what was happening to his notes once they left the bank. Were merchants accepting them? He wanted to see for himself. He took a midmorning break and walked to a newsstand to buy a paper. The stand used to be made of wood, but it had burned and was now a small tent. Almost all downtown businesses were operating out of such tents, even ones that had not suffered from the fire. Tents, it seemed, were fashionable.

The news tent had two young women wedged inside. An assortment of other goods Barton could not remember the old stand selling were laid out on a desk before them: hairbrushes, belt buckles, three taxidermic mice. He took a copy of the daily paper and gave the woman nearest a note for one dollar. She looked at it, then turned to the other woman. "It's another of these things," she said. The other woman just nodded, then the first made change and Barton left smiling.

His good mood didn't last. On his walk back to work, he saw someone who made him very uncomfortable. She was two blocks away and with her back to him, but there was no mistake. She was as familiar to him as if she were his own mother.

It was Roslyn, not dead at all.

His first instinct was to hide. But of course she wasn't looking for him, probably wasn't thinking anything of him. That is, unless someone had asked her about him. The police, say.

Barton felt it was best to get out ahead of the problem. He ran as fast as his body would allow, overtaking Roslyn while she waited to cross the street at the corner of Second Avenue. He tapped her on the shoulder to get her attention, but then the strain of his exertion forced him to bend over, holding his knees for support until his breath returned.

"I thought maybe you died," he said, by way of a greeting.

She gave him a squinty look. He knew what he'd said was rude, or at the very least strange. But now was not a time for niceties.

"Is your hair different from the last time I saw you?" she asked.

"No. It was like this already."

"I think I would have remembered something like that," she said, then, "Why did you think I died?"

"In the fire. I heard a person died. I thought it might be you."

Here, her expression changed, her eyes wide, almost pleading. "Who? Who died? Do you know who it was?"

"No. I thought it was you, like I said."

"But it wasn't me." She was crying a little now. Barton hadn't anticipated this. He felt he was losing control of the situation.

"Have you spoken to anyone since the fire?" he asked. "Anyone official?"

"What do you mean, official?"

"The police? The firemen? The National Guard? Just for example."

"No. Why would I speak to any of them?"

Barton had to scramble for a lie. He repeated what he had heard from the policeman who'd addressed the crowd at Wolfe's: that shelter was being made available for those who'd lost their homes to the fire. Was she in need of such shelter?

At this, Roslyn nodded. She wiped at her eyes and drew a deep breath. She said she'd spent the past couple of nights with an acquaintance on the South Hill, but didn't know the woman well and wasn't sure how long she'd be welcome. She told Barton if there was a place set up for people to stay, she'd likely go there instead.

"Is it just a matter of visiting the police station?" she asked.

Barton felt his throat tighten. How to now get out of the trap he'd sprung on himself? By continuing to pretend it was her he was worried about, not himself.

He shook his head and told her he didn't think she should stay at such a place. That it was, in fact, the very situation he was trying to warn her against.

"The police are saying the fire might be arson or an accident of negligence and that there is an investigation to determine who's responsible," Barton said. "Aren't you worried you might be a suspect?"

This nearly doubled the poor woman over once more. "A suspect? I hadn't thought . . . but, oh. Maybe I should go to the police, then. If there's any information I could provide."

Barton noticed her speech was quicker than usual. He was used to waiting a long time for her to answer questions, and then only sometimes getting the answer he actually asked for. He wondered if she had not yet been able to drink that morning.

"They won't believe you," he said. "Whatever you tell them, they'll assume it's a lie."

"How do you know that?"

"Because of your profession," Barton said. "People always assume the worst."

"It's true," Roslyn said. "I've been blamed for things before. People think poorly of women like me. What should I do?" She was crying a little again.

"I don't know," he said. "But you ought to make other plans about where to stay. Someplace where you can lay low for a while."

"Where?" she asked. "I don't have any real friends."

"You can stay at my house," he said.

Roslyn nodded a frantic yes. She dabbed her eyes with her sleeve and gave a little smile. This eagerness made Barton feel sad for her. Her desperation and lonesomeness were so acute. But he also felt pleased. And just a little horny. Like he held some bit of power over her—the power to invoke fear, and then, magically, to relieve it.

"Okay, let's go," he said.

They didn't speak again until they reached the house. Barton opened the door and ushered Roslyn into his parlor.

"It's nice and cool in here," she said.

Barton agreed it was.

"I think you'll find the house is always a very pleasant temperature," he added. But after that, he didn't know what to say. It was the first time he had ever had another person inside his home.

"Would it be all right if I sit?" Roslyn asked, and Barton realized the thing to do when a woman comes to your house is to escort her to a chair and offer her something to drink, especially if she's just endured a long hot walk. But she said, "No, thank you, I've got my own," and pulled a flask from the recesses of her boot.

"Would you like some?" she asked.

Barton had never drunk with Roslyn before. He was always in the middle of his workday when he saw her and thought it imprudent to return to the bank smelling of alcohol. But now he accepted. He went and got two glasses from the kitchen and held them out while Roslyn poured. The liquid that emerged from the flask was a milky gray color.

"What is it?" he asked, seating himself in a chair opposite her.

Roslyn only smiled, then drank. Barton drank too. It smelled chemical, but the taste was musky, like an animal. It was very strong and he could feel the effect right away. He understood why she spent all her time sleeping if this was what she drank.

"I have to go to work," he said, standing up for fear that if he didn't, he would sink into the chair and never leave it. "You're free to do as you like here until I get back." Then, he looked around for ideas of how a woman in his home might entertain herself. "There are some books," he offered, pointing to the shelf behind him. That was all he could think of.

Roslyn nodded, but in a way that suggested she had no intention of reading. Her eyes had already drifted from Barton to other parts of the room, sizing things up, perhaps. What would she do in his absence, he wondered. Still, he'd said he should go and that was true, so he left. But once outside, he found his sense of unease did not diminish.

This woman he'd invited into his home, Barton thought, was someone he'd known for six years, but really hardly knew at all.

What had he done, bringing her there? She was a prostitute. She was in his house, alone. She could do damage. Rob him. Then run to the police and tell the whole sordid story—that she knew a man who'd been at the hotel the day of the fire, and for some reason he'd tried to shut her up about it.

But no, Roslyn would not do this. She wasn't cunning or quick enough to see through to his true intentions. He was certain he'd spooked her so badly, she would not leave the house on her own. And who else would ever come to his home to find her? Roslyn could stay safely kept away there as long as he wanted. Forever, if need be.

While he was gone, she mostly slept. At first, she slept in the armchair where he had offered her a seat, upright with both feet on the ground. She didn't dare even use the ottoman. She was afraid to let her guard down there in his house. It didn't seem safe. But she was so, so, so tired. Just to sit in the fine chair in that cool, quiet room felt an unearned luxury. And after several hours, when Barton did not appear suddenly to spring a trap on her, she allowed herself to move to the couch, and a lying position. Though still she kept her shoes on, feet dangling from the cushion. She could run if she needed to, she told herself. Then eventually she did have a look around the rest of the house and found the spare bedroom, with just two pieces of furniture: bed and nightstand. The bed was large and carefully made. It looked like a picture in a magazine. Had anyone ever slept in it? She felt she was in an undiscovered land, a forest primeval of bedrooms. She took her shoes off.

8

When he returned home that night, Barton found Roslyn asleep. He thought it strange to see something so familiar in a different setting: Roslyn dozing, not in her apartment in Wolfe's Hotel, but instead in his own house, in the guest room that had never held guests before. He decided it was not an unpleasant sight. It gave the place a homey feeling—having another person there, enjoying its comforts. At the same time, Barton was grateful Roslyn was asleep. After the awkwardness of the morning, he was unsure what to say to her.

And the next day, she was still asleep when he left for work. So, it wasn't until that evening that he spoke to her for the first time since she'd gotten to his house thirty-six hours earlier.

Meanwhile, Barton wrote banknotes by the dozen, his hand steady, penmanship precise. *Good handwriting is the mark of an honest man*, his father used to say. If only he could see Barton now. Barton had always been a dutiful servant of the bank. Diligent and precise in all matters. He took pride in his good work, but it earned him nothing except ire, suspicious stares as he walked the streets, mean names behind his back. Once, at a café, someone spit in his omelet. Now he was throwing all that good hard work out the window. He felt no guilt. Why should there be guilt? He owed no one his loyalty, his diligence, or his precision.

All he felt was the thrill of the taking. Thirty percent loans were on offer for anyone who came into the bank with so much as a look of wanting to borrow money. No one questioned him. The Dwellers, if they overheard these conversations, ignored them. He found this to be an exceptional time for him. A radiant time. As if the shimmer he had seen the night of the fire had taken him over, making his whole being bright. Brilliant. That was the word. He felt brilliant, in all ways.

On his way home from work that night, Barton walked through Trent Alley, thinking to do something kind for his houseguest. The street—mostly small wood structures in close quarters—had been almost entirely gutted. The only shop Barton found open sold an odd amalgam of items: boots, paint, flour, mugs, pillows, seeds in packages with no labels. Barton asked the shopkeeper if he had liquor. The man began to pull jars of liquid from behind the counter until Barton saw one the color of what he'd drunk with Roslyn.

"There," he said. The shopkeeper smirked like he knew something Barton didn't.

Though he came bearing a gift, upon first entering his house, Barton could not find its recipient. He searched the parlor, bedrooms, and hallways, calling her name. Pinpricks of anxiety clustered at the nape of his neck. What if she had left and gone to the police after all? What if she told them who she was and where she lived and who she'd been with the day of the fire? But why would she do that? Guilt? Fear? Wasn't it in her best interest to stay hidden with Barton? Why give up such safety?

He sat in his chair and tried to work through the situation. There was no need to give in to irrational thinking. He was a newly brilliant man, after all. The key was simply to get Roslyn back to the house before she had a chance to speak with anyone, and if she'd already done so, to find a way to intercept that person as well. Surely, everyone involved could be reasoned with. And if not reasoned with, perhaps bought? Barton had extra money. Why not wield that power? That was how he should have handled Roslyn to begin with. No need to keep her with him at all times when a simple bribe would do.

It was then, still and quiet for the first time since entering the house, that Barton heard something. He followed the sound out to the backyard. There she was—on her knees, her face dangerously close to a blackberry bramble. The sound Barton had heard was a guttural sound, a retching sound. It was Roslyn vomiting into his bushes.

He stood and watched her. He'd never seen a woman be sick before. He'd never considered the possibility that women were capable of such things. But then, other than his own mother, Barton had spent little time with women, and this made it difficult for him to picture them engaging in many normal, human activities. When he did think of women (who were not his mother), it was almost exclusively for masturbatory purposes. These fantasies had not, in the past, involved anyone puking.

He didn't want to interrupt. When she was finished, Roslyn pushed herself up from her hands, tipping immediately to the ground on her right side. Her knees remained as they were, but now her torso was twisted in such a way that her head and one shoulder were also touching the grass. She looked toward Barton.

"I didn't want to make a mess inside," she said. "So I came out here."

"That's all right. I don't like those blackberries anyway. Too sour."

He could tell she hadn't heard his response. Her face was red from her exertions and her eyes had gone dim. Barton wondered if she might throw up some more, but after a moment it became clear that she had passed out in that strange posture.

Barton observed her a moment longer before deciding the thing to do was to help her inside. He knelt and wrapped his arms around her. He found her body awkward and heavy, and he was afraid he might not be capable of moving her anywhere. This was upsetting to him mostly for the thought of the neighbors discovering an unconscious woman in his yard. But eventually he did get Roslyn up to a standing position, and from there she was able to walk with his assistance.

She was hot to the touch, feverish. Anyplace Barton's body connected with hers instantly bloomed with sweat. She muttered things that were not words. Barton wondered if she had acquired some sort of disease. More likely, though, she'd just made herself sick with drink. Perhaps she did this exact thing every evening, only normally she would have vomited in the alley behind Wolfe's Hotel, instead of in Barton's blackberry bushes. But how much alcohol could she have consumed? The flask they'd shared the day prior had been almost empty already. Barton had no alcohol of his own in the house.

Maybe this was the problem. Barton had heard that a drinker who stops drinking all of a sudden can become ill. He laid Roslyn on the bed, then went for the jar he'd bought in Trent Alley.

"You should have some," he said, holding it out to her.

"No," Roslyn said, with a sudden lucidity. "I don't want that."

Barton offered food. She declined. He brought a glass of water instead. She took a few tentative sips before returning it to him. She closed her eyes, head to pillow. He picked up the blankets and arranged them on top of her. This was not something he had ever done for another human being—tuck them into bed—but here, it felt right.

After that, Barton went back to the kitchen and had his dinner, which he ate quickly and hardly tasted. Then, he retired to his parlor as usual to read, but the book he was currently engaged with could not hold his interest. He set it down and looked over his bookshelves for something different.

He couldn't concentrate on the second book either. He found he could think only of Roslyn. This was new. In the past, when he'd thought of her, it was always in a practical light. What time might he visit her at Wolfe's Hotel? Was he able to spend a whole hour, or did he have to get back to the bank sooner? And even in the past two days, he'd thought of her in terms of his own preservation. Roslyn's place in his mind had always been a matter of business.

Now he thought of her in another way. It was a sexual way. This had been, of course, Roslyn's role in his life from the beginning. But normally, when Barton had sexual thoughts, they were focused on himself. His needs, and how to get them met. Roslyn was merely the vehicle. Suddenly, he was thinking of her separate from him. He was thinking of her body and the heat that had radiated from it when he helped her in from the yard. He was thinking of her hair, wild on the bedroom pillow. He was thinking of how she had looked pitched toward the blackberry bushes, and how that image had disgusted him, but it was also, now that he reviewed it, somehow enjoyable. Was it enjoyable because it was disgusting? Was it her weakness in contrast to Barton's strength? Was it the odd posture of her body, affording him a new view of parts of her he did not usually consider, even when naked and on top of her? He had no idea. He could not sort it out and quickly stopped trying. He allowed himself instead to enjoy the images of her as they arrived in his mind: heat, flesh, sight, smell, sweat, hair, blankets. He sat and thought these thoughts until he was very aroused and decided he would like to go join the real Roslyn in the spare bedroom. He saw no reason why he shouldn't.

Heydale Versus
Heydale Versus Love

B arton was fourteen the first time he had sex. The woman was older than him—a friend of his parents and a widow. Or maybe not a widow. Maybe just a woman who did not like her husband much and never brought him to parties. That's where it was—a party at the Heydale home, thrown by Barton's father, who, though Barton found him terribly unlikable (always had and always would), was popular among his own peers, and even regarded as jovial and entertaining. The party was dull. Barton was drunk off alcohol he'd been sneaking from the guests' glasses when they abandoned them. The maybe-widow also looked drunk. She was sitting alone and Barton got the idea she'd rather do anything than be alone at a party. He approached her and said, in what he thought was a suave way, that he found her to have an exotic air about her, and he wondered if she would like to join him somewhere private for a more intimate conversation.

In hindsight, Barton could not recall what had made him think this was a good strategy for seduction. He might have read it in a book, or heard another boy tell a story where he claimed to have used such a line. More likely it was something he'd misheard, or misread. Morphed and shaped in his teenage brain into a notion that seemed to him both original and clever. Or at least plausible.

But as soon as he said this, the maybe-widow began laughing. She laughed so hard and for so long, Barton turned to leave. She clasped him by the elbow to keep him in place, then laughed some more. Then, as abruptly as she'd started, she stopped and said, "All right. Where should we go?"

He led her with a sweaty hand to his father's study, which was on the opposite end of the house, and where no other party guests would venture. Once there, the maybe-widow sat in his father's chair.

"We're here," she said. "Now what do you want to do?"

Barton, flustered by the success of his plan, admitted he didn't know.

"Come on then and I'll show you," the maybe-widow said. And she did.

In the days following the party, Barton existed as if in a dream. In his memory of this time, there was no school, no work at his father's downtown office, no dour family dinners, though surely he must have continued with these things as normal. There was only the constant reliving of his minutes in the study with the maybe-widow. He did not see this preoccupation as a problem. His conquest had been tremendous, and he felt he'd earned the right to obsess over it. Besides, what else in his life was as interesting, or as pleasurable even by half? He dwelled, revisiting details, revising the scene, replaying and reconstructing until it was perfect in his mind. His erection was nearly constant.

He became certain if he knew where the maybe-widow lived, he would go to her home and break down her door in demand of more lovemaking. Instead, he found a moment alone with his father to ask when there might be another party.

Mr. Heydale was occupied in some way, as always, only giving his son his half attention.

"Another party? Why? So you can fuck Mrs. McCall again?"

Barton had never heard his father say *fuck* before, had never heard him mention sex in any way.

"I didn't," he said, already a liar even as a child.

"Yes, you did. I know what goes on in my own home."

Barton said nothing to this, but for the first time in many days felt himself fully and immediately un-aroused.

Mr. Heydale set aside his papers. "The thing you must know about sex is . . ." he began.

Barton shoved his hands in his pockets and braced himself for diatribe. *Sin*, he thought the older man might say, though they were not a religious family. Or, *dangerous*. Or, *improper*.

"The thing you must know about sex is," Mr. Heydale said, "that it's everything."

Barton looked up, thinking finally, fourteen years into his relationship with his father, he was being told something honest, something real.

"What I mean is," the senior Heydale continued, "for a man like you, it's everything. To a weak man. Sex consumes a weak man. He can't see any life outside it. I only hoped you might wait awhile before you threw yourself into that pit. But, now, here you are."

"I don't even like her," Barton lied again.

"It doesn't matter if you like them," his father said.

"But what about love?" Barton asked.

His father laughed and told him there was no such thing. Love was only an illusion, again belonging to weak men. Later, Barton would wish he'd asked what this meant about his father's feelings toward his mother, but he was pretty sure he got the picture regardless.

"And what is sex for strong men?"

"It's whatever they want."

Then his father went back to his work, signaling the conversation over. Barton decided he did not agree with his father about love. Love was real, and not just for the weak. As for being called weak by his dad, well, that was fine—almost all his father's advice came with insults. But it was the notion of strong men making sex into whatever they wanted that lodged most prominently in his teenage mind.

Barton went to his spare room and found Roslyn just as he'd left her, groggy and red-faced. She did nothing to encourage or discourage him as he got under the blankets beside her and wriggled out of his clothes. Her breath on his face was warm and sour. Barton did not linger once he was finished. He picked up his clothes and shuffled out of the room, saying a quick "Good night," which he was not certain Roslyn heard. But alone in his own room after, he felt different. Even though the mechanics were the same, this was like no sex he'd ever had before, with Roslyn or anyone else. The reason, he thought, was affection.

That night with Roslyn was bright and brilliant, just like Barton's day at the bank had been. He was a man with money and power and love. What other wonders might fill his world, now that he had opened himself up to them?

She would not drink again. For Kate, she had decided, Kate and everyone else. She wished she could have come to the decision faster, an immediate epiphany. But then, she had many other regrets as well. Though she was unable to set them right, this was one thing she could do. For Kate, she thought, over and over, as sickness overtook her. She had never shown the woman any real kindness in all the years they had known each other. Small talk in the hallways, some meals together in the Wolfe's lunchroom, a shared joke here and there. That was all. But now Kate was the foundation on which she built a promise. She would keep it, no matter how difficult.

She did not think Kate was the one who had died at Wolfe's. And that was almost worse. What kind of life was left to a woman like Kate in the world outside the hotel?

9

The next evening, Barton once again stopped after work to run an errand in service of his dear Roslyn, this time at the pharmacy. The pharmacy was, of course, now a tent. The whole of the store had been transferred into it, including a collection of roustabouts who hung around for reasons unclear to Barton. Perhaps the pharmacist gave them some medicines for free. But what would be the benefit of this to him? And now here they were still. Barton couldn't imagine the guardsmen would have issued such people passes, which meant they'd been stowed away in downtown streets since the fire, never leaving even at the worst of it. One such individual—a woman with matted hair and dirt on her face, but wearing a surprisingly stylish dress—lolled in a chair by the pharmacist's counter. When Barton approached, he thought he heard her hiss.

The pharmacist himself, however, was a pleasant and clean-cut man. He asked what he could do for Barton.

"What would you recommend for someone trying to quit alcohol?" Barton asked.

Before the pharmacist could answer, the woman in the chair leaned forward and leered at Barton. "Oh, ho!" she said in a kind of half laugh. "Nothing to be done for you, banker. You're already dead!"

Barton locked eyes with her and found he could not look away. So confidently and quickly she had spoken.

"Don't mind her," the pharmacist said. "She's"—and here he gave a swirl of his hand, palm up, a gesture Barton hadn't seen before and couldn't decipher—"a certain kind of woman."

Barton nodded, but he could not free himself from the chair-sitter's gaze.

"What sort of alcohol? Sir? What sort?" the pharmacist asked, clearly ready to move on.

"I don't know. Some moonshine."

"I would recommend laudanum, then. Or balsamroot oil." He pulled two brown vials from under the counter.

Barton nodded again and bought both. He did not realize until later that he didn't know which was which, or even what the difference between the two was.

A quick survey of the house proved Roslyn had been up, at least briefly, to be sick again out in the yard and also once in the washroom, though it seemed she'd done her best to clean it up. Barton assembled a plate of food and took it in to her along with the little vials from the pharmacy, all of which he left on the bedside table. He also left a copy of the day's newspaper. The headline read, "The Most Devastating Fire in the History of the World." Barton had not been present for any other catastrophes, but he suspected this was hyperbole. Although Roslyn didn't stir during this visit, she did make some sounds and movements when Barton returned later to make love to her. He took these as signs of gratitude as well as shared intimacy.

Barton thought of all the things he'd like to say to Roslyn once she was well and coherent. He imagined the two of them sitting together on the couch in the parlor, with her hand resting upon his knee. He would tell her about the bank and the Dweller twins. He could do a pretty good impression of them and he thought that would make her laugh. He'd tell her about his childhood in Portland and his mother, whom he'd loved but had not seen or spoken to in six years. He didn't think he'd talk about his father because it made him angry to even think of the man, but maybe he would, after a while, and it would feel good to get it out in the open. She'd be so understanding about everything. These were things he could have said to her before, of course. He'd had years to say them, to speak personally and intimately with her, but he never had. He did not regret this. He thought of the Roslyn who was in his home as an entirely separate person from the Roslyn he'd visited at Wolfe's Hotel. He could not account for this and didn't try.

10

The appearance of Zane Zeeb, owner of the First Bank of Spokane Falls, always made Barton nervous. And so he hoped,
when Zeeb arrived at the bank on the morning of August 10 without warning (he was always, much to Barton's dismay, arriving
without warning), that he, Barton, did not seem suspicious in his
nervousness. Just the normal amount of nervous.

The thing that made Barton generally nervous about Zeeb was
that Zeeb was exactly the sort of man Barton himself wanted to be.
He was wealthy and, as a result, powerful. But he was also respected, and not just because of his money. Zeeb was respected
because he commanded respect. Even in Spokane Falls, where no
one cared for the bank, he was treated with deference. More people
knew him than knew Barton and he didn't even live there. Zeeb
was not only married to a beautiful woman but had two mistresses
as well. Barton knew this because Zeeb bragged about them. And
he had all his hair, which was shock-white and glorious in its appearance.

He was also a bore and, in Barton's opinion, an asshole. Barton hated himself for wanting so badly to be like this man.

On the morning of August 10, Barton found Zeeb in his own office, sitting in his chair, looking through his ledgers. It was early and the bank wasn't open yet. At the sight of him, Barton thought he might vomit.

"Well now, Heydale," Zeeb said without looking up, "looks like you've been very busy here indeed."

Barton was certain this was a wry observation about his various misdeeds over the course of the past five days. He believed Zeeb had the power to look at his cooked ledgers, read the neat lines of tallies and numbers, and see each and every inflated loan and faulty note Barton had issued.

"I'm not sure what you mean, sir," Barton said.

Now Zeeb did look at him. The look suggested he thought Barton very dumb.

"Good God, man. The bank hasn't seen this much traffic in a decade. Haven't you noticed? Fire and finance. Finance and fire. They always go together."

Barton nodded. Relief washed over him. Zeeb didn't see anything wrong after all, didn't suspect Barton of a thing.

Zeeb closed the ledger, bored already with the "business of his business," as he might say, and suggested they get breakfast. Barton took him to a restaurant called Tiny's on Third Street, one of the few downtown eateries operating out of its original building rather than a tent. As they walked, Zeeb offered commentary on all he saw. Though he said he'd come to Spokane Falls to speak with the insurance men, and also the mayor, it was clear his personal interest was in sightseeing—to view the fire's aftermath firsthand, and to delight in the horror of it.

"This is a good thing," he said. "It may not seem like it now, with everything in shambles and that awful smell, but a phoenix is going to rise out of these ashes. This city is too important not to build back up and when it does, it will be better. It was such a hole before—could hardly be worse."

Barton, who'd never had any love for Spokane Falls himself, felt a twinge of slight at Zeeb's remark. Who was this man, an outsider, to come in and pass judgment?

"Take Seattle, for instance," Zeeb continued. "They burned two months ago and they're already doing big things. The area where their fire happened was like hell incarnate before, just bad hotels and brothels with ugly whores. Now it's going to be a real part of the city—the sort of place folks actually want to go and conduct business. It will be the same here. Why, I wouldn't be surprised if many of the city's struggling residents take the disaster as an opportunity to remake themselves as well, if that makes any sense."

And here Barton agreed, genuinely, that it did.

Zeeb did not stay long. He ate fast, talking of his beautiful wife, of his fun-loving mistresses, and of large breasts. Barton had let his mind wander and didn't know who the large breasts belonged to—the wife or one of the mistresses. He was thinking of things he would like to say about Roslyn. He could talk of her shy beauty (which he saw more clearly each passing day) and maybe also of her breasts, though he was modest and unlikely to reveal as much even to a close friend. Zeeb was no such friend. Then, as quickly as he arrived, Zeeb was gone, strolling down the street toward city hall to meet with the mayor. Spokane Falls, Zeeb had told Barton, was about to be inundated with monies from other cities in the name of charitable relief funds. The fire had made national headlines and people all over the country were keen to lend a hand. "Such generous times we live in," Zeeb said, though his voice was thick with sarcasm. The mayor wanted to speak with him about the best course of action for holding and spending these funds, the first of which—fifteen thousand dollars from the recently fire-ravaged Seattle—would be arriving that very day. Barton tried not to show his hurt that the mayor had sent for Zeeb rather than asking Barton's counsel on the matter.

"Why would Seattle send so much, when they have such a need for it themselves?" Barton asked Zeeb before he left.

"Because they need something else more," Zeeb said. "Statehood."

Zeeb said the fire was going to be good not only for Spokane Falls as a city, but for the whole of Washington Territory. These disasters gave civic leaders a chance to stand up and show their best selves to the nation. Look how strong Washington is: We can suffer and we can rebuild. We can help our neighbors in need. We can be brave and charitable, triumphant and selfless, all at once. What better for a region whose fate was to be decided by Congress that very fall? Seattle, Zeeb explained, as the territory's largest city, had the most to gain from statehood. And so they were willing to give the most to make it happen.

"I thought statehood was all but assured," Barton said. "That was my understanding. Montana, and the Dakotas, and us are all to be states by the end of the year."

Zeeb shook his head and his torrent of white hair ballooned to a wave of cloudlike beauty, then resettled perfectly in its place. "Nothing is ever a sure thing," he said. "I was there in Olympia in July when they ratified the constitution. I know the newspapers made it sound like a happy time for all, a real triumph of Western democracy. Oh no. The situation was tense. The delegates are a nervous lot. So much opposition for so long—no one trusts it will actually happen. Those of us in Walla Walla have been working toward this for nearly thirty years. But there are others who've got no need of the federal government and say so. They fear the oversight that will come with it—as if men from Washington, D.C., will be looking in their windows at night. Stupid, to give up not just the money but a seat at the table. Statehood doesn't put us under Congress's thumb, it gets us out from under it! Gives us a voice of our own. Anyway, Vancouver had a fire of their own in June and it's rumored theirs was arson. An anarchist expressing his views, or some such thing."

"Oh, yes. Of course," Barton said, though he'd known none of it.

"So, Seattle's doing their part. I imagine you'll see money from your other neighbors as well soon. Though perhaps not so much. It's all about who stands to gain. Who's going to come out ahead and all that. Like everything else."

Who's going to come out ahead, indeed. Barton had been rattled by Zeeb, fearing his schemes would be exposed. But there was no cause for concern. He'd been right all along. The chaos of the fire continued to provide cover for his actions. Zeeb, distracted, was looking everywhere except at his own bank.

Barton got a second unexpected visitor that day. It was Sam Flint, come to make the first of his loan payments. Flint held cash in his hand. "See, I told you I was good for it," he said, grinning proudly. Barton could not help grinning too. This, he thought, was a good thing.

Another good thing was waiting for him back home. Roslyn had emerged from her delirium. Just like in his fantasy, she was sitting in the parlor. She looked clean, with her hair pulled into a bun, but Barton could see when he got closer to her that her face was still pale and she appeared to be trembling slightly. When he leaned in to kiss her on her lips, she pulled away. Barton attributed this skittishness to nerves. He likewise found himself a little riled.

"It's good to see you up," he said, sitting beside her on his couch. "Are you feeling better?"

"Yes," Roslyn said.

"Did you take the medicines I brought you? They are from a druggist I know. He has an excellent reputation and suggested those remedies specifically for your case."

"No, I didn't."

After that, Barton didn't know what else to say. He tried talking about the bank, as he'd imagined in his daydream he might, but Roslyn did not nod with interest or put her hand on his knee in a supportive fashion. Instead, her eyes took on a kind of glazed-over look and her light trembling turned to fidgeting. He didn't bother with an impression of the Dwellers, thinking it would not be well received. He tried to turn the conversation back to her instead.

"Why have you stopped drinking your alcohol?" he asked. "Is it because of the fire? Are you feeling guilty you may have started the fire?"

"I didn't start the fire," she said, her eyes becoming alive again.

"I didn't say you started the fire. I said 'may have.' That's no certain indictment. I'm on your side here." His old lawyer habits— how quickly they returned when called upon.

At this, Roslyn dropped her gaze. "Are people saying I started the fire?"

"People are saying a lot of things. Many rumors, but no certainty yet. Don't worry though. I've been doing my best to keep them off your trail. Every time your name comes up, I say, 'No, not her.' But not so often as to suggest I have any connection to you at all. No one knows you're here. That's our secret."

Roslyn nodded. She seemed to be considering this. Barton thought she would thank him. Surely, if nothing else, now was the time she would put her hand on his knee to acknowledge his bravery in protecting her identity and location from whatever people she might believe he had been speaking to. But there was no such hand.

"I think I should go," she said.

Barton felt as if a hole had opened up in the middle of him and all his guts had fallen out at once.

"No, no," he said. "Why would you do that?"

Roslyn pressed into her eyes with her palms. "It just doesn't seem right," she said, "to stay here."

"But where would you go?"

She only shrugged.

"You can't go," Barton said. "I don't want you to go. I don't think you should. It's not a safe choice, with all that's going on out there. I don't want anything bad to happen to you."

Tears came into his eyes as he spoke, and he realized that what he'd said, while not based on real facts, was still true. If something were to happen to his Roslyn, he would surely die. He would kill himself—for real this time.

Roslyn's face had turned a shade paler and was devoid of expression entirely. She had her hands up like she'd just encountered an animal in the woods and was backing away slowly. But she wasn't backing away. She wasn't going anywhere. She stayed right in her seat next to Barton on the couch and said yes, all right, she would stay a while longer. Until it was safe.

———

She remembered a story her father had liked to tell her when she was small. It was a story from his own childhood, or so he said. It went like this. He had been out hunting with his cousins and got lost. He thought to stay put and call for the older boys, but he wanted to prove himself brave and resourceful. So, he set off in the direction he thought was camp. It was not. He walked for many hours, even as it began to snow. The snow grew thick and he could no longer see the ground beneath him. He sought shelter in a cave and felt himself lucky to have found it. But of course the cave was not empty. There was a bear in it, a sole bear with no cubs or companions. Her father feared he would be eaten, but the blizzard outside scared him more. He sat at the edge of the cave and looked at the bear. The bear looked at him. For two days they did this. He watched the bear and the bear watched back. He had no food or water and was too weak to leave even once the snow stopped. A search party from a nearby town found him and told him they could not believe he had passed the days with the bear. The bears in that region were ferocious and several villagers had suffered disfiguring injuries from them. "I always thought we had an understanding, that bear and I," he said. "A beautiful animal. I only wished I hadn't lost my rifle in the snow. I would like to have shot him and brought him back as a trophy."

At first, she did not believe in the bear. Then, she did not believe in the blizzard. Eventually, she questioned whether her dad had even been hunting. But still, she thought of the tale from time to time—of the things a person might do in extreme circumstances, and of the stories a person might tell themselves afterward.

———

II

The Dwellers were late again.

There was trouble with Jim's pass at the checkpoint even though it was the same guard who'd issued him the card a few days earlier. This time the guard had refused to acknowledge the document or let him through until some proof could be offered up of Jim's true identity and station. The brothers were explaining the trouble with proving this when Barton told them to shut the hell up, which they did, boring into him with their identical eyes a look of pure hate.

All day long, Barton seethed. He made unreasonable demands of the Dwellers, like insisting they polish the outside of the bank vault, deeming their work shoddy, making them start over, and spitting on the vault door to prove his point. The atmosphere in the bank became so tense that several people, upon walking in, stopped to look around as if sensing danger.

This was Roslyn's fault. Barton knew he was in a foul and cruel mood, as bad as days before the fire when he'd loathed himself completely. He was furious at Roslyn for not returning his affection. He had spent so much time thinking of her, imagining what it might be like when they would finally speak. And then, when they had, the very first thing she'd told him was that she wanted to be away from him. This rejection made him want her more. He was propelled forward in his love by the panic of not being loved.

Around noon, Del knocked a bottle of ink off the teller's desk and Barton threw a letter opener at him. After that, he retreated to his office, announcing in a voice that sounded wild even to him that he did not wish to be disturbed the rest of the day.

But not five minutes later, he was disturbed—by a familiar and unwelcome face. Bill Wolfe, the owner of the scorched lunchroom and hotel, stood in the doorway.

"Mr. Heydale," Wolfe said. "If I might have a moment of your time?"

This man was here for Roslyn. Barton was certain of it. He knew Barton was harboring her. Barton had given his heart to that woman and what did he get in return? Rejection, and now trouble from an angry pimp.

"I have nothing of value to you, sir. And now if you don't mind, I am very busy and will ask you to be on your way," Barton said, determined not to show his fear.

Wolfe gave him a look of concern. "I'm sorry to disturb you. But I need to discuss the matter of my insurance check," he said, producing this item from his shirt pocket.

Barton flushed. Just as with Zeeb the day before, he had misinterpreted the situation. Wolfe went on to say that he was eager to begin rebuilding his hotel. The new version would be much improved. It would be larger and classier. In fact, in a certain light, he felt the fire had actually been a blessing—a chance to start fresh. The old hotel, he'd be the first to admit, had grown a little ramshackle in recent years.

"So now it's just a matter of getting the funds secured, which I am thinking I would like to keep in an account here. Does that seem wise? I'm embarrassed to say it, but I've never been much of a bank person before. I suppose you already knew that. Anyway, I want to get back to business as soon as possible.

"And then you can get back to seeing your girl," Wolfe added.

"She's dead," Barton said.

"No, she's not," Wolfe said.

"If she's not dead, then where is she?"

"Well, I don't know. Staying with a friend, I assume. Is that what's making you uncomfortable? I can ask around. Or find you another girl in the meantime."

Barton wondered what this man's relationship to Roslyn had been. She'd lived in his hotel and he'd arranged clients for her. He'd been the one to send Barton up to her when he, a nervous new arrival in Spokane Falls, was first looking for a particular sort of company. Had anything ever exchanged hands between him and Roslyn besides money? Had he ever been unkind? As Wolfe spoke, Barton was beset by an image of him and Roslyn together, having sex, Wolfe on top, and then behind her, grunting, talking, saying things about insurance and construction costs. Reality and fantasy crashed together in his mind. He shook his head in an effort to rid himself of this picture.

"You should reconsider," Wolfe said, taking Barton's headshake for an answer to his question. "It's really no big deal. I'm happy to help. Just like you can help me here, with my money and such."

Barton would be of no such help. He told Wolfe he couldn't take his check, or open an account for him at the bank. He gave vague excuses, cited various processes thrown into disarray by the fire and whatnot.

"But might I offer you a loan instead?" he asked.

Wolfe, irksomely unfazed, declined. He said he would try back in a day or two. He took his leave of Barton's office then, but not of the bank entirely. A moment later, Barton heard the man's laugh carrying from the lobby. When Barton went to his office door, he was met with another unsettling vision: Wolfe, the Dwellers, and a uniformed police officer all standing together, cackling like witches.

Barton made for the teller's desk, thinking he might be able to overhear their conversation if he pretended he had work to do there. But he was quickly sighted by Wolfe, who waved him over.

"Heydale, we were just talking about you," he said, his voice too loud, too friendly.

For once, Barton hoped the laughter had only been for his bad haircut.

"This is Police Chief Hornsweller," Wolfe continued. "He and his men have been a tremendous help to me these past few days at the hotel, with the investigation and all."

"We're helping too," Del added. "We're going to be deputized."

"Well, now, that's not exactly what I said." Hornsweller was a thick man and he extended a meaty hand that engulfed Barton's when he shook it. He seemed, like Zeeb, comfortable in his largeness.

"And you've come here with Mr. Wolfe today to talk about his insurance settlement?"

"Nah, we just bumped into each other," Hornsweller said. "The

mayor asked me to visit our city's institutions to make sure everything's still smooth sailing since the fire. Your assistants were giving me a tour."

"And are you finding it to be? Smooth sailing?" Barton asked.

"Are you?"

Barton looked into the police chief's eyes but could read nothing
in them. He decided this meant the man was either very smart or
very dumb.

"Absolutely," he said. "Please let me know if there is any further
information I can provide to you."

"We're already doing that for him," Del said.

"That's what I'm afraid of," Barton said, and forced a laugh—to
show he too was the sort of man who could laugh amiably in the
lobby of his bank. A helpful fellow with nothing to hide. But neither Wolfe nor Hornsweller took the bait. The only one to chuckle
at Barton's joke was, inexplicably, Del.

12

Roslyn was waiting for him in the parlor. Just like the night before, she was sitting in a way that looked uncomfortable, but this time, when he entered the room she gave him a little smile. It was such a small gesture, but for Barton it contained all the light in the world and he was, for a moment, struck near blind with the joy of its brightness.

"You look so lovely," he said. "You should be in a museum."

"I went to a natural history museum once in Tacoma," Roslyn said. "They had animals that had been shot and stuffed for everyone to look at. Is that the sort of thing you mean?"

Barton balked, ashamed she could think him capable of such a horrific suggestion. But no! He realized that wasn't really what she meant. She was teasing him. Teasing was good in a romantic relationship, wasn't it? Like flirting? He smiled but didn't know what to say. Roslyn broke the silence.

"I'm feeling rather hungry," she said. "Is there anything I could eat?"

Of course! Barton told her to wait right where she was. He hustled himself to the kitchen. He had a woman who cooked for him every other day. She delivered the meals while he was at work, leaving them in a wooden icebox on his back porch. He'd seen the woman only a handful of times in the years he'd employed her, but he liked her food just fine, so he saw no reason to augment their arrangement. He paid her by leaving money in the icebox.

That night's dinner was pork with beans and bread. Barton heated the food on his stove, then put it on plates and found there was more than enough for two servings. He wanted his first meal with Roslyn to be nice, so he lit a candle on the dining room table. Then he went and retrieved her from the parlor as if he were a waiter at a restaurant. "Right this way," he said, and was pleased when she followed.

Barton had thought after so many days without food, Roslyn would be ravenous. He was expecting to see her devour her plate. He'd been looking forward to that—watching her do something animal-like again. Instead she ate slowly, taking her time, her face slightly pinched, as if she did not like the food but felt obligated to consume it.

After a while of this slow, unenthusiastic eating, she paused.

"What's it like downtown now?" she asked.

"It's a smoldering hellhole," Barton said. "Whatever wasn't burned up in the fire, the looters and vandals have gotten to. It's gang warfare in the streets, practically. Very dangerous. Very awful."

"Is it true it's the worst fire in history like the paper said?"

"If anything, I'd say that's an understatement."

"That's terrible," Roslyn said, her hand to her mouth. Barton was pleased to hear the wavery tremor of fear in her voice.

"Don't worry," he said. "You're safe as long as you're here with me."

"What about your bank? It wasn't harmed?"

"No, no. The bank was saved. You and the bank, the two things most precious to me, safe and sound. I feel God must truly be watching over me. I think he'll continue to do so. To watch over both of us, together."

He was sawing with a knife at a piece of pork when he said this and did not look up to see Roslyn's reaction. But he was confident that had he done so, he would have found her face alight with pleasure.

The woman who had nearly broken his heart the night before—that Roslyn was not the same person as the Roslyn seated before him now. Barton felt sure the previous evening's Roslyn was still suffering the effects of her alcohol withdrawal and that had put her into a state of mind not quite her own. It had forced her to say things she didn't mean—like that she should leave. Illness had made her paranoid. Or modest. Or ashamed. Barton wasn't sure what feeling might have led to her desire to leave him. But he was certain now it was not a dislike of him or his home. Surely, right-minded Roslyn was fond of him. She felt indebted and grateful to him for all he had done for her these past few days, and now that she was well, she was excited to become a more active participant in their domestic life together, and their budding relationship.

All of this was confirmed for Barton when, after dinner, Roslyn took him by the hand and led him into his own bedroom. She took her clothes off and lay on his bed, a place where no one except him had ever been. He stood and stared for a moment, almost not believing what he was seeing. "Come on now," she said, gesturing for him, welcoming him to join her. Just like the maybe-widow had that night in his father's study. And for a second, he felt a rush of all the loneliness of his whole six years in Spokane Falls pulse through him, as if it were trying to leave his body. He thought he might cry. Never before had anyone known so completely and perfectly what he wanted. Not even his own mother when he was a little boy with simple little boy needs. He felt it possible that Roslyn could read his mind. That she knew him through and through.

―――――

The trains, which had marked her days at Wolfe's Hotel, could not be heard from Barton's hill house. Nor any of the other downtown sounds. Only the sawmill. Was there anywhere the sawmill could not be heard? The mountaintop? The middle of the ocean? The face of the waxing moon creeping out from the clouds?

Barton had clocks, but she did not wish to look at them.

―――――

13

At home with Roslyn, Barton fell into an easy routine. He came back from the bank each evening and she was always in the parlor. They would chat for a while. Rather, Barton would chat, telling her about the bank and his day, just like he'd imagined when she was sick. He also gave her reports on the status of post-fire Spokane. These he always embellished. Accounts of general lawlessness. Visible corruption of city officials. Orphans begging in the streets. A swarm of rats, grown fierce and canny, terrorizing local businesses. He said these things not because he still feared Roslyn might leave; that anxiety was gone. But more because he wanted her to feel he was very courageous, braving the feral, blackened streets each day.

They ate dinner together. Barton had left a note for his cook saying he would have company indefinitely and that he would adjust her payment to account for the extra portions if she would make them. Lavish meals began to appear in the icebox on the back porch—much more inspired than anything he'd known the woman to make when she was feeding only him. There was poached fish, large steaks of both beef and venison, greens with a tangy dressing, clever arrangements of fruit and nuts, and cakes and candies to accompany every meal. Barton took this as a sign that even this relative stranger was happy for him, and wished to help him celebrate his new love.

After dinner, there was more sitting in the parlor. Sometimes they talked, other times they read, and some nights they played cards. Roslyn could play a little piano and tinkered with the one in his parlor—mostly the same tune, which was both cheery and sad at once and which was somehow so familiar to Barton, though he was certain he had not heard it before. "Won't you play your song again?" he would ask, trying to place it, and she always complied. Some nights, also, there was sex. Like before, Roslyn would, out of the blue, take his hand and lead him to his bedroom, disrobe, and beckon. Other times, she would retire to her own room without him. He was not disappointed when this happened. And on evenings when she bade him good night this way, he always resolved that he would stay put in his parlor and respect what he now saw as her very reasonable desire for time to herself. After all, even history's greatest lovers could not be with one another every second. But then, some nights his more base impulses would get the better of him and he'd follow Roslyn into the guest room and make love to her anyway. These times she'd lie still and let him do what he liked, just as if they were in his bedroom. Just as if they were in her old apartment at Wolfe's Hotel. Afterward, he went to sleep right beside her, content, thinking nothing at all.

––––

His contentment carried into his daytime hours at the bank. He went about his daily tasks of serving customers and keeping his ledgers. He gave usurious loans and Barton-certified banknotes at every opportunity. He kept his books straight as could be, hoarding a separate pile of money in the smallest of his desk drawers to keep the balance accurate, taking that excess home at night tucked securely in the pockets of his pants and vest. He whistled as he did these chores. Smiled at all visitors. Gave supportive slaps on the back to the Dweller twins, who scowled at this, thinking he'd invented some new way of mocking them. "What's the big idea?" one or the other would ask. But Barton only shrugged and smiled. He paid no attention to customers skeptical of his banknotes, the way they would fold them, hold them to the light, even smell them. Some grumbled at being given nonstandard currency. Barton didn't hear this. Didn't hear when the grumblers took their grumbling to the Dwellers. Took no notice of the occasional presence of Jep Hornsweller or, more frequently, his deputies, in and around the bank, talking to the Dwellers, or leaning against the building, smoking cigarettes. He sent telegrams to Zane Zeeb every few days. ALL'S FINE IN SPOKANE. EVERYTHING GREAT. THE BUSINESS OF BUSINESS IS THRIVING.

14

S am Flint had been the first person to take a 30 percent loan and the first to make a payment, but he wasn't the only one. Barton was pleased with the rate of return he was getting from his borrowers. They were honest, the people of Spokane Falls. More honest than he'd given them credit for in the past. Even the man who'd wanted a loan to sell his fraudulent and probably dangerous lung medicine had begun to make payments. "Can't make the stuff fast enough," he'd said when Barton asked after his business. "I sell out by noon every day." The banknotes were fun, Barton felt, but outside of the insurance check cashers, most people weren't asking for large amounts, which meant Barton wasn't taking large amounts home. Just a little walking-around money—someone needing to pay the grocery tab or the milkman, a dollar to slip inside a beloved child's birthday card. It was the loans that really thrilled him.

Only once had anyone questioned Barton's terms. It was a husband and wife who'd come into his office together, nice-looking folks. *They'll ask for something big,* Barton had thought, and he'd been right. Anyway, it was the wife who'd gotten in his face when he said 30 percent.

"Now wait a moment," she said. "My father's in finance and I happen to know—"

But the husband cut her off. "Dear, perhaps this isn't your place." She was quiet after that and the husband signed everything he needed to sign with no further trouble, not even a look of concern on his part. They'd made their first payment already too, with Barton calculating his cut as soon as he saw them enter the bank.

Initially, Barton had no plan for what to do with his stolen money. The money itself was never the point. He wanted the power that came with the money and the satisfaction of taking it from a place that had rendered him small, pitiful, and childlike for more than half a decade. It was his Big Man money. Something to stand upon and feel himself taller.

But it was currency, still. And shouldn't it be used as such?

Roslyn was the one to make him think this. He had someone else in his life to consider now. He decided he'd use the money to make his escape from Spokane Falls. He wasn't going to be able to stay forever anyway. It was the chaos of the fire and its aftermath that had allowed him to steal from the bank in the first place. Once that chaos had subsided, Spokane Falls would take stock of its institutions. There'd again be oversight and attention to detail. He'd be caught. So, before that happened, he needed to be long gone. And that was what the money was good for. He and his lady would head out on a marvelous adventure.

He'd take Roslyn and they'd go east, back to one of the country's truly great and established cities. There, they'd start a new life, together. They would pick new names, rewrite their own histories. He'd claim to be a baron, and adopt an accent. Roslyn could be an artist. Or better yet, an heiress. It didn't matter what she was an heiress to. In fact, best perhaps not to specify. Let the neighbors guess. They would come up with far grander assumptions than anything Barton and Roslyn might invent.

If he could do this, Roslyn would be beholden to him not just for saving her from trouble in Spokane Falls, but for providing her with a lavish and wonderful lifestyle. Love is always strongest when it's based in debt, Barton the banker thought.

"Have you ever imagined what you might want your life to be like if you were rich?" he asked her one night.

She seemed to consider this question seriously. "I think if I were rich, I'd like to use my money to help people. Children especially. I'd like to help children who need it in some way."

"You are so wonderful and kind, always thinking of others," Barton said. "But don't you feel now is the time in your life when you ought to think of yourself? To take care of yourself first? For example, have you ever dreamed of living someplace other than Spokane Falls?"

"I have lived someplace else," Roslyn said. "I'm not actually from here, originally."

Barton nodded but did not hear this answer. He had slipped into a daydream in which he and Roslyn were riding in a carriage through some stately and well-lit city. They were wearing very fine clothes and their hands were clasped together as he imagined all lovers clasped their hands when riding in carriages. They were laughing. Barton did not extend his daydream so far as to know what the joke was, but in his mind he and Roslyn were having a grand and hilarious time.

"Me too," Barton said. "But don't worry. Someday I'll take you there."

*She looked in the mirror in Barton's bathroom and her face was familiar
again. For days, her face had looked washed out, gray and ghostly. Then,
for a while, it seemed smudged. She had cleaned the mirror, thinking it
dusty, but the mirror was fine. Her sickness had wracked her inside and
out. At first, she had vomited, lost consciousness, awoken only to vomit
more. She struggled to stand, moving on hands and knees instead. She was
always hot, her heart thudding too fast. She thought she might die. But then
the violence of the illness had given way, replaced by heavy fatigue and
disorientation. She slept all the time, unable to separate dreams from reality. Now that too had passed, but she remained unwell. Her thoughts came
too slowly. Making decisions was like walking through mud. She was nauseated even when she was hungry. She could not imagine navigating the
streets of Spokane Falls in this state and so she gave in to inertia. The days
in Barton's home fused together. Every morning, she woke and took stock:
still sick.*

*But here the mirror said otherwise, and that was almost as troubling
as when she'd looked as deathly as she felt. A lie. Though there was no one
to see it. No one to see it but Barton, whom surely the mirror also deceived
with regard to his own well-being.*

15

In spite of all his new grand plans, Barton's stolen cash soon posed an unexpected problem: he ran out of places to store it.

At first, it fit fine in his dresser. Then he moved on to wedging bundles of it under his mattress. This made his bed lumpy and uncomfortable. Also, it would take a thief only a matter of seconds in Barton's room to find a small fortune. He needed something more discreet. He decided the best way to secure money in his house was to keep it literally inside the house—in its very structure.

So, early one morning, Barton began the process of knocking fist-size holes in the walls of the parlor and adjoining hallway. He'd filled every bag and sack he could find in his house with cash, and when he ran out of those, he wrapped wads of money in towels, then shirts.

Roslyn emerged from the guest room while he was stuffing these bundles into the holes. She regarded him with a sleepy look he thought charming.

"Sorry for all the noise, dear," he said. "Just fixing up the house a little."

Roslyn assessed the bundles on the floor. She kicked at one with her big toe. When the money spilled forth, she nodded. As if it were exactly what she'd expected.

"Where's it from?" she asked.

"The bank," Barton said.

"Shouldn't it be at the bank, then?"

"Well," he said, "most of the money is at the bank, but for various reasons of law and bureaucracy, I am also required to keep some here. It's somewhat complicated, so I won't bore you with the specifics."

Roslyn nodded again. "My father was a grifter," she said.

Barton tried to conceal his surprise, and then his horror.

"It's not grift," he said. "I know it may seem odd, but I assure you any banker in the country has such holes in his wall for the very same purpose. It is the most common of practices."

Roslyn shrugged. "Who am I to judge how another person makes their money? Everyone does what they need to do to get by. That's what my father used to say."

Then she disappeared back into the guest room, leaving Barton to his chore.

He didn't like the idea of Roslyn believing him a criminal. He wanted to maintain what he thought to be his carefully crafted persona of the white knight: her prince and her savior. He couldn't be that if he was a thief.

There was something else that unsettled Barton about this interaction. He was struck, more than anything else, by the sense that Roslyn had known immediately what he was up to. Even before she saw the money, she'd known.

16

The Dwellers, all of a sudden, were acting like they knew things too. They began peppering Barton with unusual questions. And when he gave answers contrary to what the brothers seemed to want to hear, they offered an unbelieving "Huh." Barton wondered if they, of all people, would be the first to cast scrutiny on his shady dealings. He was almost proud of them for figuring him out. He took their newfound canniness to be a sign of his own success as bank manager. Until it became clear to him the questions were all circling around a different topic: the fire.

Del: So, you know Bill Wolfe pretty well?

Barton: No, not well.

Del: Huh. I thought he was a friend of yours.

Barton: No, not a friend.

Del: So then he's your enemy? Like Chief Hornsweller?

Barton: What's that? My enemy? No. Chief Hornsweller and I are on very collegial terms. What makes you think otherwise?

Jim: Huh. No matter. Bill Wolfe said you used to spend a lot of time at his hotel.

Barton: I used to eat lunch there, yes.

Del: Is that what people are calling it these days?

Barton: I don't take your meaning.

Jim: Say, when was the last time you went by the hotel? Before it burnt up, I mean?

Other times, they said their *Huh*s when Barton confirmed something the Dwellers already knew. Barton couldn't decide if this was better or worse.

Jim: You're not from Spokane Falls, are you?

Barton: No. I moved here from Portland.

Del: Huh. Why would anyone come to little old Spokane Falls from big-city Portland? Don't people usually go the other direction? Do you find that odd, Jim?

Jim: A little odd, yes.

Barton: I had my reasons.

Del: Oh, I'll bet you did.

Del: Say, Jim, wasn't there a fire in Portland too? Wasn't Portland destroyed by a fire?

Jim: I believe it was, Del.

Barton: Yes. It was in 1873. Downtown was mostly wiped out.

Del: Downtown wiped out! Just like here! Imagine. And you were there for that?

Barton: Yes. I was a child. I lived at home with my family.

Del: Huh.

Jim: Huh.

After a few days, he learned to read a threat in those *Huh*s. They

were the sound of someone biding his time—biding their time—
until they found the right moment to use the information they'd
gained. Even if the information was false, nonsensical.

Jim: You were in Seattle in June, weren't you?

Barton: No. I was here. I've been here every day for the last six
years.

Jim: Huh. That's funny. I thought you went to Seattle. The way
I remember it, you'd gone to Seattle in June. I'll have to ask Del,
but I bet he remembers it that way too.

Barton: But that's not possible. It isn't true.

Jim: It's not? Huh.

One night, Barton, flustered and seeking pity, told Roslyn about his
problem with the Dwellers.

"My employees are conspiring against me," he said.

"Is that so?" she asked.

Barton realized his mistake immediately. He could not tell Roslyn he feared scrutiny over the fire. It undermined so many of his
previous lies to her—namely that she was the one in danger of being
charged with the crime.

"Yes," he said. "I think they know I'm harboring you here. I
think they aim to blackmail me."

He looked Roslyn in the eye when he said this and expected to
see some fear in her as he had seen in the past when he mentioned
her being a suspect in the fire investigation. But he could not read
her reaction now, one way or the other.

"Is that so?" she asked again.

"They've been asking a lot of questions. All circling around you.

They haven't made any demands yet. But I presume they will shortly. Don't worry, though. I won't let them know the truth. As I've said before, I will continue to do all I can to protect you. You are very safe here. This is only a mild inconvenience to me."

"If they haven't asked for anything, maybe you aren't really being blackmailed," Roslyn said. "Maybe they're just collecting information for someone else."

She said this so calmly, like it wasn't speculation so much as fact. The Dwellers weren't suspicious of her in the slightest. It was all Barton's trouble, and she knew it.

It cracked him right through, this revelation of hers. She was not the caged bird, eating only from his hand. She could form conclusions of her own, based on information beyond just what he offered. She might even know things he did not. He loved Roslyn and always would. But she was no longer a joy and a comfort to him. From here on out, she was back to being a source of real concern. And so too entered a whole host of other concerns, both old and new.

―――

Then, miraculously, one morning she felt better. The fatigue, the nausea, the slow-wittedness—gone. She did not feel new in her skin; she simply felt like herself, which was best anyway. She breathed deep, stretched her limbs gone weak from days of inactivity, and for the first time since arriving at Barton's home, made a thorough assessment of her surroundings.

―――

An Event from the Unreal Past

B arton was a boy and dressed as a devil. His costume was the homemade kind of devil: long johns dyed red, with a strip of tail-shaped fabric attached to the back and a headband with horns, also red. He felt he should have a pitchfork. He thought he used to have a pitchfork. He'd lost it somewhere. The red long johns were comically large on him. The collar slumped off one shoulder and the crotch hung to his knees. Underneath the long johns, he wore his regular clothes. In the pocket of his regular pants was a book of matches. They were stolen from his father and he took pleasure in patting his pocket every so often to remind himself.

He was out in the streets of an unfamiliar neighborhood, hot sweating in his sad devil outfit. It was not his birthday or any other occasion when he might have been encouraged to dress up. It was hot like summer.

Also, there was smoke. The air swirled with it. Chunks of flaming ash matter fell from the sky. Barton delighted in these projectiles. He prodded at them with the toe of his shoe when they landed nearby. There was a big fire somewhere close. He wanted to see it. That was why he was in that neighborhood. It had a tall hill and he wanted to get to the top so he could look down below.

Barton was a husky child. He wheezed through the smoke and sweated in his inexplicable costume. He didn't mind. He was too focused on his goal of getting to the top of the hill—too excited by the disaster unfolding around him.

After a while, he found he was not alone. He hadn't seen anyone else on his walk. They were all inside, away from the smoke and falling ash. But now there was someone with him, a woman, walking at his side. He wasn't alarmed by her arrival. He thought it fine to have company.

"Do you like this?" the woman asked.

Barton nodded his head.

"That's good," she said. "I'm very proud of you."

He didn't know what she meant by this. The woman was also wearing a devil costume, but unlike his, her costume was professionally made and included a mask that hid her eyes and nose. Barton was jealous. Even with the top of her face hidden, she was quite pretty—younger than his mother but older than the oldest girls at his school. Her voice was deep, throaty even. He wanted to hear it again.

"Do you like the fire?" he asked.

"Oh, yes," the woman said. "You did a great job."

Barton still didn't know what she meant and this time said so.

The woman only laughed. Then, in a motion that seemed both casual and violent, she lunged toward him, reaching with a red-gloved hand for the crotch of his devil outfit. Barton, afraid she was grabbing for his genitals, jumped back, though not far enough to escape her grasp. It wasn't his little-boy penis she was after. What she got was the book of matches, holding it through Barton's double layer of clothes.

"Clever, clever boy," she said through her smile. It was a friendly smile and it scared the hell out of him. All around them, flaming ash fell until it looked to Barton as if the whole sky was on fire and it was coming down upon him.

These images infested Barton's mind during his waking hours. It was not a dream because he was not asleep. And it was not a day-dream because he wasn't in control of it. It felt like remembrance. But there was nothing real in the memory. Not the devil suit or the matches or even the vision of the fire in the distance. The day Portland burned, Barton had been working at his father's office. He kept messing up his assigned project, resulting in constant scolding and nasty name-calling from his dad. He didn't even know the fire had happened until the end of the day when he walked home through the sooty evening, feeling choked by both the air and the oppressive discontent of his father's company. This true memory sat side by side with the new false one.

The scenes and sensations of the false memory upset him. He could not control when they entered his mind. He feared something sinister was taking hold of him.

The false memory was hooked into his brain the same as the song Roslyn played on the piano. Like it had been buried only to be revived, never really belonging there in the first place.

17

B arton took what Roslyn had said about the Dwellers to heart.
They weren't bright enough to come up with a scheme to blackmail him on their own. It seemed obvious now that they were trying
to collect information for someone else. Was it Bill Wolfe? Zane
Zeeb? Or were they reporting directly to Hornsweller? Barton
thought back to Del's claim that he and Jim were to be deputized,
perhaps not so absurd now after all.

Barton imagined Hornsweller and his men gathering evidence
as part of an elaborate endeavor to trap him. He envisioned a plot
that went far beyond Spokane Falls—officials from across the territory working together to prove his guilt. Zeeb had said the fire
was good for Washington because it would show how the region
could work in a statelike manner. Well, what would be better for
that than snaring a crooked banker? He might end up the crown-
ing achievement of Washingtonian collaboration. Hundreds of
uniformed men closing in on him, and politicians eager to hold him
up to the federal government as proof of a territory ready for state-

hood. *If we can capture Barton Heydale together, we can do anything,* they'd say.

Surely, now was the time to go. Get out of Spokane Falls before the dragnet was sprung. That was always his intention. But there was no plan behind the plan. It was only an idea, a daydream. Where, exactly, would he and Roslyn go? How would he ensure they weren't followed? How would he transport his stolen money safely, and where would he store it once he arrived, and how would he spend it without raising suspicion? How would he explain all this to Roslyn? He needed time to work it out. But what if he was out of time? What if he was already caught? What if he was not caught, acted too soon, and got himself caught as a result?

He worked himself into a fever of anxiety thinking of all this. The shimmering lights that had appeared to him the night of the fire, where were they now? He wanted that confidence back, that decisiveness. He was lost without it.

He sat in his office at the bank with the door closed and rocked himself in his chair. His mind circled the possibilities that awaited him with each choice he could make. All seemed to end in jail or worse. And then, intermittently, there was the devil woman from his false memory, making him feel guilty. Guilty for something he had not done.

How strange, when the crimes he had actually committed evoked in him no such feeling.

Each knock at the door jarred him. The Dwellers noticed this and deliberately exacerbated the situation by banging with fists as loudly as they could whenever they wanted his attention.

Worst of all, on the way home that evening, Barton had a vision of Zane Zeeb. It was another hot day with the temperature rising as the day went on. Downtown still stank of smoke, char, and rot. Plus, there was ash again, this time from nearby mountain wildfires. These fires turned the sky orange with smoke. Forest animals had been spotted in town, driven out of their dens and burrows. People were warned to be vigilant of wolf packs. A black bear had been seen sleeping behind a butcher shop. In earlier weeks, Barton would have delighted in repeating these horrors to Roslyn, embellishing details to make the scene even more awful than it already was. But he no longer had energy for the charade. He kept his eyes on his feet as he walked. He felt weak from the strain of the day's anxiety, and had to pause every few blocks to clear spots from his eyes. He worried he was not breathing in a regular fashion. It was during one of these spot-clearing stops that he saw Zeeb. Barton was bent at the knees, trying to regain balance and composure. When he felt it was safe to stand straight, he was nearly doubled over once more by the image of his employer, sauntering with all his usual poise on the next street over. The vision of the man wavered in the horrible heat, but Zeeb's regal white hair seemed to defy this phenomenon. It radiated a kind of still clarity, even as the head it was attached to moved out of Barton's line of sight. Barton was certain he was hallucinating.

Once home, he told Roslyn he felt ill. She nodded in a way he interpreted as sympathetic, then disappeared into the guest room and returned with the two vials of liquid Barton had bought weeks earlier from the pharmacy. He'd forgotten what they were, or if he'd been given instructions about dose. He took both in their entirety and let Roslyn lead him to his own bed.

"My dear Roslyn, I feel myself slipping down into madness.

You're the only thing holding me up," he confided as the medications wrapped his eyes and ears in a gauzy hug.

He'd hoped she would lie down with him, but he fell so quickly into sleep that he could not tell if she was beside him or not.

She wasn't.

In the morning, Barton woke feeling as if he hadn't slept at all. He went to work anyway. He had never missed a day before. He didn't consider it an option.

———

She used to think Barton was an important man. He was the manager of the bank, always dressed nice and speaking coolly in his deep voice. The other women at the hotel chided her for keeping him as a client. "Gah, the damn banker! What's wrong with you? You might as well be fucking a cop," Kate said once.

But she didn't see him that way, not as bad as the cops, no. After all, no one ever forced anyone else to keep their money in the bank. She herself kept what little money she had in a can with a screw-top lid inside her dresser. So what? But of course she knew that wasn't the issue. The existence of the bank reinforced the power of those who could use the bank over those who couldn't. Money always makes more money for the people who have the money. And then they wield it to hold down everyone else, to foreclose on houses, hike up rents, raise interest, raise prices on things people need just to live.

When she first moved to Spokane Falls, there was no bank yet, and no rich people. Well, there were a few rich men, the ones who owned everything. But no big houses on the South Hill or in Browne's Addition, no nice restaurants, no trouble from the police about who could live where or do what kind of work. People from the Spokane tribe still came to camp by the river sometimes then, before the cavalry made them go elsewhere; Roslyn didn't know where. She had tried to tell Barton once that Spokane means Children of the Sun, which she thought was a beautiful name, but he didn't seem to understand. He was a good deal younger than she, though he acted like he knew more. All the men did. "Have you ever considered cutting his dick off?" Kate asked another time, and she'd laughed along with her. Still, she had taken some pride in having him as her client. As if just by associating with that cruel sort of power, she could have a little of it for her own.

Now, though, he did not seem powerful or important. Nor did he seem young, for that matter. Everything about him was suddenly slightly askew, his hair and clothes and even the way he walked. His voice had taken on a tinny quality. Something had happened to him between the last time he'd come to Wolfe's and the day he'd met her on the street and taken her to his home. She was certain of this, though she could not guess what. It had made him desperate, and maybe dangerous, like a baby rattlesnake full of venom and easily spooked.

But she had known this kind of man before and was not afraid. Like with snakes, the key was to move slow. Disguise yourself to make him believe you are neither predator nor prey.

———

18

B ut again, there was Zeeb.
Over the next two days, Barton sighted him repeatedly—
strolling through downtown, perched on a stool in a tent bar, eating
a hot dog from a vendor's cart, and even riding along the river on
a very tall horse. Barton was now certain Zeeb was no psychic
illusion. He was the real flesh-and-blood man. But he never entered the bank, at least not during business hours when Barton was
there.

This wracked Barton. Zeeb never came to Spokane Falls without visiting the bank. Popular as he was, the bank was always his
first stop. It was his most pressing place of interest, and normally
the reason for his travel. Zeeb was fantastically devoted to all his
banks. For him to come to Spokane Falls and avoid the bank entirely could only mean that something was very wrong.

Barton, of course, assumed the thing that was wrong was him.
If only he could act. Pick a direction, any direction, and go.

He could not. And if he could not act, he at least wanted confirmation that his fears were rooted in fact. Though he knew in his heart they'd be no help, he asked the Dwellers.

He skulked out of his office and pulled the twins away from the teller's desk and into a corner, where their conversation could be more private, even though there was no one else in the bank.

"Has either of you seen or spoken to Mr. Zeeb in the past several days?" Barton asked, his voice low, head tipped a little more conspiratorially than he intended.

"Who?" It was Del who spoke first, his face twisted in mock confusion.

"Mr. Zane Zeeb. The proprietor of this bank. Have you spoken with him?"

"We don't know who you're talking about," Jim said. Then both Dwellers gave elaborate childlike shrugs.

"Goddammit," Barton said. "Stop this. Whatever it is you're doing, stop it and answer my questions. Have you seen the man who owns this bank recently?"

"Yep," Jim said. "I've seen the man who owns the bank."

"Okay," Barton said. "When did you see him? Did he talk to you?"

"I'm looking at him right now. I talk to him all the time."

Barton turned around, expecting to see Zeeb just behind him, ready to pounce. But there was no one.

"What are you talking about?" Barton asked. "What the hell do you mean?

"It's Jim," Del said. "Jim's the owner of this bank. I'm looking at him right now. I talk to him all the time. Every day."

"Nah, I'm not the owner of this bank." Jim said. "Del is. It's my brother Del that owns it."

"No, it's Jim."

"No, it's Del."

"No, it's Jim."

Barton's eyes spotted over, as they had walking home in the heat two days prior, then, for a moment, he saw only blackness. Through the blackness, he thought he saw flames.

"Please stop this charade," is what he tried to say. But the sound that came out of his mouth was something entirely different. A jagged garble of noises, not his voice at all. It frightened him. He thought it would frighten the Dwellers as well. Though when his sight returned to him, they were smiling. Whatever was happening to him, they were pleased by it.

19

For Barton, the final straw came on a Friday afternoon. It was five days after he first started seeing Zeeb (who had yet to visit the bank) around town, ten days since the Dweller twins began their campaign of psychological terror against him, and almost four weeks since the city of Spokane Falls burned and Roslyn came to live in his home. This was the moment when the trouble he'd brought upon himself finally slipped from his control and he knew for certain he could not carry on with his life as it had been any longer.

It didn't happen the way he'd imagined. Instead, it was a woman he did not recognize at first, standing in front of his desk like a person with normal banking business to conduct. She was small and slim, about his mother's age. Her face was pleasant. But when Barton asked what she needed, she leaned in close and hissed, "I want more money," with a voice he was certain must have come straight from hell.

This person before him looked nothing like the devil woman

from his false memory, and did not sound like her either. But somehow he knew in his heart it was her. She seemed so familiar. He could not imagine who else it might be, this harbinger of evil.

"You don't even know who I am, do you?" the woman said in her horrible voice.

Barton took this as further confirmation of his suspicion.

"Fuck you," she said. "I'm only the person who's been making you dinner for half a decade."

So, then, not the devil. Instead, his cook.

"I'm sorry," he said, "I don't follow. You're asking for a raise?"

"In a way, yes," she said, and smiled.

In the past, Barton would have told her no and sent her quickly on her way. His father had always said one must take a hard line with the help. This was one of the few points on which the Heydale men had agreed.

But on this day, Barton felt he did not have the energy for the hard line. He wanted a quick resolution to this conversation and no trouble. Even though he now knew this woman was not the devil, she still made him very nervous.

He asked her how much more she would like.

"A thousand dollars," she said without hesitation.

It was such an outrageous sum. All Barton could think to say was, "I believe that's too much for a week's meals."

"I don't want to cook meals for you anymore, you idiot," the woman said. "I want you to give me a thousand dollars and then I'll go away. Otherwise, I'll tell about the woman in your house."

Barton, dumbstruck, said nothing.

"No one's supposed to know about her, right?" the woman said. "She's not your wife. It's a big secret."

Someone had gotten to her, Barton thought. Asked her to do a little snooping on him, to see what she could find. How easy! Get his cook to spy; he'll never suspect! And sure enough, she had information worth telling. But, crooked bitch, here she was, trying to get something extra out of the deal—a thousand dollars not to report back what she knew.

"And if I give you the money, you will keep this to yourself?" he asked.

"Yes, that's the deal," she said.

"What assurance can you give me of this? That you won't just take your money and then tell anyway?"

The cook shrugged. "Can't, I suppose."

Barton stood up from his desk and went to the vault. He gathered the cash, counted it twice as he always did, and returned to his office. When the cook saw what was in his hands, she made no effort to conceal her pleasure.

"Just tell me one thing," Barton said. "Who are you working for?"

The cook looked at him like she didn't understand the question. "I work for myself. I always have."

She took the money from his hands, put it into her purse, and left the bank. Barton sat in his chair for five minutes. He counted the seconds to make sure. He did not want to arouse suspicion by moving too quickly. What he would do, he thought, was go home and get a thousand dollars out of his walls and return it to the vault, covering the bank's loss to the cook. It was fine. He would take it all back again later via his tried-and-true methods.

But as he stepped out of the bank, he saw, finally, something he'd been expecting for the better part of a week. Zane Zeeb was heading toward him, his gait showing the purposeful confidence of a man on the way to visit his bank, to check his ledgers, to make sure the business of business was well and sound after all.

Barton turned and ran through the bank and out the back door.

He realized he might as well have taken the rest of the cash in the vault for himself while he was leaving. But by the time he thought of this, it was too late. He was already sprinting toward home. Later, he'd regret this oversight.

20

There was no way to hide what he'd done for the cook, and once that was discovered, no way to hide the rest either. There was a freedom in this, his options winnowed down to just one path.

Get Roslyn, pack clothes and supplies for both of them. Hire a coach out of town to Coeur d'Alene, pay double for the driver to keep his mouth shut if asked about his passengers. Get train tickets. Go east. Proper east. He'd let Roslyn pick the place. Wherever she thought would make her happy, that's where they'd go. And in that new place, he would thrive. He would find the success and the power and the health and the happiness he had so wanted but never gained in Spokane Falls. After all, he was a man in love. He had Roslyn and he had his money. What more could he need? The rest would follow. He was confident. He was not afraid anymore.

He ran. And as he ran, he laughed, overwhelmed by excitement for what would come next.

He crossed the Post Street Bridge at a gallop and headed up the hill. He was slick with sweat, his clothes and hair sticking to his skin.

He was certain this was the farthest and the fastest he had ever run in his life. But he wasn't tired at all. In fact, he was so shot through with energy, he didn't feel he could stop even if he had to. People gave him odd looks as he passed. He waved to a few and hoisted the middle fingers of both his hands to others, whatever he felt in the moment. Their reactions all seemed the same, dull slack faces a blur, indistinguishable in their stupidity. How pathetic everyone in that sad, burnt-out city was. Thank God he was on to bigger and better things.

He formulated a script in his mind for what he would say to Roslyn when he got home. How he would tell her of their new adventure, and how she would respond with equal excitement.

Barton: Darling! I have fantastic news!

Roslyn: Oh, what is it? Do tell.

Barton: I have taken steps to secure for us a new and better life.

Roslyn: It's just what I was hoping you'd say! When do we leave?

Barton: Right now! This very day! Gather your things!

She would kiss him then, deeply and passionately, but he would pull her free. They must move swiftly. He'd assure her there would be plenty of time later for her to show her gratitude in the form of fantastic lovemaking.

Then what? A lifetime of lovemaking, of course. A lifetime of everything with Roslyn. Their new world, built together from the spoils of Barton's hard work. Wonderful, wonderful. He felt this was surely the greatest day of his life. He was to be reborn a free man, a loved man, a big man.

He reached the front of his house—his former house!—and pulled open the door, already talking, already explaining his plan.

"Get your things together! Sweetheart! New life!" This was not the order in which he'd meant to say these words. He didn't think it mattered. He knew he would be understood. After all, his Roslyn always knew what he meant—better than he could ever say it himself.

She wasn't in the parlor, so Barton continued, ricocheting from room to room. "Leaving! The east! Money! Love! I've done it!"

The bedrooms were also empty of Roslyn, as were the kitchen, the backyard, the washroom. He was breathless now from his efforts. His limbs trembled. "Let's go! Sweet dear! You and me!" It was only as he made a second dash through the house that he noticed anything amiss. The holes he'd put in the hallway wall, filled, and then patched had been reopened. The job looked hasty, done with some crude tool like a kitchen knife. He forced himself to stop his running, to hold still and try to make sense of what he was seeing. He put a sweaty, jittery hand into one of the holes and found it empty. His bank money. All his Big Man plans. It was gone.

So, of course, was Roslyn.

———

A pleasant day, in spite of the heat and the rot in the air. She walked through town at a leisurely pace. No one noticed her. Just as no one had ever noticed her. Why should they?

———

Interlude I

B etween 1851 and 1853 a magician known as Irwin the Incendiary traveled the new state of California and the Oregon Territory performing his act. He delighted audiences with small displays of pyrotechnics. There was the lighting of a match on the opposite side of the stage, fireballs from his own hands, snapping firecrackers from seemingly nowhere. It was the sort of act that, developed thoughtfully, could have garnered real attention, earning him spots at theaters around the country. Instead, it had a carnival sideshow feel to it, all novelty but no substance. And indeed, Irwin was often on the carnival circuit. He also frequented mining and logging camps on holidays, when liquor flowed and he was free to practice another kind of magic after his shows—sleight of hand. Irwin was also a pickpocket. Between the commission from his shows and what he took on the side, he made a fine living. He had no grander ambitions.

Irwin was aided in his act by an assistant, Sweetheart Sheila. Sheila was young, barely out of her teens, and onstage it was her role to prance and gesture, to whip her long hair and smile her just slightly gap-toothed smile. She had freckles, which accentuated her youthfulness, and which the miners and loggers seemed to like, much to her chagrin.

"Sweetheart! The bowling pins!" Irwin would cry mid-show, and Sheila would arrange a half dozen pins for him to ignite one by one. This was the sort of thing the audience saw.

What they did not see: it was Sheila who made the flames.

Irwin met Sheila in the fall of 1850. She was standing on the bank of the Rogue River, setting fire to the tail feathers of passing ducks with only her fingertips. Irwin, who had been scratching out a career with card tricks and some clowning, saw an opportunity. Sheila, desperate to get away from her family and her childhood home, accepted an offer of work from him.

"What sort of magic will I do?" she asked.

"None," Irwin said. "A woman can't do magic. People will think she's a witch. I'll do the magic. You will help."

Still, Sheila went along.

But after two years, she had grown tired of Irwin's schtick.

The man was charming onstage, but a dullard and a bully once he was out of the spotlight. He treated Sheila less like an assistant and more like a bratty little sister he wished he could have left at home. She resented this. Also, though Sheila herself was no saint (as many a singed duck could attest), Irwin's penchant for petty theft grated on her. Didn't the men who came to their shows, seeking a rest after a long week of work, deserve to keep what they earned? Sheila sewed her own wages into secret pockets in her bedclothes to keep Irwin and his sticky fingers from taking them back.

She felt itchy, ill at ease, as she often had at home before she'd left with Irwin. But Irwin was not family and she owed him no grace.

"Tomorrow, how about I be the magician and you be the sweetheart?" Sheila asked Irwin one night after a show at a logging site outside Corvallis.

Irwin laughed. "Do you think they'll drown you like the old witches back east? Or just run you out of camp with saws and hatchets?"

It should be noted that Irwin, like many men, was inclined to overlook obvious danger when doing so served his own worldview.

"I think people will like the show," Sheila said.

"Don't be dumb, girl."

She nodded and Irwin assumed that was the end of it.

Just after midnight, Sheila crept from her own tent and went to Irwin's, where she dragged her fingers across the canvas, tapping lightly at the wooden posts for good measure.

Security men from the logging camp and, later, the Corvallis sheriff, declared the fire an accident. Most likely, Irwin had fallen asleep smoking a cigarette. No mention was made of his assistant, whose own tent had disappeared during the night—not burned, just gone. It wasn't until three nights later that a man who had been at the show sat up in bed, bolted from a deep and unrelated dream, to shout, "What's become of Sweetheart? Is she okay?"

A frantic search was made and when no sign of the girl could be found, a diminutive grave marker was set for her at the camp's edge next to Irwin's. It gave the loggers some peace to know they had remembered her, had acknowledged her small, short life.

—

A decade later, Sheila was apprehended by law enforcement in Oakland, California. Not for what she had done to Irwin. No one had ever connected her to that event, and never would. Her arrest was instead for the immolation of two other men, at a hillside bunkhouse. It seemed she had been doing business with them for the past six months, and was involved romantically with one or the other, though jurors at her trial were never clear which, and Sheila, even under oath, would not say.

A deal gone sour? A lover scorned? A tale of abuse? Sheila's lawyer begged her to give a reason, hoping he might plead for a light sentence if there was a sad story to go beside her innocent face. Sheila grinned. She leaned in and whispered, "I've burned nine men. Nine before these."

After that, the lawyer made only minimal efforts on her behalf, though he never repeated to anyone what she had said. A smarter man than most, he feared her.

PART II

QUAKE

I

Quake Auchenbaucher arrived in Spokane Falls by train on the afternoon of September 5, 1889. He stepped out of the passenger car and looked around with the expression of a man sizing up a place he'd never been before. Quake had, in fact, been in Spokane Falls previously. But he wanted to pretend he hadn't. He wanted to look upon the place with fresh eyes and see it as new. Indeed, much of Spokane Falls was new since last he'd visited. He could tell by just a quick survey that the city's boundaries had grown. The downtown, scarred by its recent fire, was more or less unrecognizable to him. The air was still thick with it—the smell of char and the taste of ash—though he soon learned this was actually the fault of wildfires that had been burning for several weeks. Everywhere he looked, buildings were hollowed out, their frames standing only from habit. Others, though, were already in the process of repair and refurbishment, bolstered with scaffolding. Even the train station at which he had just arrived had burnt and was mid-reconstruction. It was like he was really looking at two cities at once: one in an eager climb for betterment, the other in desperate decline. There was a confusion to the place and he was glad for it. He thought it would serve him well.

The police department was just three blocks from the train station, but Quake took a circuitous route. He wanted to see more of what had become of the city. He wanted to arrive knowledgeable, with a clear lay of the land and sense of the damages. But as he walked, he found he could not get a scope of the fire's path. The destruction went on without end, but it was sporadic. A scorched structure here, a perfectly fine one there. A street charred on one side and clean on the other. Nothing like in Seattle, where the fire had swept through that city's skid road, taking everything in its path. Here, it seemed the fire had been selective, deliberate in what it chose to consume. Quake liked this idea—fire as a sentient being with its own wants and desires. It was not an idea he'd share with anyone else, though. For everyone else, there would be structure reports, forensics, maps and charts, the role of heat, wind, and time of day. There would be process and procedure. Then there would be answers and there would be justice. That's what he was there for. That's what they would want from him.

At the police station, there was no one to greet him. Quake tipped his lean frame against the front desk, crossed his arms, and waited for someone in the depths of the building to feel his presence. He did not call out. After a moment, a stout man in a faded uniform appeared. He seemed flustered.

"Oh, oh you're here," the officer said. "I thought maybe someone was here. And yes, it's you."

Quake gave a quick nod.

"Mr. Auchenbaucher? Inspector Auchenbaucher, right?"

Quake extended a hand, which the officer took, shaking it too vigorously, his grip too tight.

"We're awfully glad you've arrived, Inspector. We really are grateful for your service. You come so highly regarded. In Seattle, they said—"

Quake cut him off. He wasn't one for hearing accolades. They rang false to him and he'd never developed a taste for that.

"Why don't you tell me what you and your men know so far," he said.

The officer—who turned out to be the chief of police, Jep Hornsweller, though Quake could not imagine the man commanding power over other police, much less the general public—told him the fire had taken place at the start of August. It began at a hotel that was known as a popular lunch spot and a somewhat less popular brothel. Because of its reputation, the police right away considered arson a high likelihood. In fact, they had just three days prior taken a suspect into custody who they felt had a clear motive for starting the fire, as well as a proven connection to the location.

"What's the motive?" Quake asked.

"He's the manager of the bank. After the fire, he started giving people loans at very high rates, then pocketing the interest. He was also printing fake banknotes and taking the real cash home with him."

"Usury," Quake said. "And counterfeit."

The police chief shrugged. "Well, what we think is, he wanted to start the fire so people would have to take out loans to repair their homes and businesses. He really had folks over a barrel for a while."

"Very forward thinking," Quake said. "Impressively so."

"It was his own employees at the bank that tipped us off. Couple squirrely bastards, but they had their fingers on the pulse of the situation. They played the long game and we got our man. They seemed to take a particular pleasure in the whole thing. Guess he was a real asshole to them."

Quake asked what the banker's connection was to the place where the fire began.

"He had a girl at the hotel."

"So why would he want to start the fire there?"

"Ain't you never had a girl you wanted to set fire to?"

Quake locked eyes with Hornsweller and waited. But there was no more explanation forthcoming. Only this flimsy joke. That was why the Spokane Falls police had seen fit to lock up the banker. Not that it mattered particularly to Quake. He just thought it was interesting, as a lifelong student of human nature.

"I'd like to talk with the suspect to start. Then perhaps one of your men can take me out to survey the damage," Quake said, and the police chief nodded like his head was on a string, grateful for the chance to be of use, and to be out from under the scrutiny of the arson inspector's gaze. This indicated to the arson inspector that he was doing a fine job in Spokane Falls already.

2

Quake Auchenbaucher arrived in Spokane Falls by train because the horse he'd been riding was dead. Well, maybe not dead. It was still alive the last time he saw it. But very near death. It was old and probably sick and definitely exhausted. He didn't know the horse well—hadn't had it for long. Still, he felt bad for it. He left it with a farmer in a place just west of Spokane Falls called Stevens, which was not so much a town, per se, as a rail depot in a field. The farmer offered Quake a dollar for the horse, but Quake waved him off, saying he only wished the animal a speedy recovery.

It was preferable, he felt, to arrive by train anyway. Not only because riding into the city on a dying horse was undignified but also because he did not want anyone in Spokane Falls to know he'd come from places a person needed a horse to get to. Better it appeared he'd come straight from Seattle, with all its metropolitan dignities. Better they thought he'd been enjoying himself in Seattle's saloons and restaurants, paddle-boating on its lakes, and strolling in its parks since his last job finished. Not riding through the state's unpeopled hinterlands, burying money under a tree in a county where he knew he would not be bothered. Men of legitimate purpose did not do such things. Men of legitimate purpose kept to the cities. They took the trains. They stored their money in banks.

Well, maybe not the people of Spokane Falls, Quake thought. They, it seemed, would have all done better to keep their money under a tree.

Quake found the banker in his jail cell, behaving oddly. He was up on the narrow bed on his hands and knees, his elbows bent so his torso sloped down. He was breathing heavily. Quake had once seen a woman give birth this way. He was surprised by the animality of it. It had reminded him of how close humans are, all the time, to being something else, and he'd appreciated that. With this fellow in the cell, there was no such reminder. He looked very human. Very human and very sad.

"How long has he been like this?" Quake asked Hornsweller.

"Just a while," the police chief said. "Earlier he was upside down."

Quake said the banker's name and the man stopped his hyperventilating and looked, but made no sign of understanding.

"Mr. Heydale," Quake tried again.

"I'd give the money back, if I could," Heydale said. "It was a mistake and I'd give it right back. Only she took it all, and I've got none left to give back."

"I'm not here to talk about the money," Quake said. "I'm here to talk about the fire. My name is Quake Auchenbaucher and I'm a federal arson inspector with the Department of the Interior."

"I keep telling them I'd give it all back," Heydale said again.

Then, turning to the police chief, he added, "Don't I keep telling you? Isn't it so? Don't I?"

"Shut up and answer the questions you're asked," Hornsweller said, though Quake hadn't asked Heydale anything yet. Heydale looked at both men with a confusion Quake thought justified.

"Perhaps you have other business to attend to while I interview Mr. Heydale?" Quake suggested to Hornsweller. "I don't want to keep you from important work."

The police chief agreed. Quake was grateful. The man was clearly an idiot, and Quake had found through the years that in his line of business idiots were the most likely to cause problems. They didn't have the social grace to know when to stay out of the way, or the mental agility to convince themselves something was all right when it obviously was not. These were attributes in others Quake relied heavily on.

Heydale was not an idiot. The scheme he had been running at the bank, as ineptly described by Hornsweller, wasn't something an idiot would attempt, or even think of. A dark intelligence spilled from Heydale's crazed eyes as he squirmed on his jail cot.

Quake had a notebook with him, which he now removed from his pocket and made a show of writing in. The writing was real, though the notes were nothing he intended to reference again.

"Do you feel like talking?" Quake asked once he felt he'd note-taken for an appropriate amount of time. "Want to tell me about how you got here?"

"I came from Portland, but I don't remember why." As Heydale said this, he dropped from his hands and knees. He was now lying facedown, his head turned slightly toward Quake to prevent his mouth and nose from being wedged into the mattress.

"I was led to believe you managed the bank here. How could you do that if you were in Portland?"

"I was in Portland before I managed the bank. With my parents. It was a mistake to come here. Everyone here hates me."

Pouting child, throwing a tantrum on his bed, Quake thought.

"I meant, do you want to tell me how you ended up here in jail?"

"Oh, because the police came to my house and said, 'Everyone hates you so you're in jail now. Hahaha!' They're mad about the bad loans and all. I know it was wrong. But also they hated me before. Everyone always hates me."

"They think you started the fire," Quake said.

"Oh," Heydale said again. He sat up and looked to be considering what Quake had said very intently, as if it were the first time he'd heard this information.

"No," he said, finally. "No, not that."

Where just a moment ago Heydale had seemed almost infantile, Quake now thought he actually looked quite old. Withered and weak, sinking into his skin. When he asked Heydale his age, he was surprised to hear him say, "Twenty-nine," two years younger than Quake himself. He wondered if the trauma of Heydale's arrest had aged him so horribly in just the past few days, or if he'd always looked old. A man whose good years skipped him over entirely.

"Police Chief Hornsweller has suggested to me that you chose to start the fire at Wolfe's Hotel because you were involved with a woman who lived there, and that perhaps things had soured between the two of you. You wanted to hurt her," Quake said.

"Hurt her?" Heydale repeated. "Why would I want to hurt her? I love her."

Quake asked if this woman was the same one he'd mentioned

before, who'd taken all the bank money Heydale was otherwise so eager to return.

"She took advantage of me," he said. "She put ideas in my mind and made me do bad things. I think she might be a witch."

Quake, who had been writing again, looked up from his notes. He wondered if the banker was fucking with him. But he could see in that man's eyes he was not. Heydale was both earnest and honest. He clearly believed himself to be speaking the truth.

———

She had been to the lake before. A number of years ago her boyfriend at the time brought her for a romantic getaway. The man's efforts at romance had been absurd—candlelight picnics, guitar serenades (though he did not know how to play guitar, or sing particularly well, for that matter), a long time spent staring together at the stars each night. She had wanted none of it, and once they'd returned to Spokane Falls she ended the relationship. In hindsight, he was a nice enough fellow, but at the time, she was only looking for a drinking partner—someone to pick up the tab and keep other men from bothering her. He'd done these things admirably. But the candles and bad guitar and stargazing were too much, and even years later when she thought back on the trip, she cringed a little. The lake, though, she recalled fondly. Blue to match the sky with pined hills on all sides. The lake was long, and from the town, she could not see the other side. She liked the possibilities in that. How far did it go? The hills, similarly, seemed endless. You could walk through those piney woods all day without encountering another person, just deer and chipmunks, the sharp smell of bears nearby but always unseen.

It was just as she remembered. Though time had tumbled forward for her, the lake and the poky little town at its shore seemed not to have changed at all. So then, the only difference was her. And the fact that this time she was, mercifully, alone.

———

3

Spokane Falls presented a new opportunity for Quake because it was the first city where he'd been invited to investigate a fire. In Vancouver, Ellensburg, and Seattle, he'd simply shown up, informing local police that he'd been sent by the Department of the Interior from its western office in Portland. And once the investigation was complete, he insisted the cost of his services be paid by the city. This was brazen, but he'd yet to encounter any resistance. By the time the matter of payment came up, civic leaders in each city were so grateful for what Quake had told them, they would have given him the moon. The mayor of Ellensburg had, in fact, suggested Quake might like to stay in town and take up romantically with his daughter.

This was because wherever Quake went, he gave people what they wanted. That was his true business. And for this service, he was always fairly compensated. At least, those were the terms in which he thought of his work.

But the Spokane Falls police had contacted him of their own volition. They'd written to him while he was still in Seattle based on a recommendation from the Seattle chief of police. So this was a different sort of situation altogether. It meant these people had been expecting him and thought they knew things about him. But it also meant they knew for themselves what they wanted: they wanted someone to blame for the fire. And it seemed they'd already chosen that person. All they were asking of Quake was to confirm or deny their choice.

It was immediately obvious to him that Heydale had not set the fire. But it hardly mattered. Quake had no means of performing a real investigation, nor any interest in doing so. He would pretend to investigate as long as was necessary for putting on a convincing show—or as long as was enjoyable. He'd found other cities treated him quite well while he worked for them, providing him with nice meals, accommodations, and even women, as was the case in Seattle, where he'd had a really excellent time and stayed so long another whole city had burned while he lingered, which was why he was still there when Spokane Falls came calling. Then, he'd announce that yes, without a shadow of a doubt, Heydale was their man. He'd hold up whatever evidence he thought they'd like, and they'd pay him what he asked and probably hang the banker on the spot without a real trial because even though Spokane Falls was a big city by Washington Territory standards, it was still as wild and impulsive a place as any frontier town. At least, that was the impression Quake got.

The tour he received of the city from Hornsweller and a small team of policemen did little to counter this image. They escorted him, as if he were some foreign dignitary, through downtown. The policemen took this project very seriously, but Quake suspected it was an excuse to avoid real police work for a few hours. The need for such work in Spokane Falls became apparent when, just two blocks from the station, Quake and his delegation saw a man push over a cart full of construction material and, in the ensuing confusion, grab whatever he could in an ungainly armful and run off in the direction of the river.

"You don't want to pursue him?" Quake asked as he stood with his escorts, watching the cart's owner and a few other workers give half-hearted chase.

"We know him," one of the policemen said. "We can just go get him later. No big deal."

The looting and rampant theft, they added, had calmed down considerably.

"At first it was so bad, the National Guard had to come in," Hornsweller said, with what sounded like pride. "They got here and set up a perimeter downtown where nobody who didn't live or have work could pass. They gave out cards."

"But there weren't enough of them, the Guard," another policeman added. "People without passes kept slipping past the checkpoints."

"So they rounded up all the veteran guardsmen and military and cavalry in town to volunteer. I swear there were guys from both the Union and the South out there together, walking the perimeter, all real crazy old bastards come out of the woodwork." This was from another officer. It was a story told in a round, as if they'd practiced it this way together.

"I'm former cavalry myself," Hornsweller said. "So I volunteered with the rest. It was an honor to serve."

"You're the chief of police," Quake said. "Aren't you always serving, theoretically?"

Hornsweller shrugged. The guardsmen had stayed fourteen days. When they left, the perimeter and checkpoint system fell by the wayside.

"No trouble, though," Hornsweller said. "We've got the bulk of the roustabouts put to work now, sweeping streets and hauling shit. My men made it clear there's work for anyone willing, and anyone not willing is no longer welcome in town, so to speak."

"We got rid of a bunch of the Chinese too!" added one of the other officers, gesturing emphatically toward the east side of downtown. "We knocked on doors and said we suspected them of arson and were gonna start making arrests in forty-eight hours. Ha! They got the message and packed up fast."

Quake sucked at his teeth to bite his tongue. Cruel men, he had found, always preferred to travel in packs. And if they could get someone to give them badges, they would wear their cruelty in public with pride.

The burn area extended much farther than Quake had walked on his roundabout path to the police station the previous afternoon. He could not tell how far, but one member of his escort said thirty blocks and Quake believed him. He made little notes on his writing pad. Later, he would ask for city maps and any other available materials related to downtown infrastructure or planning. Again, not to actually look at, but just to have made a show of procuring.

Most of what had been destroyed, Quake was told, were businesses and offices. Not much housing beyond hotels and tenements, for which the general consensus of the policemen was: good riddance. Dens for drunks and gamblers, whores and immigrants. Insurance covered the loss of most legitimate establishments.

Repair and new construction were in full swing, as Quake had already noted. There were also the tents. White and canvas-color army-style tents on every street, even in areas where the fire had not gone. These tents always came out after fires, Quake knew. They were how businesses stayed open until they could rebuild their physical structures. But in Spokane Falls, he felt there must be more tents than there ever were shops to begin with. Some were small, like a closet-size space with a sign that read NICE THINGS above the door. Others were more spacious. There were tents as bars, tents as doctors' offices, tents as grocery stores, even a tent museum, though when Quake asked what this meant, Hornsweller said, "It's just a lot of somebody's old junk."

There was one incongruously large tent—seemingly two stories, if such a thing were possible with a tent—that sold only waffles. There was a line of men and women out the door and down the block.

The citizens of Spokane Falls looked to be treating the whole scene as if it were a bazaar. Surely, Quake thought, there could not normally be so many people out in the streets of downtown on a weekday morning. But here they were, folks of all kinds. Some with clear business, others just milling about, shopping, eating, stopping from time to time to kick soot from their shoes. Animals, too, ambled through the streets with a kind of ease Quake found both endearing and unsettling. He saw a family of white-tailed deer crossing the street at an intersection. Then, a sturdy mountain marmot chewing on a corncob. An unsettling number of snakes wriggled in gutters and potholes—garter, rattle, bull.

"Is there always so much wildlife?" Quake asked, and was told no, the animals had fled the mountains to escape the wildfires. They were a minor nuisance, causing property damage and startling citizens unaccustomed to a rural lifestyle.

"It's ironic if you think about it," one officer said. "People who lived down here had to leave because of one fire and then a bunch of animals moved in because of another fire."

"It's not irony," said another. "It's stupidity. Dumb animals. How is this better than what they left?"

"Sometimes animals have knowledge we don't. Watch them close—they'll show you," Quake said, forgetting himself momentarily. But if any of his companions thought this remark out of place, they gave no sign.

Hornsweller named the buildings not destroyed by the fire as they went past. A hotel, a church, an attorney's office, a dry goods store. When they reached the bank where Barton Heydale had perpetrated his crimes, the procession stopped. Even if Heydale had set the fire, there was certainly no way he could engineer it to protect his own place of business. Still, the preservation of the bank did not look good for his case. The policemen standing to either side of Quake shook their heads.

"Never trust a man with a head for figures," one said.

Hornsweller nodded his agreement. Two doors down, a young boy used a brick to smash through the window of a burnt storefront, then collected the larger chunks of glass with his bare hands and put them gently into his pockets. He was within clear sight of Quake and the police but apparently did not care. And none in Quake's party made any move to stop him or question his actions. Seeing this reminded Quake of his own childhood, which had been equal parts directionless and dangerous. It sent him momentarily to distraction—a fit of unwanted nostalgia. This feeling was aided by the arrival of a smell, sweet and pleasant, cutting through the rotting-ash air. It made him think of home cooking and warm kitchens—the luxury of other people's lives.

Quake's companions smelled it too. The police lifted their heads to sniff. Smiles emerged on faces.

"Oh," one of the officers said. "The waffles must be ready."

At the end of the tour, when the other policemen, grown weary of even their excuse to avoid real work, had drifted away, Hornsweller offered up a piece of information that gave Quake pause. Heydale, Hornsweller said, was thought to have been in Seattle in June. There were rumors, in fact, that he had done quite a bit of travel that summer, and he may have been connected to other fires in the territory as well.

"Might be a serial arsonist," the police chief said in a low voice.

Quake nodded. He did not ask for any further information. He had gone momentarily cold with a kind of fear he'd never felt before in all his days running schemes and scams: the fear of being caught.

4

That night, Quake lay on his back on his hotel bed and thought of Barton Heydale, who was likely lying pensive on his jail bed, though perhaps in a much stranger position. The sad banker who claimed he'd been duped by love. Quake himself had never been in love. In fact, he'd only ever been intimate with two women who did not require payment after sex. The first had been a sweetheart of his adolescence, whose face and name he could no longer remember. She'd been fond of him, but he was so mired in his own dissatisfaction for his young life, he had no emotional energy left to give back in the form of love. The second woman he'd met in Bellingham while he was there pretending to be a geologist, offering up his services to convince the nervous people of that hillside burg that their nearby volcano was not actually on the verge of violent eruption (a nervousness he himself had planted in the first place). She was kind and pretty, and seemed genuinely interested in him. But of course everything he told her about himself was a lie. So this too could not be love, only a temporary balm for loneliness.

He could use such a balm now. The task set before him in Spokane Falls was clear: to proclaim Heydale's guilt. But everything around it seemed murky—the dumb and potentially dangerous Hornsweller and his apathetic men; the fever of crime and industry mingling together in the burn zone; the sad humanity of Heydale himself. On top of all that, Hornsweller's remark about suspecting Heydale of involvement in other Washington Territory fires made him exceedingly uncomfortable. Because Quake, in his "investigations" of those fires, had deemed them unconnected. In Seattle, he'd blamed a drunk brothel patron who'd fallen asleep after sex with a cigarette in his mouth (and had, it should be noted, died in the fire). In Vancouver, he'd pinned the fire on a man who'd been arrested shortly thereafter on an unrelated murder charge and was likely to be executed anyway. In Ellensburg, where the mayor could not bear to think ill of any of his citizens, Quake blamed a lightning strike. These findings were a matter of public record. They had been printed in newspapers. And so he worried that the police chief was setting him up in some way, calling Quake to town to make him a scapegoat as well as Heydale. Worse than a scapegoat, a tool for publicity. *Look*, Spokane Falls could say, *we've got the arsonist responsible for all the fires right here in our custody, and the man who's thrown everyone else off the scent.* They'd both be hanged side by side, Quake and Heydale.

All of this Quake would have liked to say to a lover, if only he had such a person with him. A companion and a confidant. He could really use a woman like that now. In response she would cluck sympathetically, run her hands through his coarse hair, kiss him on his forehead, and tell him he was being a paranoid twat. She'd say it gently, teasingly. Hornsweller was not trying to trap him. The man was not quick enough for such a scheme, and if he were, how would he even know Quake was trappable? Quake had, after all, come with the highest recommendations. Much more likely, Hornsweller had thought up his serial arsonist theory precisely because he was so out of the loop that he'd never heard anything about the previous fires' resolutions. It was entirely possible, Quake's imaginary girlfriend would say, that Hornsweller could not read and so even the region's biggest, boldest headlines would pass before his eyes uncomprehended. The man, she'd insist, was merely thrusting his cock into the dark, hoping he struck pussy. Then she and Quake would both laugh at her cleverness and her crudeness. And Quake would feel better.

Did she not also deserve reassurance in this difficult time? She couldn't even imagine the sort of person who would be suited for the job. So she did not let her mind drift in such a way. She kept her attention instead on the mundane and the practical. Remembering to keep the drapes closed during the hottest part of the day. Walking without stepping in horse shit. Learning to cook a whole trout. She had time for cooking now, and she thought she'd like to improve upon her skills. Her clothes were the cleanest they had ever been, her hair brushed twice daily. She did not conjure scenarios in which she might remark upon these things to anyone else.

Still, she wondered what had become of the people she'd known in Spokane Falls.

Where were the other women of Wolfe's Hotel? Had they found new homes, new places to work? And did they think of her, or had she disappeared from their minds? She had often felt herself an ethereal presence, floating through her days. It took so little for her to vanish completely.

Where was Bill Wolfe? The man was a son of a bitch, as a lot of people liked to say. He was crude and gruff. She had seen him drag men out of his hotel and beat them in the middle of the street with an uncommon ruthlessness even in generally ruthless Spokane Falls. But he'd always been straight with her. He'd never raised her rent and the clients he'd sent to her were trustworthy sorts. Would he rebuild or was he left in ruins?

And of course she wondered, daily, about Kate. Was she safe? Or in trouble? Had she been caught? Or did they find someone else to blame for the fire?

These were the people she thought of, these and no one else.

5

Quake: Tell me about the woman who's got the bank money.

Heydale: She's the most beautiful woman in the world.

Quake: Any idea where she might have gone when she left?

Heydale: She's got red hair and she knows me better than I know myself.

Quake: Did you two have a plan for getting out of town? A rendezvous point?

Heydale: We didn't need to make plans. She could read my mind. She has abilities like that, you see.

Quake: All right. And where did your mind tell her to go?

Heydale: No, no, that's not how it worked. I had no control over her. It was the other way around. She's a certain kind of woman, that's for sure. She can make men do things by implanting ideas in their brains. She used to put music into mine. And scary images. And the idea to steal from the bank, I'm pretty sure. Though she wasn't even with me yet at the time. Still, it was her that did it to me, that made me a criminal. I was a very law-abiding person before she exerted her influence over me.

Quake: Very law-abiding. I'll make a note of it.

Heydale: Yes. If you find her, please arrest her and put her in this cell with me.

Quake: Will do, partner. How did you come to know her?

Heydale: I rescued her.

Quake: Is that so?

Heydale: She was being held captive by an evil man. He kept her locked up and made her do foul things. I got her away from him. I was keeping her safe.

Quake: Like a knight in a fairy tale.

Heydale: Exactly! You understand. If you find Bill Wolfe, please arrest him too. But put him in a different cell.

Quake: Anyone else you'd like me to arrest while I'm at it?

Heydale: Yes. Several. Jim Dweller and Del Dweller. You can find them at the bank. Also, the bitch who used to cook food for me. Also, the barber who gave me this terrible haircut. Also, all the policemen who have been quite mean to me.

Quake: What about the fellow who really started the fire, and then framed you for it? Shall I arrest him too?

Heydale: Absolutely!

Quake: Any idea who that might be?

Heydale: Oh, it's not any one person.

Quake: A conspiracy, then?

Heydale: It's the whole city. They've always been against me, ever since I got here. It's because I work at the bank and everyone in Spokane Falls hates the bank. Until they need something from it, that is. So what happened was, all that hate, it built and built and built until one afternoon it exploded. Combusted. That was the fire. Hate was the kindling and the spark. All of it for me. Then, when people wanted to know how the fire started, they turned and blamed the person they hated the most. Also me. Even though it was all their fault for hating me in the first place. If this city had any love in it, we could have had a nice summer. Very temperate.

Quake: That's quite a theory.

Heydale: It's simple science. I'm certain your investigation will reveal it correct.

Quake: So really your only crime here is being unpopular?

Heydale: Yes. None of this would have happened if I'd had a different job.

Quake: What job would you want instead?

Heydale: Any kind! As long as it's clean and respectable. Like your job, for instance. A government job. That's a good job. How'd you get that job?

Quake: It was a long path. Lots of training.

He also thought—though did not say—that it helps if you used to be someone else entirely. Someone with a different name and from a different place. Ideally, someone you did not like, and did not miss.

Bored in the West

The earthquake wasn't anybody's fault, but Archibald had the idea to blame the rich man. Archibald was living in the only hotel in Ainsworth at the time, trying to look like a rich man himself. Or if not a rich man, at least the sort of man who could stay in a hotel and not seem out of place. At this, he was failing. The front desk clerk eyed him with suspicion every time he left his room or returned to it. The restaurant attached to the hotel served him with visible reluctance, always seating him at a table farthest from other customers. And only one of the whores at the brothel across the street would even talk to him, much less do anything else.

This, Archibald assumed, was because he'd been living in a tent in the desert for the past six months and looked it. Even though he was clean and shaved, with a new suit, new money, and a new name, everyone he met could see right through him. They could tell he wasn't fit for living indoors or for any of its related luxuries. Archibald did not begrudge the people of Ainsworth their perceptions. After all, he knew who he was and who he'd most likely always be. All he wanted was the chance, for just a little while, to be otherwise.

Archibald had been in Ainsworth a week when the earthquake happened. This was in June 1880. He was in his hotel bed, awake but with his eyes still closed, when he felt the shaking start.

Begrudgingly, he opened his eyes and went to the window.

The rest of Ainsworth had felt it as well.

People appeared in door frames and stuck their heads out of windows. A banner that hung across the street and read AINSWORTH: A REAL AMERICAN CITY had fallen and was now being pushed and twisted down the road by the wind. Three horses tied in front of the hotel turned tight nervous circles, tangling their leads, bumping into one another as if very drunk.

These sights cheered Archibald. He had no idea what had occurred, but he thought it delightful. This was, without a doubt, the most interesting thing to happen in Ainsworth since he'd arrived. He imagined it might be the most interesting thing to happen in Ainsworth ever.

Before Archibald came to Ainsworth, he was restless. This was a chronic problem in his life. He'd grown up in a small mining town in South Dakota, raised by a woman he was certain was not his mother. When Archibald thought back on his childhood, he pictured indistinguishable days filled with purposeless wandering through town and into the nearby woods and hills, sometimes with friends, sometimes with his various pets—dogs, a mule, and for a short while, a trained fox—but mostly alone. The woman who raised him expressed no concern for how he spent his time. Her name was Anna Klemmick. Archibald's real name was Dan Kite. Not even Daniel. Just Dan. Anna never explained her relationship to him. He did not call her aunt or cousin. He called her Anna. He had never met another person with the last name Kite. At sixteen, he left Anna and South Dakota not because he was unhappy or because he resented his lawless orphan upbringing, but because he could not stomach the thought of every day of his manhood looking the same as every day of his childhood. He went west, as he understood all men at the time with any ambition were meant to do. South Dakota was already west to many, and he knew this, but he vowed to go west-er.

In Montana he quit job after job almost as quickly as he was hired. Each was unbearably soul sucking, like in the town that endeavored to pave all its streets in brick. Like Europe. The Europe of Montana. They were hiring young men by the dozen to lay brick. Archibald lasted three days. Though the other workers complained of the pain from hunched backs and sore arms, Archibald was bothered only by the repetition. So he left, again, as had become his habit.

In Idaho, there were no jobs, only criminals. Archibald indentured himself to a seasoned train robber but did not have the resolve for the tasks this man demanded of him. He'd wanted, as a boy, to be an outlaw. But when he came face-to-face with real acts of violence, he balked. Embarrassed, he moved west again.

It was in Washington Territory that he joined the cavalry. He thought (wrongly) that rule of law might be his style after all. The first task assigned to his company was delivering 500 Paiutes to the Yakama Reservation, the last leg of a long and undesired journey. They had been expelled from their home in Nevada and forced to march hundreds of miles north. The other cavalrymen were edgy and mean with their charges, always looking to fight. But the Paiutes would not engage. They accepted their lot in grim silence. Whoever had come before Archibald and his unit had already stripped the fight from them. This was the worst of all his jobs.

Archibald lasted nine months with the cavalry before he defected. One morning, when his company went east, he turned and went west. Or the direction he thought was west. He called it west and there was no one to tell him otherwise. After that, there would be no one to tell him otherwise for quite some time.

It didn't take Archibald long to learn the name of what had caused the shaking. Once he learned it, he thought he'd heard it before and was ashamed not to have remembered and applied it right away to the situation. *Earthquake.* He was sitting in the bar below the brothel when the bartender asked one of the whores what she thought of the *earthshake* and she corrected him. "Earthquake, you mean." Archibald saw the bartender blush and felt his own cheeks color too. He reminded himself he had not been the one to speak his ignorance out loud. No one in the bar knew what words Archibald did or did not have, *earthquake* or otherwise. He could be a goddamn expert on earthquakes, for all they knew.

"What do you think caused it?" This was the whore again. She asked in the voice of a curious child and Archibald figured she was trying to make the bartender feel better after having embarrassed him a moment ago.

"It was God, obviously," he said. "Punishing this town for its sinful, sinful ways." Then, grinning, he leaned over the bar to swat her across the ass with his hand.

"Nothing caused the earthquake." This was from another woman sitting at the bar. "Nothing causes anything. Everything that happens is random and unconnected. No God, no purpose, no reason." Archibald liked this explanation and thought it was probably the correct one. It was not, however, an interesting one. He decided to offer another.

"An earthquake is caused by people," he heard himself say. "When humans tamper with the earth by digging into it—mine shafts or tunnels, say—it can respond violently."

They were all looking at him, everyone in the bar.

"How do you know that?" the bartender asked.

Archibald thought back to his earlier revelation: for all these people knew, he was an earthquake expert.

"Earthquakes are my field of study. At the University of Washington. I'm here doing research."

A collective *oh* seemed to pass through the bar.

"You knew the earthquake was going to happen this whole time?" the bartender asked. "Why didn't you warn anyone?"

"No," Archibald said. "In science, we rarely know anything for sure. I had a hunch, though. That's what brought me here. Besides, no one was hurt." He said this last part even though he had no idea if it was true.

Again there were *oh*s. Archibald could feel the room warming to him.

"So, you're saying some people did this," one of the women asked, "by disrupting the ground?"

No one in Ainsworth had wanted to see Archibald as a rich man, but apparently they were willing to take him for a smart man. He thought he should have just started out that way from the beginning, pretending to be smart. He could have saved himself some lonesome nights, if nothing else. But he didn't care for being smart; would rather be rich. So, he thought he'd split the difference. He'd be a smart man who got the better of a rich man.

"Well, a person did this, yes."

Of course, everyone at the bar wanted to know who that person was. And Archibald was happy to tell them.

After he walked off from the cavalry, Archibald didn't know where to go. He thought of continuing farther west, but he worried he'd be identified as a traitor as soon as he set foot in any town. So he stayed in the desert. He tucked himself into shallow canyons, followed streams, camped in his tent, ate marmots, little brown birds, and sometimes lizards if he got desperate. He used the skills he'd learned as a boy in South Dakota to stay alive. He didn't care for the desert, but he had a hard time imagining a scenario in which he would enjoy a normal, civilized life. Every job he'd ever had put him under somebody's thumb, and results were mind-numbingly dull or unfathomably brutal. He could not abide dullness or brutality just to help someone else grow rich, be it one person or the whole government. He wanted to live on his own terms. If that meant eking out an existence alone in the wild, so be it. At least in the desert, Archibald was beholden to no one.

His hair and beard grew thick and tangled, his fingernails turned the color of the reddish dirt in which he lived, and he forgot what his own face looked like. Some days he minded these things, but most days he didn't. After all, he could think of no alternative that would make him any happier. Until he found the other soldier. Even then, he always thought he'd eventually return to the desert, or if not the desert, some other unpeopled place. But with the other soldier, he could at least have a little break. He could pretend to be someone else.

The other soldier was dead. Archibald knew this as soon as he saw him. He wore a cavalry uniform, like Archibald's, only cleaner, and he had two hundred dollars in cash in his pocket. His identification said his name was Robert Welsh. Archibald had no idea where he had come from, or how he died, but he guessed Welsh, like Archibald, had walked away from his unit. Unlike Archibald, Welsh— who probably had not spent his entire childhood outdoors—had then wandered like an idiot in the hot and cold desert without food or water until he fell dead on his face. Poor Welsh. Archibald took his uniform, his identification, and his money.

After that, he packed his few possessions and walked until he bumped into the tiny town of Digby along the bank of the Snake River. In Digby, he found first a bathhouse, then a tailor. At both locations, he loudly proclaimed his name was Robert Welsh and that he'd just run away from the cavalry. He'd got it into his mind that the best way to avoid being suspected as a defector was to pretend to be a different defector. But no one cared.

Archibald then continued on to Ainsworth, just across the river—the big city compared to Digby—feeling flush and new. The cash he'd found on Welsh had made him rich by his own standards, and though he knew it was not enough to start a new life (and even if it were, he still couldn't imagine that life), it was enough to afford

him a while of a different life. On the way into Ainsworth, he picked
out his new name, the most rich-sounding name he could think of:
Archibald Auchenbaucher. It was ridiculous, he knew. But no more
ridiculous than calling himself Robert Welsh. No more ridiculous
than calling himself Dan Kite.

Archibald did not know the rich man's name. He told the people in
the brothel bar that the person responsible for the earthquake was
the person responsible for sinking pylons into the river just outside
town. One of the other patrons provided the name for him: Atlas
Stern. When he heard it, Archibald thought, *Yes, of course, that is a
real rich man's name*, and decided the next time he had occasion to
change his name he'd pick an object to go by—something that
sounded worldly but also tangible.

Archibald had first seen the pylons three days earlier. He was
walking along the bank of the river when he came upon a very involved project in progress. He went to one of the workmen standing
on the shore and asked what was being built.

"A bridge," the workman said.

"When will it be finished?" Archibald asked.

"Doesn't matter to you," the workman said. "It's a private bridge.
Even when it's done, you won't be able to use it."

Archibald asked who it belonged to.

"Him," the workman said, pointing over his shoulder to as big a
house as Archibald had ever seen. It was partially obscured by a very
uniform row of trees that rose incongruously from the otherwise
barren scabland hillside, but still he could tell it was immense. He
was impressed. And he was jealous. If there was one thing Ar-

chibald thought he knew for certain about his life, it was that it would never look like this.

He told the patrons at the bar that his department at the University of Washington kept tabs on all digging projects around the region.

"We got wind of Mr. Stern's bridge. This is such a volatile area. I was sent to check it out. And now here you've had an earthquake."

"It was him that did it," the bartender said, nodding.

"Are you certain, though?" This from the woman who had previously expressed skepticism about cause and effect.

Archibald said yes, he was certain. He had been conducting experiments daily, down at the river's edge, since he arrived in Ainsworth. The data he had collected provided irrefutable evidence.

"Will there be more earthquakes?" someone asked.

Archibald fixed his face in what he thought to be a grim expression and nodded. Yes, he said. There most certainly would.

Everyone else in the bar nodded. Not only willing but happy to go along, to believe. As if they'd been just waiting for someone like Archibald to come along and lie to them.

That night, he found himself with new options at the brothel. It wasn't just the one woman who was willing to spend time with him, but several. He took his pick and enjoyed himself immensely. He was no longer a pity case. In Ainsworth, his stock had risen. This made him wonder what else he might be able to get.

By the time Archibald got to the brothel's bar the following evening, everyone was already angry. He sensed the hostility in the room right away and assumed it was meant for him. They'd figured out his deception from the previous night and were now ready to run him out of town—liar and upstart that he was. He braced himself, not for a fight, but to run.

But the anger wasn't for him. It was for Atlas Stern. For Archibald, the people in the bar—and it was a packed house that night—had nothing but praise.

They made way for him. The bartender pulled out a chair at a small table in the middle of things and brought him drinks he didn't have to pay for. All of a sudden, everyone knew his name.

"That Stern," the bartender said. "He's got more money than God, but he never does anything good for anyone with it. Now what he's doing, he's putting us all in danger."

"All for a bridge no one but him is allowed to use," someone else added.

Archibald nodded. "It does seem . . ." He paused as if searching carefully for the right word, though he'd had it the whole time. "Selfish."

"Yes, it's very, very selfish," another echoed. Archibald heard murmurs of agreement all around him. After that, he did not feel he needed to say anything else. The men and women of the brothel bar carried things along just fine on their own. How quickly his lies had moved beyond him and were taking on a life of their own in the hands of Ainsworth's citizenry.

It turned out all of Ainsworth had been waiting for something to blame on the rich man. Archibald was just the first to provide a feasible option. He was not from there and did not know what had gone on before he arrived. The previous night, when Archibald first heard Stern's name spoken in this same location, it was said with a kind of respect, even pride for knowing the name of such a rich person. But the facade of respect had fallen away. No one needed to pretend anymore. Now they could resent openly. Stern had caused the earthquake. Suddenly, there was a reason for feelings that had already existed, and the people of Ainsworth grabbed for that reason like candy.

"Friends," the bartender said, now speaking to the room at large, his head thrust back to project his words to the far corner of the bar, "if what Mr. Auchenbaucher has concluded from his experiments is true—which I think we have good reason to believe it is, coming as it does from such an authority—then our city, our property, and our very way of life is at risk. And so it is our right—nay, our duty *and* our right—to see that justice is done."

It was a surprisingly bold statement from a man who just the day prior had learned the word *earthquake*. All around him Archibald saw heads nod in agreement, shadows of nodding heads bouncing around the thinly lit room. Murmurs and *damn right*s, but none so loud as to interrupt. Archibald found himself holding his breath, waiting to see what would be said next. In the quest to demonize Atlas Stern, the bartender had found his voice, and he was moving the crowd. Like Archibald, this man seemed to be reinventing himself for the occasion.

"And so," the bartender continued, "since it seems we can do nothing to stop Mr. Stern from building his bridge, I propose that we extract from him some financial assurance that will compensate the town for any damages caused by his earthquakes, both this first one, and any that may occur in the future."

"How much?" someone demanded from the back of the bar.

This time it was not the bartender who spoke, but a man standing behind him.

"As much as we can get." These words came slow and heavy, a promise and a threat.

"Anyone who wishes to accompany us to speak with Mr. Stern is invited to stay," the bartender said. "We are requesting the company of at least ten able-bodied men for this venture, in addition to myself, Mr. Wyatt"—he gestured to the other man—"and Mr. Auchenbaucher."

So, a plot had been hatched in Archibald's name. He nodded as if he'd been a part of it all along.

The men who remained in the bar numbered closer to twenty than ten. Archibald expected more discussion. An outlining of plans. A strategy. At least a clarification of the general activity proposed. But the bartender, done with his oration, said only, "All right, then, let's go." And they did.

Walking through the dark streets of Ainsworth, then down along the riverbank, Archibald heard the men whispering and shifting around him.

Suddenly faced with the prospect of real violence, the kind he hadn't had the stomach for in Idaho, he grew nervous. His heart beat too fast and a bile taste appeared in his mouth. He allowed himself to be swept along.

Until, that is, he was told to stop. The man who had been walking in front of Archibald turned, placing his hand out.

"You should stay here, Professor," he said. "I don't think you'll want to come any farther."

Archibald nodded, relieved. It hadn't occurred to him that he'd be omitted from whatever acts the men were planning to commit, but now it made sense. After all, they still thought him a man of great learning and culture. Of course a person such as him would not be invited to, or even wanted in . . . whatever this was. A burglary? A murder? He stood still and the other men patted him on the back as they passed, as if for good luck.

He thought maybe he should hide. But that was too cowardly even for him. Instead, he sat where he was by the river and squinted at the cluster of lamps that marked Stern's property, trying to make out what was going on at the house.

Archibald wondered again about the man building the bridge. What had he done to this town that was so terrible? Was he a known crook? A highwayman who'd made a fortune through violence and deceit? Was he an oil baron who'd poisoned the town's water supply? Was he a man who took advantage of his wealth, making offers to young women and men alike that they could not afford to refuse but did not wish to accept? Archibald remembered another rich man. In South Dakota, nearly everyone he knew worked in a silver mine. The town was built up around it, in fact. The man who owned the mine lived in a big house on a hill. He wasn't the mayor, but what he said was law. Archibald remembered Anna Klemmick cursing this man's name, saying Archibald (still Dan then) should never work for him. Though Archibald could not recall what, in particular, the man had done to upset her. He hadn't thought about that memory in a long time and he wondered now, sitting in the dark beside the river, if this was the real reason he'd left for the West. Not because he was restless as a boy at all, but because Anna had told him to go.

Archibald didn't hear the men returning until they were practically upon him. At first, he thought something had gone wrong, or that they had changed their minds and not gone through with their plan at all. But when he asked, someone told him everything had gone just fine, real easy.

"Here's a fee for your services, Mr. Auchenbaucher," someone said. "We're awful grateful to you for your help." Then a crumple of bills was thrust into his hands. More than he'd taken off the dead Robert Welsh. More than enough, certainly, for a second suit and another stay in a hotel.

"Thank you," Archibald said.

He waited until all the others were out of sight before he began to run, not back to his hotel downtown, but instead toward the public bridge that led to Digby. He was anxious to put some distance between himself and what had just transpired. He knew, regardless of their confidence, they'd all eventually be caught. Someone, law enforcement or otherwise, would come for them. And in the hashing out of all that had gone on, the people of Ainsworth would realize they'd been taken for a ride, duped by a charlatan pretending to know about earthquakes. Their anger would flare anew, this time at Archibald. Fake anger. He'd been their excuse to do something they'd wanted to do all along, and once they'd finished, he could be their scapegoat too. But by then Archibald would be long gone.

He spent the night at an inn that was really just a single room in the home of an elderly couple. They fed him soup and asked him polite, unobtrusive questions. If they thought Archibald's lack of luggage odd for a traveler, they didn't let on. In the morning, he paid cash for a ride on a coach going out of town. Any direction. He didn't care where in particular. Any little town would do. His time in Ainsworth had turned out to be a great success. The more he thought about it, the more he felt confident he could replicate that success almost anywhere. All he would have to do was let himself be the vehicle for whatever it was people most wanted: revenge or justice or answers or hope or prophesy. He could be a scientist, but he could also say he was a politician, a preacher, an inventor. An outsider with some knowledge. The key, he'd learned in the past few days, was a willingness to relinquish the control that had at first so thrilled him. Once he'd offered himself up as the holder of information—whatever it may be, it didn't matter—to then let those around him decide what they wished to do with it. And take what he could from the arrangement. As much as he could get.

In this way, he found a new vocation. It seemed to him something he would not grow weary of, would never find tedious or dull. Something he could do over and over and over again, all across the isolated, lonely, angry places of the West.

Archibald kept his promise to himself from Ainsworth. When he took a new name, he picked an object. Well, not an object, but certainly a noun: Quake. In honor of the event that had brought him to his new way of life. He kept the last name Auchenbaucher because he'd grown used to it. He'd been Quake Auchenbaucher for almost a decade and the title had served him well in his many and varied occupations since. He'd been Quake the pastor, Quake the newspaperman, Quake the cartographer, Quake the census taker, and so on. Now, Quake from the Department of the Interior, Quake the man of the law.

There was a song her father liked to sing. It went like this:

Up from the banks of the muddy Mississippi / A woman did climb blind and drippy / She said I come from the shallows, I come from the deep / I come with the power to see you in your sleep.

It was the sort of thing he'd hum to himself while he worked in his shop or cooked at the stove. Sometimes as he sang, he would chuckle a little, and other times he would sigh. She came to think of the song as a defense of sorts, a tool her father turned to when the trauma and tumult of his life overran him and he wished to clear his mind. It was like a prayer, a mantra. And when she heard its melody, equal parts peppy and dreary, she felt herself grow melancholy and think, Poor Dad has suffered so much. I only wish I could do more for him.

But then one day near the end of his life (an event he had not antici-pated, though she had), she asked him on what occasions he sang his song. And he said it was in times when he was thinking nothing at all. It was just a way to fill his empty head with something nice. And wasn't that just like him? *she thought.* Happy as a duck, to whom water never sticks, no matter how much of it there is. *Then he taught her the other verse, which he had not sung aloud during her girlhood, believing it inappropriate for a young lady.*

I'm a creature of horror and total despair / Water snakes and toads jump from my hair / When I get to your house you'll know I'm meaner / 'Cause I'll point and laugh at your crooked little wiener.

She had taken the song as her own. She sang it both when she needed to push something unbearable from her mind and also when her mind was good for nothing else at all, an empty place that required filling. She sang it frequently now and could not always discern which occasion it was for.

6

"Inspector Auchenbaucher, do you know what an anarchist is?" This question was from Chief Hornsweller. They were in a tent saloon, sitting at a rickety table, drinking what the bartender insisted was beer. But Quake feared it was in part made of some other, less palatable substance (dishwater, maybe). For this reason, Quake left his beverage untouched. Hornsweller had indulged in several.

It was only early afternoon, but Hornsweller had insisted Quake come with him for a little "walk and talk" concerning his thoughts on the fire. Though it had turned out to be more of a "sit and drink." They'd been at the bar an hour and the topic of the fire had yet to come up.

"I believe an anarchist is a person who refuses to acknowledge the legitimacy of an established government, or the notion of a ruling order in general," Quake said.

"An anarchist," Hornsweller said, clearing his empty beer glasses to the side of the table, leaning forward as if he himself were about to offer up an anarchical conspiracy, "is a person who wants to fuck shit up for no good reason."

"All right," Quake said.

"Have you ever met anyone like that?" Hornsweller asked.

"I can't say that I ever have."

Hornsweller nodded in a way Quake thought was meant to look sage, but of course it did not.

"They're all over the place," he said. "More and more each day, I hear. They've got no respect for human life or personal property. In fact, they'll destroy whatever they can just to make their point."

"And what point is that?"

"It's that they don't want any federal government out here. Statehood is what they're fighting. Tooth and nail. Like weasels in a sack. That's what they are. Nasty vermin, these anarchists."

"You're saying you're having a problem with anarchists here in Spokane Falls?" Quake asked, though he felt he knew where this line of discussion was leading.

"An anarchist is our whole problem. That's what I'm saying. It's Heydale! He's trying to undermine everything the good citizens of this territory are working for. He set the fire here. And, as I've said, I do believe he may have set the other fires too, in the other cities. To fuck shit up!"

"I thought you said Heydale started the fire at Wolfe's Hotel because his relationship with a prostitute who lived there had soured."

"Sure. That's why he started the fire at the hotel. But he was going to start a fire somewhere anyway. Just like he did in Seattle and wherever else."

And wherever else. This suggested to Quake that Hornsweller was just grasping at straws. He didn't even know the names of the other cities that had burned that summer. He probably didn't even realize he was treading on Quake's turf with these claims. But others would realize it if Hornsweller started sharing this around, which clearly was his intention: to become a rising star of the new state by protecting it from the previously unseen threats of anarchy and Barton Heydale.

Either way, Quake felt he needed to put a stop to Hornsweller's blathering.

"Okay," Quake said. "Let's find out."

Quake led on long legs. Hornsweller had to take little jogging hopsteps every few seconds to keep up. This pleased Quake. It made Hornsweller seem like a pet—a dog, easily trained and desperate not to get left behind.

"What are we going to do?" Hornsweller asked in a gaspy voice.

"We're going to ask Heydale if he's an anarchist."

"He'll lie. He's unscrupulous. You know how unscrupulous he is."

"No, he won't," Quake said. "When a man takes action in the name of a political cause, he becomes a champion of the cause, does he not? He needs people to know his reasons. What good is championing a cause if he lies about it when asked? None at all. He may as well not have acted. So, if he is really an anarchist, he will admit to it readily. Otherwise, his anarchism has been in vain."

Hornsweller conceded this made sense.

Back at the jail, the scene Quake had engineered played itself out. Hornsweller jammed his face against the bars of Heydale's cell and demanded to know if he was an anarchist.

Heydale, of course, said no.

Hornsweller looked to Quake, disappointed.

"Mr. Heydale," Quake said, "what do you think about the prospect of Washington Territory achieving statehood? Are you for or against it?"

"Oh, I'm very much for it," Heydale said. "Who wouldn't be? Isn't everyone tired of living in this filthy backwater?"

"Don't call my city a filthy backwater," Hornsweller snapped. "You're the filthy one." Then the police chief walked off, leaving Quake and Heydale alone, presumably convinced that Heydale was not an anarchist and that to continue to suggest as much publicly would do no good. Quake allowed himself a rare smile.

"What was all that about?" Heydale asked.

"Hornsweller believes the Spokane arsonist may have set the fire as a result of his feelings over statehood," Quake said.

Heydale's face took on a knotted look. "Oh dear," he said. "He'll think it's my fault for sure now."

"Why's that?"

"Because fire is good for Washington. He'll think I set the fire because I wanted to accelerate its becoming a state."

When Quake asked for further explanation, he was treated to one of the more lucid statements he'd heard from Heydale, who offered up a theory that he said had been imparted to him by his former boss, the owner of the First Bank of Spokane Falls. The man's name was Zane Zeeb. Heydale admitted to disliking him for personal reasons, and that in his darker moments before his arrest, he had even become somewhat obsessed with Zeeb, convinced he was seeing him everywhere, though Zeeb never acknowledged him in any way and seemed, in fact, to be avoiding him.

"I was hallucinating him. I know that now," Heydale said.

But in spite of this dislike, Heydale said he had the utmost respect for the man as both a banker and a student of politics. The Zeeb doctrine of fire, apparently, was that the disasters gave the territory a chance to show off its best self in the face of adversity, and that this would help assure it a place in the union. Surely, Congress could not deny them now.

"That's why so many cities donated money after the fire," Heydale explained. "To make a public show of Washington being unified."

"How much money?" Quake asked.

"I've no idea. Quite a lot, though. It was coming in from all over. Mr. Zeeb was assisting the city with it."

Quake took a moment with this information, rolling it around in his mind, melding it with what he already knew about Spokane Falls.

"It doesn't seem odd to you that as the manager of the city's only bank, you never saw that money?" he asked. "Where would it go, if not to the city's bank?"

"I didn't think of it," Heydale said. "It never occurred to me."

Quake suspected this was just one of many, many things that may have slipped Heydale's notice. "Well, I imagine that's what your old boss was doing, slinking around town and avoiding you. You weren't hallucinating him. He was helping someone embezzle it. Making the money disappear in a way that looked all nice and proper."

Heydale looked as if he'd just been punched in the gut. Quake couldn't tell if his shock was from learning his employer was not the upstanding citizen he'd once admired, or from the news that he, Heydale, was not Spokane Falls's greatest fire-born con man. But then, given that he'd spent the past two weeks in a jail cell, he'd probably figured that out for himself.

7

Quake believed there were no honest men in Spokane Falls. His work had taken him to so many cities and towns across Washington Territory, and in most of them he found people to be just as they were: straightforward, trusting, and trustworthy. But here in Spokane Falls, he'd yet to meet or even hear of a single person who fit that description. It seemed everyone was out to get one over on someone else. There was Heydale, of course. Then there was his story of the woman who ultimately got the upper hand on him. There was Heydale's boss, Zeeb, yet another crooked banker. And then whoever Zeeb was working for, presumably city officials— councilmen and the mayor. There were the brazen thieves in the streets, and the only slightly more highbrow thieves selling fraudulent or overpriced goods from tents. Then there were the police, who were charged with keeping the peace but seemed on the take just like the other crooks.

And there was Quake himself. Never honest, never trustworthy, never straightforward. He had no illusions otherwise. Still, he did not think himself the worst person in Spokane Falls. Not by a long shot.

The worst person was Chief Hornsweller. Quake decided as much the day after their conversation about anarchists. He was leaving the police station, intending to get a meal at one of the tent restaurants before heading back to his hotel for the night, when Hornsweller called out to him.

"Inspector Auchenbaucher? Could I have a word with you in my office?" The police chief's voice had a nervous edge to it, but when Quake turned to meet him, he found him smiling. Further proof of the man's lack of self-control. He was so clearly up to something, even a child would have known it.

Quake followed him into the space Hornsweller called an office, but it was really just a room. It had no desk or bookshelves. There was only one chair. Quake couldn't imagine what Hornsweller used the office for. He probably just sat in it and called that work.

Hornsweller lowered himself onto the chair. Quake leaned against the wall, reaching out with a hand to close the door. Though it was Hornsweller who had summoned him and not the other way around, he wanted the police chief to feel a little trapped with him. Intimacy, Quake found, had a way of stripping away insincerity. There was no one for Hornsweller to put on a show for.

"Seattle told us you need to be paid," Hornsweller started. "For your services and all. We intend to make good on that."

A pleasant surprise. It had, in other cities, been Quake's least favorite part of the arson inspector scam: explaining why a fee needed to be tendered by that municipality—expenses not covered by his salary, and so on. But here, Hornsweller was relieving him of that discomfort. Too good to be true, Quake decided.

"Trouble is, the mayor says the city's short on cash."

There it was. Quake fixed Hornsweller with a deeply impassive gaze.

"The cost of making repairs since the fire, it nearly cleaned us out, assets-wise," he continued.

A lie. Spokane Falls was bursting at the seams with cash and goods from other cities. Though Hornsweller had no idea Quake knew this.

"And then there's all the money Heydale stole from the bank. Well, with all that, we just don't have the funds. But don't worry, you'll still get paid! The mayor's got a plan for that."

Still Quake said nothing. Kept waiting.

"What he says we can give you instead are banknotes. We've collected most of the ones Heydale issued before we arrested him. We don't need them for evidence anymore, so we're putting them back into circulation. Just until the city gets its cash situation sorted out. They're certified from a bank, by a banker."

"You intend to pay me in forgeries made by a man currently in police custody for those very forgeries, among other crimes?"

Hornsweller looked at his shoes. "Well, Heydale says they're good as cash. The mayor says the same."

What a truly awful place, Quake thought, where the highest-ranking civic leaders were perfectly comfortable using the logic of their most hated criminal.

Most men in Quake's position would call bullshit. But the brazenness of this bullshit Hornsweller was trying to sell him gave him pause. It meant someone in Spokane Falls—Hornsweller or the mayor or someone else—thought Quake of so little consequence, they were willing to cheat him with no fear of repercussion. Again, he wondered if his scheme might have been discovered. But if that were the case, wouldn't he already be under arrest? Spokane Falls, he'd found, was not a place to hesitate. He couldn't be sure one way or the other. Not that the reason mattered. Success was never a result of perfect understanding. It was only about shifting the balance of power back into his favor. But he had become exhausted by this game he felt himself playing with Hornsweller—nearly every day a new problem for which to devise an elaborate fix. A lesser con man would have given up. Quake had never done that before on a job. He wasn't going to let Spokane Falls be the first to get the best of him.

So, with no more than a quick nod, he agreed to what Hornsweller had told him. Then he left the room before Hornsweller had the chance to say anything else. Then he closed the door behind him. He did this to show he was the one having the last word, but he pushed too hard and it slammed, betraying his anger.

An Event from the
Impossible Present

Quake was in a forest that had burned. Everything was still black and charred, but the smoke was gone, replaced by the smell of fir trees and rain. Nothing crunched under his boots. The earth was soft now, waterlogged. Rain had come heavy to this place and there was new growth everywhere. Saplings and ferns and fungi all sprouted up from the ground at the same time. Quake looked down as he walked, searching for morel mushrooms, his favorite. They loved burn areas, growing up in pockets of threes and fours, sometimes a half dozen. Soon, he was seeing them all over, more than he could possibly pick.

"If I was a mushroom, I'd be a morel," Quake said.

"Because you show up after fires. These are the conditions in which you thrive." This from a woman standing at his side.

"No. Because I'm delicious sautéed in butter."

The woman laughed. She wasn't touching Quake. She didn't need to. Even standing away from her, he knew she loved him. They were a couple, engaged with plans to marry soon. He was showing

her this thatch of woods because he knew she'd find it just as wonderful as he. Not the destruction, but the signs of what comes next.
And he was right. She was delighted. She sprinted ahead, then back
to him, reporting what she saw: newts and salamanders emerging
from inky puddles; a family of beavers damming a stream; a whole
grove of new saplings, already as high as her waist. Quake smiled
so wide and for so long, his face hurt. He had gone many years allowing himself only the barest signs of any outward emotion. But
now, here, he was happy. Happy to see her happy.

"Nature is always reinventing itself, just like people do," he said.

"Some people more often than others," she said. Then she winked.

The woman was not anyone Quake knew in real life. She was a
composite of other women he'd met and liked, and also of Heydale's
description of his own mysterious love. If Quake were a more forthcoming person, he would admit to Heydale he found the same attributes attractive: red hair and a knowing smile. Mysterious—*a
certain kind of woman*, to borrow a phrase from Heydale. Plus, she'd
pulled something over on the man, and that meant, whoever she
was, she was smart. Quake liked smart. So, he folded this person
into his own image of the fantastic woman he might one day be
with. She was clever. She was old enough and observant enough to
know the hard truths of the world, but had not been made bitter by
them. And most important, she knew all about Quake's past and
about how he made his money, and she didn't care.

They followed the path of the fire's destruction, all fresh and
new with life. A fox kit popped its head from a den, and the woman
bent down, making clicking sounds until the creature came to
her, letting her feed it berries from her hand and stroke its fuzzy
back.

"That little babe says this is a good place," the woman said, as the fox bounded back to its home. "Can we stay?"

"I don't know, can we?"

She smiled and Quake took her by the hand and led her across the stream and down a little path to a cabin, tidy and theirs. A surprise for her. Upon seeing it she kissed him again and again and again.

This was a daydream. A mental refuge Quake crafted for himself in Spokane Falls. He let this fantasy play through his mind on a loop. He'd daydreamed of women before—like the imaginary girlfriend who consoled him about Hornsweller when that man first began to worry him, and also, really anytime he was lonesome, which was often. But this daydream was unique in its consistency. He kept returning to it. Always the same story, the same scenes and dialogue. From the depths of his displeasure in ash-mired Spokane Falls, he conjured deep lonesome woods and a secluded cabin. And, most important, love—one of the few desires in his life he felt truly powerless to achieve.

———

She'd spent a fair amount of time in wooded places, and had found she preferred the city.

———

8

Did you know that fires are good for forests?" Quake asked Heydale. They were sitting at a small table behind the police station. Quake had grown tired of "interviewing" Heydale in his cramped, foul-smelling cell, so he'd told Hornsweller that criminals were more forthcoming with confessions when in the outdoors. Now they conducted their talks at a table set up for that purpose. Quake leaned back in his chair as he spoke, his arms up, hands hooked behind his head, a posture Heydale could not mimic even if he wanted; he was handcuffed to his chair.

Quake had stopped asking Heydale about the Spokane Falls fire, however, unless someone else was within earshot. Such questioning was all for show anyway. This day in particular, frustrated with Hornsweller—and everyone else in Spokane Falls, for that matter—he preferred to talk of almost anything else. He had let himself spend his morning in his forest daydream and he wanted to stay in that world. Heydale could come along if he wanted.

"Like the fires that are happening in those mountains, just outside town." He pointed south. Heydale, without speaking, pointed north. Quake adjusted north.

"Anyway, did you know that those forests need fire?" Quake asked. "It's important. It clears out all the dead stuff, makes way for new growth, new life. There are certain types of trees whose spores won't open until they get heated up. They need fire to spread their seeds. That's how essential it is. People are generally opposed to fire because it's an inconvenience, or they're fearful of it. But it's natural. It's a good thing. Did you know that?"

Heydale seemed to consider this question carefully before speaking. "Did you know more than half the money in circulation in the United States is counterfeit?" he asked. "Did you know that?"

Quake stopped thinking about his forest fantasy then. He unhooked his hands and leaned forward in his chair. No, he said, he didn't know anything about that at all.

Well, not half of all currency, Heydale corrected himself. Maybe 10 percent. He didn't know for sure. But there was a time when it was more than half.

"Go on," Quake said.

Heydale told him that before greenbacks became standard, all banks printed their own notes. And because there were so many different versions of currency around the country, there was no good way to tell what was real and what wasn't. So, there proliferated a vast counterfeit industry, to the point that most ordinary merchants and citizens never had any idea if the money they'd been given was genuine or fake. Banks still had the power to print their own notes, Heydale explained. But it was no longer a necessity, and so most, like his bank in Spokane Falls, chose not to as a general rule. Though they did continue to accept notes from other banks, which meant there was always the possibility of taking and giving counterfeit bills.

"We have books at the bank called counterfeit detectors. They describe every legitimate banknote in circulation and its known counterfeits," he said.

"Do you know a counterfeit bill when you see one?" Quake asked.

"Sometimes," Heydale said.

"Then what do you do?"

"Wad it up and throw it back in the guy's face!"

"Really?"

"No. I take the bill, I guess," Heydale said, his expression turning hangdog. "It doesn't matter anyway. Money is worth money as long as everyone agrees it's worth money. I'm the bank. If I take a bill and then give the bill to someone else, well, that makes it money, even if it's not."

"Just like the banknotes you were giving out."

Heydale slumped into his chair. "I said I was sorry for that," he said. "You know I said I was sorry," and Quake agreed he did.

"Now, tell me something else," Quake said. "At the time of your arrest, how much real cash was still in your bank?"

9

It was early evening by the time Quake returned Heydale to his cell. He left the police station and walked through the maze of downtown to the tent saloon Hornsweller had taken him to, where, he knew, the police chief and other officers frequented after work. Quake stepped through the little canvas opening and found the interior of the structure humid and musty. He didn't know why anyone would ever want to spend time in such a place. It made him anxious for the outdoors—the true outdoors, forests and hills and plateaus and canyons. He comforted himself with the knowledge that he would leave the city soon and could go where he liked.

He found the police easily. They were the loudest group, taking up too much space and making the other early evening drinkers uncomfortable. Quake had to tap Hornsweller on the shoulder to get his attention.

"I'd like you and your men to return with me to the station. I'm afraid it's regarding a fairly pressing matter."

Hornsweller stood and signaled his subordinates to follow him, which they did with a measure of precision Quake had not previously seen from them or thought them capable of. It was only once they were outside that he realized the brisk, uniform exit was a trick the police must have used at bars all over town—a way to leave without having to pay for their drinks.

Back at the station, Quake led the policemen into Hornsweller's office and then gestured for them to circle up around him. He hadn't planned on speaking to the whole force, just Hornsweller. It was better this way. Later, they would all have the same story to tell. There'd be no hearsay or rumors to gum up the works.

"Barton Heydale has made a confession to me," Quake said.

"I knew he would!" Hornsweller said, slapping his hands together. "I knew he was the one!" All around him the other officers shifted and murmured.

Quake shook his head. He kept his movements slow and his speech steady. He wanted to be a counterweight to the other men's excitement.

"No," he said. "Not the fire. He's made a confession about his activities at the bank."

"We already know that stuff," Hornsweller said. "He's been confessing to that since the beginning. I've heard him confess it so much, I wish he'd shut up."

"This is new," Quake said. "And I'm afraid it's much more serious than his other transgressions, which only impacted the particular patrons who received those loans or banknotes. This impacts the entire city."

This was met with silence. The men were listening, waiting.

"Heydale has admitted to me that those crude banknotes he gave out were merely intended as a decoy—a way to keep as much cash in the bank as possible. At the same time, he was creating much more elaborately forged bills, ones nearly indistinguishable from genuine American greenbacks. He says he has books that demonstrate how to do this, and he followed their models."

Quake paused here for a moment and looked around the room, briefly locking eyes with each man present. He knew there were some who would not be able to follow what he said, but he wanted to convey to all of them that this was very serious business.

"He then switched out his forgeries for the real money. He won't say how much he ultimately took, but he was working at this for quite a while, it seems. It is my assessment that nearly all the money currently inside the vault of the First Bank of Spokane Falls may, in fact, be counterfeit."

Again, pause, eye contact.

"I'm not a specialist in this matter, and I have no way of telling which bills are real and which are fake. But as an agent of the federal government, I am obligated to confiscate all of the money in the bank and turn it over to the Office of the Treasury where it can be examined more closely."

"Bullshit," Hornsweller spat, and Quake's pulse quickened, though he kept his face neutral and his breath even.

"We don't need no treasury to tell us what's real money. We'll get the banker to tell us. We got ways. He'll tell real fast."

Quake felt the men turn hungry for violence. But he'd gotten better at this part over the years—managing bloodlust. He'd been lucky in Ainsworth. He knew that now and wouldn't take the risk again.

"I'm afraid I can't allow that," he said. "The United States of America does not condone the torture of its criminals. And if you wish to prove you are capable of being officers of police in the *state* of Washington, you would do well to follow the rules of the nation which you are about to enter as full citizens. There are changes coming, boys. You don't want to be on the wrong side of it. Believe me, that creep Heydale isn't worth it."

Smiles vanished. Eyes on the floor, shamed and compliant.

"Though, what you do to the man once I'm out of town, that's your own prerogative," Quake added, and then immediately regretted it. He had them. He could have told them to do anything in that moment. He could have told them it was in the goddamn constitution that they had to set Heydale free and if they didn't, President Harrison himself was going to come see they were all stripped of their badges.

But, as always, Quake had acted with his own best interests in mind. If it made his last days in Spokane Falls even the tiniest bit easier to remain in the good graces of the police force—to have them think him on their side, rather than some bully lording his power over them—that was worth the sacrifice of Heydale. A man's whole life in exchange for Quake's temporary comfort and convenience.

"And what about the fire, then?" Hornsweller asked, his voice tentative, his eyes just barely lifted to meet Quake's.

"My investigation does point to Heydale as the likely culprit, yes."

After that, Quake walked south from downtown far enough to finally find the end of the fire's destruction. It gave way to a pleasant neighborhood on a hill, big houses surrounded by leafy trees. Quiet streets cooled by a breeze that never made it to the bowels of downtown. He wished he'd found this section of the city sooner. It would have done him well just to know he could escape to such a place if need be.

He walked until he found a bar—tiny and wedged between a neighborhood grocery and a tailor's shop. It was made of brick and looked as if it had been in its place for many years. He sat a long time, nursing a drink and thinking about what he'd observed that day with regard to money and the deceits surrounding it. He'd been in the deceit-for-money business himself for quite a while. But that didn't mean he couldn't still learn a thing or two.

He decided now that he was himself a kind of counterfeiter. He'd made his life's work creating out of nothing situations that people wanted and were therefore willing to believe sound. Words not backed by truth were no different than paper not backed by coin. The key was only that everyone had to agree. Just as Heydale had said. And, for one reason or another, people always agreed to believe Quake. They looked at his bastardized currency and, out of desperation or just blind optimism, proclaimed it of great value.

But he couldn't go on like this forever. The Spokane Falls scheme, with its many trapdoors and complications, had shown him as much. His line of work was growing more dangerous. Quake didn't think this was a failing in his own methodology so much as an indication of changing times in the place where he chose to conduct his business.

Eventually, Washington Territory would catch up to him, just as the nation ultimately had to the counterfeiters. Lives would stop being so remote and desperate, and he wouldn't be able to win confidence so easily. Statehood seemed like the first step in this new and unfortunate direction.

On his way back to his hotel, he spied a fox and three kits playing at the base of a maple tree. Seeking companionship, he crouched low and clicked to them, like the woman in his daydream. They ignored him. And when he ventured closer, clicking louder, they spooked and scampered out of sight.

"Oh Quakey, what have you done?" he heard the woman from his daydream ask, and he was ashamed.

"I didn't mean to scare them," he said out loud. He knew it was a one-sided conversation, but the voice sounded real, the voice of this woman he loved. He wanted to stay in its good graces.

"Not the animals," she said. "All the rest. You're a wildfire grown too wild, you know that? You take more than your share."

"What would you have me do instead, then?" he asked. But there was no answer. Unnerved and oddly chastened, he returned to his hotel and tried not to think of her again.

There was a trick her father liked to show her. He was keen for little stunts with sleight of hand. Most of them weren't very good. But there was one that worked well, and as an adult she had learned to do it herself in order to delight children, back when she led the kind of life in which she was often in their company.

It went like this. She would hold out her hands as fists, then turn and open them, showing both hands empty. Then she would make them back into fists. "Tap the left three times," she'd instruct her audience member. He or she would do this, slowly and deliberately, the way kids are apt to when faced with something mysterious. Then she would knock her fists together and open the left hand. In it would now be a coin, which she would give to the child. The tapping was a distraction. The child was looking to her left while she moved her right to her pocket for the coin, then she moved it from one hand to the other with the knocking. Then it was in the left like magic.

One day, in the town by the lake, she saw a little boy, maybe five years old, sitting on a curb outside a store. He was likely waiting for a parent shopping inside. He looked bored and she thought he might like to see the trick.

"Can I show you something?" she asked, bending to his level.

He nodded.

"Look at my palms. Nothing in my hands, right?"

Again the boy nodded.

"But you can make a penny appear if you wish it. Tap my left fist three times."

Slow and gentle, he obeyed, just as she'd known he would. But when her fist opened, she was the one surprised.

"Oh no!" the boy cried upon seeing the coin. "Witchcraft! Conjuring! She has trapped me into doing the devil's work! I didn't mean to, forgive me, forgive me!"

He ran off down the street. She had thought once the trick was done she would give him the penny so that he might buy a treat for himself at the store. Instead, she went inside and got a little bag of taffy for herself. She was sad to have frightened the boy. It was not her intent. But it was a little funny too, the way a fake trick could seem so convincing. But if she had told the boy what she could really do, he would never believe it. No one ever did.

———

10

The next morning, Quake watched as Hornsweller and three of his men pulled money from the vault at the First Bank of Spokane Falls, counted it, and then placed it into steel lockboxes the size of lunch pails. The cash filled thirteen such boxes. The police officers worked in silence with a professional efficiency for which Quake could not account, and so he took credit himself. He felt that the focus with which he approached his own work in Spokane Falls had set a good example for these men and perhaps encouraged them to take their roles a little more seriously. Every so often, an officer would stop to inspect a bill, turning it over in his hands. One man did this several times in a row, then held the stack up, looking to Quake with approval-seeking eyes, and said, "I'm pretty sure all these here are fakes."

Quake gave him a nod and a "Good work, son."

The bank's two employees stood nearby, watching. They were identical twins, rumpled and slack-jawed, who'd introduced themselves to Quake as "co-managers" of the bank, a statement that made even Hornsweller roll his eyes, and it gave Quake a pretty good idea of the amount of attention he needed to pay to these two: none at all.

They remained silent through the city-sanctioned pillage of their place of employment until all the cash had been stored, ready for travel. Then one of them tapped Quake on the shoulder—such a tentative touch, Quake felt he could have just ignored it. But everything was going well for him, and he was feeling generous.

"What can I do for you?" he asked.

"What should we give to people who come to the bank to withdraw cash?"

Hornsweller and his men looked up, as if this issue had not occurred to them.

Quake smiled. "The banknotes your former employer wrote. You can use them for the time being. Chief Hornsweller assured me they have been safely housed in his care and are ready to return to circulation for use in your fine city."

Hornsweller and his team escorted Quake to the train station. The police followed him in nearly lockstep through downtown, looking over their shoulders with grave expressions, as if they were protecting some visiting dignitary. It was quite the send-off and Quake was pleased. Things had turned out just fine for him in Spokane Falls after all. His patience had paid off.

He thanked the police and shook hands all around. A private car had been arranged for him on a train bound for Portland, where he'd told them he'd be returning to his home office at the Department of the Interior. The private car was to help ensure the safe transit of the cash, and also for Quake's comfort and pleasure; he was now a very respected person in Spokane Falls, not only for having figured out who started their fire but also for uncovering the most complex counterfeit scheme the city had ever seen. They were treating him well on his last day in town, but unlike in Seattle, he did not want to linger and bask in Spokane Falls's hospitality. These were not people to be trusted. This was not a place he ever planned to return to.

He got on the train to Portland, but two stops later, he slipped off with his cash at the sleepy Stevens depot. Then he went looking for someone from whom he could buy a horse.

Interlude II

In 1920, eastern Washington received a visit from its first barn-stormer. A man who went by the name Trap Erickson flew his biplane in loop-the-loops, upside down, and high overhead only to swoop down fast. This show took place on a farm just outside the town of Spangle, to the amazement of local folks who had gathered in the fields. After the show, Trap shook hands and signed autographs. He was a good-natured guy, generous with his time, and more than happy to spend the afternoon chatting up the people who came to see him. One young woman in particular caught his eye, and he had hoped she might ask for an autograph, or maybe even a kiss. It was not uncommon for women to want to kiss him after shows, a request he gladly obliged, regardless of their age or appearance. But this young woman—one he would genuinely have liked to kiss—made no such request. She stood apart from the rest of the crowd, a girl of ten or eleven at her side. Trap kept stealing glances until finally the young woman said something to the girl and took her by the hand, and both turned to leave.

"That's all right," Trap said to himself. "Something tells me I'll see her again."

And he was right, he would.

The woman's name was Susan Edgings McLaughlin. She was twenty-two and newly married to her childhood sweetheart, Thomas McLaughlin. They lived and worked together on a wheat farm with Thomas's parents and his younger sister, the girl Susan had been with for the barnstorming. Susan loved Thomas and his family. Unfortunately, since starting her life with them, she had been beset by melancholy. She did not know what to make of her unhappiness. But when she saw an ad for Trap's show, she felt the woolen blanket of her depression lift slightly. She asked the older McLaughlins if she might have some money to take her sister-in-law, an impish tomboy who would certainly love to see a flying show. They agreed. And the youngster had indeed enjoyed Trap's tricks, but it was Susan who felt herself truly moved.

"Do you think you could ever do something like that?" Susan asked her sister-in-law on the way home.

"Sure," said the girl. "Sure, I could fly like that. Maybe I'll learn when I'm older. More fun than driving a tractor, that's for certain!"

"I think I could too," Susan said.

This remark must have struck the girl as odd. Susan was not the daredevil type. She did not even care for galloping her horse. But the girl was too immersed in her own imagination to give it much thought, her arms spread wide to form wings as she walked in a zigzaggy fashion.

"Perhaps your arms ought to go back, not to the sides," Susan said, but the girl did not heed her, and why should she?

That night, when the rest of the family had gone to sleep, Susan snuck out to the fields. She reached her arms back as she had suggested to her sister-in-law. Then she started to walk. No need to run. She did not feel running was required. She sensed in her arms a certain upward pull. She struggled to keep them behind her, straight and strong. Then the pull extended to the rest of her body. It lifted her from the ground, into the cool night air.

Just a quick flight, Susan thought, as she circled the McLaughlin property, *nothing fancy*. But she couldn't help herself. She dipped and looped. She corkscrewed and barrel-rolled. She returned to the farmhouse smiling and the joy stayed with her throughout the next day. The family, so surprised to see her happy, did not dare question the change. Thomas kissed her on the lips in front of everyone while his sister giggled.

Susan continued to fly at night, but the thrill did not last. She wondered if real barnstormers like Trap Erickson also felt the excitement of their trade fade over time.

Some months later, Susan's little sister-in-law came to her with a page torn from a newspaper. Trap Erickson was coming back for another show, this time with two other pilots.

"A real flying circus!" the girl said. "Can we go?"

Susan assured her they could.

———

This show was bigger. In addition to Trap, there were Anders Eir-meyer, a WWI flying ace, and Shelly Gunn, who garnered interest for being a woman pilot, and a good-looking one at that. The crowd was three times larger as well.

Susan hadn't been planning to do anything, only to go and watch like before. But almost as soon as she took her seat, she felt she could not keep it. Her arms compelled her. Susan, who was normally very reserved and eschewed all public attention, thought to herself, *I guess this is happening*, and found she didn't mind.

Gunn had just finished her flight and Trap was on the makeshift runway when Susan took flight. It was a beautiful and startling thing, this woman with long hair, in a beige dress and boots, sud-denly zipping above the crowd. Many present assumed it part of the show, a trick involving wires. There were whistles and catcalls. But as Susan went higher, the sounds of encouragement faded. There was no trick and people didn't like it.

"That bitch is really flying!" one man shouted.

Only Susan's sister-in-law continued to clap and cheer. She, and Trap Erickson.

Susan, sensing her performance may not have been well received, did not return to the show. Instead, she landed in a field two farms over. Then, when the rest of the audience had left, she walked back to collect her young charge. Trap was waiting for her as well.

"Fly with us again sometime?" he asked. Susan blushed.

LEYNA KROW

"I mean it. The whole team loved what you did."

This was untrue. Gunn had dismissed Susan as "some bored housewife looking for attention." Eirmeyer had been defecating in a goat trough and missed the whole thing. It didn't matter. Trap was the most popular member of the troop and the big draw for audiences. So, what he said was law.

Trap and Co. had three more shows in eastern Washington before they left for a tour of the Midwest. Susan joined them for these as local talent. Trap kept her original place in the lineup, right between Gunn and himself. The announcer introduced her as "the Flying Mother," though she had no children.

"A real hometown girl!" he'd shout. "She can cook your bacon, then fly off with your pig!"

Susan was unclear what any of that meant, but she relished her role in the show right from the start. And because she'd received the announcer's booming approval, and a hug from Trap in front of everyone once she'd landed, the crowds were more committed in their support of her now. They whooped and crowed. People she had known from school called to her by name, but she pretended not to hear. The thrill was back, same as the first night, alone in the field. When the three shows were over, Trap implored her to follow them to Kansas. He made it clear his interest was not in her talents alone.

"What's that husband of yours got I don't?" he asked. He took her rebuff well. He had never overstepped her boundaries when they were performing together, and he vowed not to do so now that they were through, either.

Susan was loyal to Thomas, and to his parents. She told herself she'd had her fun. It was time to return to her life.

194

But her life would not allow her return. She found her relationship with both Thomas and the older McLaughlins had measurably cooled. There were no words spoken on the matter of her flying. They had not attended any of her shows, and now that it was done, a pall seemed to hang over the household. And in town, people pointed and whispered. These were the same people who had called her name during the shows. She could not understand it.

By winter of that year, the narrative surrounding Susan had become unkind.

"She thinks she can fly," people started to say.

"Poor dear."

"She always seemed so bright, so normal."

The trouble reached a head one December night when, leaving a grange meeting with the McLaughlins, Susan was tripped by another woman. The act was clearly deliberate.

"What's the meaning of this?" she asked.

"I knew you couldn't fly," the woman said. "That proves it. If you could fly, you would have done it now to avoid falling."

"That makes no sense," Susan said. She tried to offer something else, but by then the men were already fighting—Thomas and the woman's husband were grappling on the dirt floor.

"Oh, if it will end all this," Susan said to no one in particular. She put her arms behind her and lifted off. Everyone stopped to watch. They were still watching when a police officer, who had been summoned when the fight first began, arrived. Thomas and the other man were arrested, as well as Susan, all for disturbing the peace.

Thomas and his fight-mate were released the next morning with stern warnings against public brawling. Susan, however, was further detained until a psychiatrist could be found to make an examination.

When the man arrived he concluded her delusional and likely a threat to her own safety. At her sanity hearing, community members testified that they had heard Susan make claims that she could fly but had never seen her fly themselves, of course. When in fact the truth was just the opposite. Susan never spoke of this talent, but everyone in town had seen her do it.

Mr. and Mrs. McLaughlin did not come to her rescue, nor did her beloved Thomas.

Susan spent the remainder of her life at Eastern Washington State Hospital for the Insane, too dismayed even to soar to freedom. She died at the age of forty-four of pneumonia.

She had few visitors in her years in the asylum. Trap would have come, but he had no idea that anything of the kind had happened to her.

Her most consistent guest left no record in the visitor log, as she never set foot in the building. Instead, she buzzed by Susan's window, a flying girl who over the years turned into a flying woman, never to be caught or shamed or maligned by anyone. She was too good, too fast. She flew, as her sister-in-law had once suggested she do, with arms stretched behind.

PART III

ROSLYN

Roslyn the Seer

Roslyn Beck first began to levitate in the spring of 1884. She had been receiving visions—exact images of real things that would happen in the near or distant future—for most of her life. But this was something new. She knew right away that what she was doing was not really called levitating, but that was how she thought of it. It was a thing that happened to her sometimes when she meditated, and she liked how the phrase sounded in her mind: *I levitate when I meditate*. A pleasing rhyme, something she might have said aloud to children back when she was a schoolteacher. Also, that's what it felt like: lifting up, off the ground, to go somewhere else. Not her body, though, just her mind. Her mind would travel up and away from her, out the door and down the street and wherever it wanted. It would travel around, looking in on other people, observing them. As if Roslyn were a ghost. But not a ghost, just a mind, out for a walk on its own. Or maybe, more accurately, a soul out for a walk. Though Roslyn wasn't certain she believed in a soul.

After a while of this, Ernest told her a different word for what she was doing: *transcendence.* "You're not levitating," he said. "What you're describing is called 'transcending.' It's entering such a state of oneness with your body that it—your body, that is—allows you to disconnect for a little while and transcend to another place."

This was the way Ernest always talked: pompous and often at great length, regardless of the subject. But Ernest was the person who'd taught Roslyn to meditate in the first place and so she took him as the authority on these things. She nodded as he spoke.

"But, you're also not transcending," Ernest continued. "All you're really doing is getting blackout drunk and hallucinating."

Roslyn could see how Ernest might think this, since it was something that happened to her fairly regularly. The getting drunk and blacking out part. Not the hallucinating. But hallucinations could happen to a blacked-out person, Roslyn knew, so she did not begrudge Ernest his assumption.

In fact, it was because of her habit of getting drunk and blacking out that she was no longer a schoolteacher. Instead, she was a prostitute, living and working out of a small apartment on the second floor of Wolfe's Hotel on Railroad Avenue. She had done some other things in between. It hadn't been a straight shot for her, from schoolteacher to prostitute, like in some church-sponsored morality play. *Ruined by the Demon Drink!* No, not quite like that. But ultimately, there she was, in Wolfe's Hotel, having sex for money in her living room, which was also her bedroom.

This was how she knew Ernest. He was one of her customers. Though he was a white man, he said he was a Buddhist. Roslyn had told one of the other women who worked at Wolfe's Hotel this, and she'd asked if it meant he was into weird stuff, "like the Kama Sutra and all that?" But Roslyn said no; Ernest's tastes were very ordinary.

Although, after sex he liked to meditate. He showed Roslyn how, and she would sit and meditate with him. She enjoyed meditating and often continued by herself once Ernest had left. It was in these times, when she was alone, that she would levitate.

She didn't tell Ernest this, though. She thought it would hurt his feelings. He could be very sensitive. They were both sitting cross-legged on Roslyn's bed, facing each other. This was after sex and also after meditation, in the last of his time with her, which he usually used to pontificate on some subject or another of interest to him, like Buddhism, medicinal teas, acupuncture, or the Far East. Roslyn suspected Ernest had few, if any, other people in his life who were willing to listen to him, and so this became one of the services Roslyn provided as well.

Ernest was still talking. He was saying transcendence took years and years of meditation and only the best people—those who were already pretty close to achieving Nirvana—could do it. The implication here being that Roslyn was not such a person.

"Have you ever transcended?" she asked.

Roslyn could see Ernest blush behind his narrow beard. "Well, once, very briefly, only for a split second," he said. "But it was truly a life-altering experience. I'm confident I will do it again soon. My meditative practice has been going very well for some time."

"Where did you go?" she asked.

"What do you mean?"

"Where did you go when you transcended your body?"

"I didn't go anywhere," Ernest said, still pink-faced.

"Then how do you know you transcended?"

"I simply had the feeling of being separate from myself. You don't go anywhere when you transcend. That's not what it's about."

Roslyn wanted to point out that whenever she levitated, she did go places, and so perhaps transcending and levitating weren't the same after all. But Ernest wouldn't have liked that. It would break their unspoken agreement that she was being paid to listen to his insights and pretend to find them sage.

After Ernest left, Roslyn decided to continue meditating. She closed her eyes and did the things with her body and mind that Ernest had told her—sitting a certain way, breathing a certain way, thinking a certain way. Or, really, not-thinking a certain way. It was more unthinking than thinking. And as she concentrated on her unthinking, she felt herself lifting out of herself.

The first place Roslyn levitated to was the dark little shop in Trent Alley she visited three times a week to buy an alcohol called Mud Drink. Mud Drink looked nothing like mud. It was a milky gray color, sometimes almost silverish when held up to the light. Roslyn had no idea what it was made of. She liked the way it looked in the shop, all the jars lined up in a neat row. She went to visit them, the jars, and thought about which she might pick the next day when she walked to the shop for real. They were all the same. The shop owner was meticulous in his pouring and measuring. Still, Roslyn always took great care in her selection. It was part of what made drinking so enjoyable for her—the little rituals that surrounded it. Picking her jar was the first ritual. There were other people in the shop, but no one paid any notice to Roslyn's mind, levitating in front of the shelves. No one ever paid her any attention when she was levitating. She assumed this was because her mind was invisible.

Or perhaps not invisible; perhaps simply not the sort of thing that someone would notice unless they knew to look for it. Might

Ernest be able to see her levitating, since he claimed to be attuned to such things? Then he would have to believe her.

Even though she did not particularly care what Ernest thought of her, there was also within her the desire for spite—to show him she was right and he was wrong, and to make him acknowledge it. Roslyn knew this desire was petty, but she felt okay about it. After all, she wasn't a Buddhist. She could be petty if she wanted.

So, the second place she levitated to was Ernest's office. She found him in a dim room, leaning over a half-naked woman, jabbing needles into her side. Ernest was an acupuncturist. This was why he wore his beard long and skinny. He was trying to look like a Chinese man. He also kept his hair in a braid. His clothes were loose cotton and he wore sandals in all weather. The reason for this, he'd explained to Roslyn once, was that Eastern medicine had become very popular among the women of Spokane Falls's upper class. They all wanted acupuncture. But they did not want to go to a real Chinese acupuncturist in the real Chinese part of town. So they went to Ernest, who was happy to provide an approximation of the experience. Though Roslyn thought he'd gone over the top with the whole thing. Most of the Chinese men she saw in town did not dress like Ernest. They wore boots and kept their hair short. They were railroad men and miners, like everyone else.

Roslyn levitated around the room, watching Ernest work. He didn't look up and he didn't notice her. He was very focused on his task. The woman he was working on had her eyes closed. A piece of fancy silk fabric was laid across her breasts and shoulders, but otherwise she was unclothed from the waist up. A collection of needles already protruded from the left side of her abdomen and now Ernest was working the right side. He was gently placing the needles in her skin. Until Roslyn, describing the scene to herself, thought the word *jabbing*. Then Ernest jabbed. He jabbed and the woman yelped and sat halfway up and they both looked surprised for a moment.

Roslyn heard Ernest say, "Must have hit a pocket of toxins there. Sometimes when they cluster up, it hurts."

The woman, seeming to accept this answer, leaned back and closed her eyes again. Ernest looked flustered. His eyes circled the room and Roslyn thought for sure he would acknowledge her, but he didn't.

That night, alone in her apartment in Wolfe's Hotel, Roslyn got drunk off Mud Drink and blacked out. In the morning, she walked the six blocks to Trent Alley for more Mud Drink. Even though she'd stared at all the jars in the shop the day before while levitating, she stared at them again now, finally picking one from the very center of the top row. She was pleased by the shape and feel of the jar in her hand, like always. She made her purchase and walked back in the dewy cool of the morning, the streets around her just starting to come alive with people. They walked on wooden sidewalks, and where the sidewalks gave out, they walked on the hard-packed dirt streets. They rode bikes and there were some horses, mostly attached to carts and parked outside restaurants and bars, making morning deliveries. Trains rattled by but Roslyn was so accustomed to the sound of them, living as she did directly across the street from the rail yard, that she no longer heard them.

Back at Wolfe's Hotel, she set the new jar of Mud Drink on her nightstand and wasn't going to open it right away, but then she did.

Ernest was the only customer who came by that day. It was rare for him to visit two days in a row, and Roslyn was going to remark on it, or maybe she did remark on it but didn't remember his reply. She was already very drunk. He didn't stay long and he didn't want to meditate. He seemed upset but didn't say why.

"I saw you yesterday," Roslyn said before Ernest left her apartment.

"I know," Ernest said. "I was here."

Roslyn shook her head. She wanted him to admit that she had learned this special trick, this thing he wanted to be able to do but couldn't. Drunk and sleepy, she felt less inclined to uphold her pact of always making Ernest feel important when he was with her. What she was going to do, she decided, was just tell him the truth. She could levitate. She had levitated to his office. She had seen him jab a woman in the side with a needle. He would have to admit that he believed her then.

But when she opened her mouth to speak again, Ernest was already gone. He'd paid his fee and slipped out the door while she'd lost herself in the fog of her Mud Drinked mind.

Roslyn slept. When she woke, it was late afternoon. She sat up on her bed, rubbed her palms into her eyes, and gathered herself into her meditating pose. Just like the day before, she followed Ernest's routine and was up and levitating in no time.

She went straight to Ernest's office. Inside, she found him with the same woman from the previous day. The woman was showing him on her right side where something red and pus-filled had formed. Ernest was explaining to the woman that this issue could be remedied with more acupuncture. No, no, he assured her, nothing had gone wrong the day before. No, no, there was no need to call a doctor. This was all part of the natural healing process.

The woman assembled herself on the table at the center of the room. As Ernest readied his needles and his bottles of various liquids, Roslyn levitated up and over and around him. He was sweating a lot, she noticed. He did not look at her. If anything, he seemed to be looking purposefully away from her.

When he settled into his task with the woman, Roslyn situated herself directly across the table from him. *You should look at me*, she thought inside her own levitating head. Ernest did not look. He was holding a long needle in his hand. *You should look at me*, she thought again. He was still sweating. Roslyn wondered if he always sweat while he worked. She had never noticed him being particularly sweaty when he visited her apartment. *You should look—*

"Stop it!" Ernest screamed. "Christ! Fuck! Stop it!" He was looking at her now. Still sweating, needle still in hand, and anger in his eyes.

"Why are you tormenting me? Why did you make me hurt her?" He gestured to the table where the woman had been. He was so consumed by his panic, he'd neglected to notice that she, at the very start of his screaming, had seen fit to extricate herself from his care. She was gathering her things and heading for the door when Ernest referenced her. At which point she glanced back once, but gave no sign of interest in who or what Ernest might be talking to, only in her own departure.

"I'm not your puppet!" Ernest continued. He looked like he might cry. "What do you want? I tried to be kind to you. What is your reason for this evil?"

Roslyn, surprised and upset, followed the woman's lead, leaving quickly without explanation.

She hadn't meant to hurt anyone. She only wanted to prove to

Ernest that she was, in fact, the sort of person capable of transcendence. He was so smug. And though, as he'd screamed in his office, he often acted as if the things he was doing while he was with her were kind—showing her how to meditate, telling her about new and interesting ideas—he wasn't kind, not really. His reasons for doing those things in the first place were selfish. But then, Roslyn thought, her desire to prove Ernest wrong was a selfish one too. So no one was innocent.

That night, back in her apartment, she had a vision. A scene from another place came to her, as they often did. Nothing was required of her to receive it. She could not decline the vision, even if she wanted to.

The scene was of the woman from Ernest's office talking to a roomful of other women. The room was nice and all the women were dressed well, and it was clear they were rich. The woman was telling the story of Ernest screaming at nothing. The other women held their hands to their mouths and shook their heads. Ernest would lose his business, Roslyn realized. All the rich women who came to him for Eastern (but not too Eastern) medicine would hear about his outburst, and that would be the end of him.

Ernest didn't come to see Roslyn at Wolfe's Hotel anymore and she never sought him out. She thought she might apologize but didn't see what good that would do.

She continued to levitate frequently. It was exciting, this new skill. With practice, little by little, Roslyn learned what she could and could not do. She found it to be quite a handy tool.

The basics were as such:

Roslyn could levitate anywhere she wanted, and was not constrained by physical boundaries like walls, rivers, and so on. But she could not travel terribly fast. She moved at the speed of someone out for a light jog.

Because she was not bound by the physical world while levitating, she also was not able to interact with it. She couldn't touch things, pick objects up, move things. She could only observe.

Levitating gave her some power over people. She could, as she had done with Ernest, influence their actions by repeating simple instructions. But she could not alter their behavior in long-term ways, or change their beliefs. This was fine with Roslyn. She had no desire to change anyone's beliefs.

Mostly, she used her power for small errands—to spy when a bit of knowledge about some situation might gain her favor in the community of Wolfe's Hotel. And to steal. She couldn't take things outright, but she could instruct others to take them and to leave them in places where she could find them. She felt some guilt about this stealing at first, but not much. After all, nearly everyone Roslyn knew in Spokane Falls was a thief in one way or another, and weren't her needs just as valid as theirs?

And then, after a few years, she didn't feel any one way or another about levitating. It was just another thing she did when she needed to, like sleeping, eating, having sex for money, or drinking Mud Drink. A person can get comfortable with anything. Until something comes along to unmask that comfort.

I

Roslyn returned to Spokane Falls one month after she'd left with Barton's money. She went back because she had seen into the future for Barton and it was not kind. She felt obligated to help him.

She hadn't gone far after taking his money. She'd ridden the train just thirty miles east to Idaho, to the grumbly lakeside town of Coeur d'Alene, bivouac for silver miners. The place was nothing but bars and hotels, so she took a room at a hotel above a bar that she found comfortingly similar to the former Wolfe's Hotel. But in Coeur d'Alene, no one visited Roslyn's room. She didn't have to work anymore. And, free of her Mud Drink habit, she had little to spend her money on. She felt if she lived simply, she could survive on Barton's money for decades. Perhaps even the rest of her life.

But without work or alcohol, Roslyn had nothing to do. She spent her days walking in the woods or along the lake. She read when she could find something to read, but there were no libraries or bookstores in Coeur d'Alene. The only way she knew to get books was to approach anyone she saw reading one and offer to buy it from that person. She acquired an odd collection of crime novels, Bibles, and pornography this way.

She didn't think of Barton. She was confident he'd make no effort to follow her. She hadn't gone far, and she wasn't hiding. She pushed him from her memory like she was sweeping out a room. She didn't even reflect upon him when she spent his money. After all, she had another, more weighty burden on her mind.

But then she had the premonition and there he was, inescapable, again. She was forced to revisit the weeks he'd held her in captivity. That was how she thought of it and so, initially, she'd framed her leaving and theft as an escape, and also getting the better of a cruel and selfish man. Taking what was owed her.

Barton had lied to her, telling her she was suspected of having started the fire, in order to get her to his house and keep her there. She was not certain why, though she'd known almost from the start that she was being deceived. Then, he had taken advantage of her, climbed on top of her while she was sick. She had only hazy memories of this, but she knew she had not agreed to it, had not encouraged it. Later, though, she'd slept with him of her own volition. This, in hindsight, made her angrier than the times he'd forced himself on her. She'd felt obligated, if she was going to remain in his home, to do what he wanted.

But as she worried over it, she found she could play devil's advocate even in all this. There was the fact that Roslyn had genuinely had no place else to go after the fire, which was why she'd agreed to stay with Barton in the first place. And it was in his home that she'd finally managed to free herself of Mud Drink. Though she'd tried to quit before, this time it seemed to her she really had. Barton was, she had to admit, in some way a part of that. Wasn't he owed some gratitude for this?

No. He was a vile man. Always had been and always would be.

These were the thoughts that crowded her mind once she saw Barton's future. In it, he was dead. He was alone and no one knew or cared that he'd died.

She would go to him, she decided. Not because she felt beholden to him, but because she could not allow herself to ignore another vision. The last one she'd ignored had far too dire consequences. The guilt was physical. It pooled behind her eyes and weighed down her chest and shoulders. She would regret it the rest of her life, this thing she had done. Or not done. Both. This thing she had both done and not done.

Roslyn didn't start the fire in Spokane Falls. But Kate did, and that was Roslyn's fault in more ways than one.

First, she'd had the vision. It had appeared to her three times in all, each time exactly the same. It went like this: Kate is in her apartment, lying on her bed reading, an oil lamp burning on her bedside table. She startles at something and her book flies from her hand, knocking over the lamp. Flustered, she does not think to extinguish the blaze. Instead, she runs from the building. On her way out, she passes several people but tells no one. The fire spreads from apartment to apartment, building to building, and in a single night, the city is burned.

Was Roslyn upset, at the time, by what she saw? Yes and no. She was almost always upset by her visions. This was, in part, why she drank. Drinking didn't stop the visions, but it did dull the impact they had on her, emotionally. They went from a pressing obligation to something more akin to watching a bad play. She'd prefer not to see them, but once they were over, they had no bearing on her. The same was true of Kate and the fire. Roslyn could have taken steps to prevent it—warning Kate of the dangers of oil lamps and so on. This was the thing she did not do.

The thing she did do was levitate. Late afternoon on August 4, Roslyn levitated to Kate's room. Kate was her neighbor at Wolfe's. She was beautiful and therefore very popular among the hotel's patrons. She was also an opium smoker, and when high, she was inclined not to pay much attention to her money. Roslyn had been making use of this combination of facts about Kate for several years. Each Sunday afternoon, when rent to Bill Wolfe was due, Roslyn would meditate until she levitated, then pass through the wall that separated her room from Kate's. Her disembodied being issued instructions to Kate: *Take ten dollars, go to Roslyn.* Then, she would return to her body and wait for a knock on the door. When she opened it, she would accept the bills from Kate's hand and say, "Thanks for repaying what you borrowed! I knew you were good for it!" before sending the confused woman on her way.

But on August 4, something had gone differently. When Roslyn levitated into Kate's room, Kate was looking at her. She was sitting in bed with a book in her hand, but her eyes were on Roslyn, on the space where Roslyn felt her presence to be. Kate said nothing. Roslyn began to give her typical instructions, but as soon as she spoke, Kate jumped like she'd seen a ghoul. She threw her book behind her. The book hit the lamp, which broke, the oil catching fire as it hit the floor. Kate ran from the room, and Roslyn returned to her body. Once there, she, like Kate, fled the hotel, not saying anything to anyone as she went.

Roslyn knew the fire's terror from her vision, but its reality was many times worse. She watched from the safety of a friend's home on the South Hill. But she had no Mud Drink to temper the image, and the friend, who had once also been a prostitute but had since found God and reformed, eyed her with rightful suspicion. In fact, Roslyn felt the eyes of the entire city on her that night, looking askance at what she'd done and not done.

Why had she startled Kate? She had no answer. It had never happened before.

Why hadn't she heeded her vision and taken steps to stop the fire? She never heeded her visions, not anymore.

Later, she learned a person had died in the fire. She'd heard it first from Barton, then she'd read the details in the paper. It was a man, a friend of the bartender at Wolfe's, and when he got drunk there, he was allowed to sleep in one of the unused back rooms, which he was doing when the fire started. The bartender had forgotten him and no one else knew he was there. Roslyn had seen deaths in her visions before, but never, to her knowledge, had her levitations precipitated one. She had never thought herself as an evil person, but wasn't this evil, this deed from her own hands?

So, she vowed never to levitate again. It was a capacity she didn't understand, and one she should not use. She also vowed to give up Mud Drink. This was the vice that nearly all her levitations served, and that dulled her so she did not care if others lived or died. She would give them both up. So far, she'd kept true to that promise.

Here now with Barton was a vision that could be heeded. A life that could be saved.

—

She went back to Spokane Falls just as she had left: by train with Barton's bank cash sewn into the lining of her clothes and also in a bag she kept in her lap. On the way, a cavalryman rode alongside the train, waving and smiling, his rifle aimed at something in front of him that Roslyn couldn't see until the moment he fired. It was a moose, felled with one shot. Everyone in Roslyn's car clapped and agreed the successful shot was a sign of good luck for all of them. But Roslyn knew this was not true. Good omens were never so gruesome.

2

Roslyn found Barton at home. Or rather, where his home used to be.

He was filthy, hiding out in a plywood lean-to, and largely incoherent. His eyes were bright with wildness, ringed red. *I feel myself slipping into madness* . . . she remembered him saying before she left. At the time, she thought it was another one of his traps, but it seemed he had been telling the truth. He sputtered winding sentences about the horrors that had befallen him.

His tale, as Roslyn was able to piece it together, went something like this: Shortly after her departure, he had been arrested and jailed. At first, he thought it was for stealing from the bank, but it turned out he was suspected in the city's investigation of the fire. Roslyn could not discern how this judgment had been made (though she did find it a pleasing irony). It seemed Barton might not have known, either. The city called in a man they trusted to be a government arson inspector to take over the case, and the man confirmed that Barton was in fact the firebug. Barton kept referring to this individual as Quake Auchenbaucher, though Roslyn did not believe a real person could go by such a preposterous name.

The citizens of Spokane Falls pegged Inspector Auchenbaucher as a fraud after he left town with every last cent Barton hadn't already taken from the bank, but not before they'd torched Barton's house in retribution for his having started the fire at Wolfe's Hotel. Fortunately, everyone had wised up before enacting any further punishments on Barton. Though there'd been no apology for what had happened to his house, or his almost four weeks of incarceration. Since his release from jail, he'd been living in the lean-to on the site where his home once stood, eating scraps scavenged from the neighbors and stewing in his rage.

All this Barton told Roslyn immediately upon seeing her, still half-inside his lean-to on hands and knees, his speech rapid and breathy. She wasn't sure at first if he even recognized her well enough to know whom he was talking to, but then once his story ended, he lunged forward and embraced her at the waist, too quick for her to dodge him, and said, "Oh, my dearest Roslyn, you've come home at last!

"It's okay," he continued, his voice eager with forgiveness. "I once left someplace without really meaning to. I didn't even know why I left it, once I did."

"No," Roslyn said, shaking herself free of him. She felt nauseated by him. "I wanted to leave. I left because I wanted your money, and because I wanted to be alone. But I've returned now to help you."

Barton nodded, but his eyes betrayed him. He hadn't been listening. "It's okay," he said again. "Women are often apt to act without thinking. You must have been so frightened, all alone. But someone has brought you back to me. We are together again and · everything will be like it was."

Roslyn took another step back and considered the version of Barton in front of her: dirty, manic, desperate. He wasn't the same as the man she'd known before, this much was certain. But he wasn't so totally different either.

She was unsure what to do with him. She'd come with the intention of giving back at least some if not all of his money. He could get food, shelter, clothes, whatever he needed to make up for the deprivation that had led to his dire condition as seen in her vision. Then what? She hadn't thought that far. She had figured the money itself would be the solution to Barton's problem. Indeed, the money had been the solution to Roslyn's immediate problem, allowing her to get out of Spokane Falls and away from the most visceral reminders of the fire. Though her escape had done nothing to lessen the guilt.

But it wasn't simply that Barton needed a fresh start. The man was ill. He seemed delirious. Roslyn suspected if she were to put a hand across his forehead, she would find him feverish. But she didn't want to touch him. Didn't want him to think, even for a second, that they had the sort of relationship where she would ever touch him again.

She wanted, first and foremost, to get him out of the lean-to. Cleaned up and fed. She was at a loss for where to take him. She believed what he said about being seen as a pariah, and she feared the scrutiny that would come from bringing him out in public. So she settled for getting him a meal and a new set of clothes and blankets. Barton made it clear he did not like this idea. Not because he didn't want food and clothes, but because he didn't want Roslyn to leave. He screeched and tried to grab her, but she evaded his grasp, and as she jogged down the street, she was relieved he made no move to follow her.

Roslyn took a hotel room downtown for the night. It was a real hotel—not like Wolfe's, which was really just apartments for the women who worked there. The space was modest, but clean and new. The hotel had been built since the fire. So had the restaurant where she ate dinner. Afterward, as she walked, Roslyn noticed a number of new structures downtown. It seemed every block of her old neighborhood was either under construction or recently had been. She thought it looked good. This helped pacify her guilt momentarily. The fire had made Spokane Falls better, had it not? Provided an excuse for growth and modernization. The city was fine, better than fine. The new brick buildings shone orange in the evening light, making downtown beautiful, heavenly even.

But as the evening wore on, she was no longer able to hold the idea of the fire as an instrument of improvement. There were new buildings, yes. But what had happened to the people who lived in the old buildings? The families in downtown's tenements would not be able to afford space in new apartments. The police would use it as an excuse to force immigrants, mostly Chinese, out of downtown as well. They probably already had, Roslyn lamented. It was probably the first thing they thought to do, before the fire was even out. Plus, there was the smell, the air like chalk. Animals she did not remember having seen in town before skittered through the streets: porcupines, chipmunks, a large striped salamander. They didn't seem happy to be there, these creatures. The city had suffered and was not whole. Any signs of recovery were merely a mask.

She found herself wondering about another section of town she'd also considered her own: Trent Alley, where she'd gone every other day for a decade to buy Mud Drink. How had it fared since the fire? she wondered. Shouldn't she go catch up with the shop-keepers she used to know, just to make sure they were all right?

No, she must not. She forced herself to walk, head down, swiftly and with purpose, back to her hotel. When she reached the room, she locked the door, vowing she would not leave again for the rest of the night. She would not allow herself to seek refuge in Mud Drink. She couldn't fix Spokane Falls, but she could keep her promise to herself. She ought not linger, though. She forced her thoughts back to Barton and the problem at hand.

"Sad man in your lean-to, what's to be done with you?" Roslyn hummed. Then she remembered: Barton had another home. He'd talked to her of his life before Spokane Falls, when he'd lived in Portland. In fact, she'd often heard him compare the two cities, with Spokane Falls always in the negative. Might he like to go back there now? Roslyn wondered. If she could return Barton to his family, he would be cared for. In his current state, it was really that or the madhouse. She couldn't imagine any other situation in which he could safely live. This was how she would help him escape the lonesome death of her vision: She would get him to Portland, to his parents. Then, she could be free of him.

3

Roslyn visited Barton again in the morning, bringing him break-fast of bread and jam. As with the day before, he reeled in delight upon seeing her, reaching out with his grubby hands, but still not crossing the threshold of his lean-to.

"Good morning! So good to see you, dear. You look lovely! The brightest star in the sky, even during the day, brighter than the sun. Are you the sun, my dear? Tell the truth. You are, aren't you?"

Roslyn refused to acknowledge any of this. She stood at a distance from him with her hands on her hips. It was her stern pose from back in her teaching days when she wanted to show children she was not to be messed with.

"Barton, I've been thinking you should go back to Portland," she said. "I can travel with you, to make the trip easier."

He cocked his head to the side like a dog. Roslyn was unsure if he understood her, and was about to repeat herself when he said, "To Portland? Yes, that's right. So I can kill the arson inspector,

Mr. Auchenbaucher. That's where his office is. I will have my revenge for what he's done to me. In Portland."

Roslyn could not follow what he meant and said so. If Mr. Auchenbaucher was a con man, then he had no office, not in Portland or anywhere else. Surely, he wouldn't be in that city. It was only part of his lie. Plus, if the man had been a real government agent instead of a fraud, wouldn't Barton still be in jail or even hanged? Oughtn't he be grateful to this person, in a way?

Barton's expression turned crestfallen. "Then why go to Portland?" he asked.

"I thought you could go home to be with your family. With your mother and your father."

"My father?"

"And your mother. It would be nice, don't you think? You could stay with them until you feel better."

"Yes. I could kill my father."

This, again, was not what she had expected.

"Why would you want to do that?" she asked.

"Because the tragedy of my current situation is as much his fault as Mr. Auchenbaucher's. Perhaps more so. Had he not been so unkind to me throughout my youth, I never would have come to Spokane Falls in the first place. I would have stayed in Portland. I'd have a fine life there. I would have finished my training in law and built a thriving practice. I would be rich and respected. But no, he was mean and so I left, and now I'm hated and poor and living in squalor."

At the word *poor*, Roslyn bristled, thinking this might be the moment when Barton remembered why he was poor. But he made no mention of the money she'd taken.

"But now I can get my revenge," he continued. "We'll go to Portland together and kill my father, just like you said. Perfect, perfect. You always have the best ideas, darling. I do truly believe you are the most remarkable woman on earth."

It unsettled her, the ease with which Barton had twisted her words to violence. But she didn't object. Because he'd agreed, at least in part, to her plan.

Roslyn returned late that afternoon, train tickets for the overnight to Portland and her meager luggage in hand. Barton, still in his lean-to, was full of energy. She could hear him rustling in the structure's depths. So ungainly were his sounds and movements, she mistook him at first for one of Spokane Falls's new wild city animals—a badger, or perhaps even a bear.

"Let's go, time's a-wasting," he said when he saw her. Then, to her surprise and relief, he stood and exited the lean-to. She'd been worried that when it came time to actually extract him from his makeshift home, there would be some sort of an ordeal involved. But no. He was more than willing to leave.

She asked if there was anything he wanted to take with him, any belongings to pack. He shook his head. He was already wearing the new clothes she had bought him, though they were dusty and rumpled from having been slept in.

She walked with him down to the river and encouraged him to clean his face, neck, hands, and feet as best he could. After that he still smelled, but not so bad he could not ride a train across Washington Territory. She knew from prior travels that the bar for male hygiene was not a high one.

What about his fear of the citizenry of Spokane Falls? Barton had painted himself as a wretched outcast, publicly hated for what he'd done, and Roslyn believed him (after all, no one had liked him much even before the fire). Walking toward downtown now, he showed no fear. He held his head high, his hands thrust in the pockets of his jacket, elbows out wide. Roslyn, for her part, was nervous. What if someone recognized Barton and tried to start trouble?

"There's nothing to worry about, my dear," he said, taking her hand, and his timing was so perfect, she wondered if in their weeks together he really had learned something meaningful about her.

"What do you mean?" she asked.

"You're anxious to be seen traveling with me," he continued, and Roslyn couldn't help but nod. "Because you think it's improper for us to do so without being wed; our actions will be seen by others as sin. But don't fret. As soon as we get to Portland and I finish the ghastly, yet essential deed of disposing of my father, we shall take his fortune and have a fine wedding. Then you will be embarrassed no longer."

There it is, she thought, and found relief in the fact that she had not misjudged Barton after all. The reality he lived in was a delusion of his own making. She shook her hand free of his and continued to lead them downtown, to whatever awaited them there.

But there was no trouble from anyone. They crossed the bridge and walked the remaining blocks to the train station. Roslyn installed Barton on a wooden bench and after he extracted repeated promises that she would, in fact, return, she went to a shop across the street to get sandwiches. He was waiting just where she'd left him when she came back, staring straight ahead into nothingness like the madman he was. Shortly thereafter they boarded the train, taking two seats in a nearly empty car. Their only travel mates were a sleeping cavalryman and a mother too occupied by her small children to pay Roslyn and Barton any attention in the slightest.

4

Roslyn's father was a small-time criminal and a drunk. Her mother died when she was very young, and she had few memories of the woman. Her childhood, as a result, had been her father's world. They lived in Steilacoom, a town Roslyn's dad boasted was the "westernmost place in the known world." Even as a small child, Roslyn found this statement nonsensical, but she liked the sound of it anyway. It was a romantic notion, to live in a something-most place, instead of a desperate frontier town populated by people who'd failed to make a life for themselves anywhere else. Her father was no exception. He was a blacksmith by trade and had a shop that he and Roslyn lived above. But business—when he bothered to open the shop at all—was slow. The reason for this, Roslyn would eventually find out, was that her dad was not regarded as a very good blacksmith.

So, he spent the majority of his sober hours engaged in various schemes. He was a crook, but a friendly one. Most of his capers did not pan out, and those that did resulted in only minor losses for the victims. There was horse trading, pig in a poke, and the solicitation of funds for can't-miss investments that never materialized. It seemed to Roslyn everyone in Steilacoom knew what he was up to, and they simply didn't care. A longtime acquaintance of her father's once remarked to her, "Someday somebody's gonna up and stab your old man if he doesn't watch out." But he said it in such a playful way, she couldn't help but laugh along with him. She was eight at the time. As it turned out, a decade later, someone would stab him. It was in a bar and he'd been caught cheating at cards. The man who did it was the very same acquaintance who'd predicted such an end.

Roslyn had a vision of her father's death six months before it happened. Though she warned him the event was coming, he did not listen to her. No one ever listened to her. And after that, she stopped trying to warn anyone about anything.

What little money Roslyn's dad earned, either from blacksmithing or grifting, he drank. He didn't drink at home. He was a social drinker (unlike his daughter, who would prefer to drink in her own company, once she found the knack for it). He spent his evenings out on the town. He wanted to have a good time and for others to have good times too. When he had the funds, he bought rounds for whoever else was available to drink with him. As a result, Roslyn's childhood was one of deprivation, sometimes even outright hunger. She didn't blame her father for this. After all, everyone in Steilacoom was poor. It wasn't until she was older and living on her own that she realized she'd been poorer than most. Still, she wasn't bitter. Her father was a kind man. And when he was present, he was a loving companion who asked her each day to tell him everything she'd learned in school. Sometimes he'd ask it twice if he was totally sauced, but Roslyn didn't mind repeating herself. Everyone had their faults, she thought. Her dad's were not the worst.

What must Barton's father have done to him that Barton did not feel the same? In the brief years when she'd taught school, Roslyn had seen the horrors adults could bring upon their children. Had Barton's upbringing been that way? And if so, did it give license, or at least meaning, to the misdeeds of his adulthood?

Roslyn considered this as the train plunged west through the fading light of the September evening. Barton had, mercifully, fallen into a deep sleep almost as soon as the train departed Spokane Falls. Roslyn was left to her own thoughts in silence. Mostly, she watched him as he slept, trying to reason out some explanation for the man and his behavior. It was too simple to write him off as insane. He was mad now, yes. But he hadn't always been. In fact, for the years she'd known him only as her customer, he'd seemed exceedingly, dully normal. Still, whatever darkness had emerged in him after the fire had always been there. It must have. Roslyn refused to believe a good person could turn so quickly, over so little.

5

Roslyn had never been to Portland before. To her, arriving in the half-light of dawn, the city seemed tremendous and imposing. Outside the train station, buildings large and small pressed together. Wide boulevards spurred off into narrow alleys that led at a slope toward the waterfront, from which a foul smell was rising. There were carriages and horses in the street and people everywhere, many of whom, despite the early hour, appeared drunk. This threw her. It was not what she'd expected. She'd expected Spokane Falls, just in a different location. It was the only city she'd ever been to, and in her mind all other cities were just like it—no bigger, no smaller, no cleaner, no dirtier. Of course, intellectually, she knew this wasn't true. But it didn't lessen her surprise.

Her plan was to get a hotel room to stash Barton away while she located his family. She thought perhaps they were prominent enough that someone might be able to tell her where they lived just from her asking around. But the activity of even this one street suggested otherwise. She was ashamed of her ignorance, her small-town sensibilities. She felt unmoored.

This was not a feeling Barton shared. The man seemed emboldened to wake up in the center of the city.

"Come along, dear," he said. "It's this way."

He led her through the crush of downtown, then out and away from it into an area less congested. The morning was mild with fog lying so low it seemed to twist around them. Roslyn felt a dampness collecting on her hair and clothes. Barton walked fast, pointing out this and that as they went, like he was a tour guide. Except the tour was of himself only. "This is where I went to school and was valedictorian." "This is the yard where us boys would fight and I always won." "This is where a man was dying and I saved his life."

Roslyn didn't interrupt. It was so easy to fall back into the habit of letting him take control, even though she knew much, if not all, of what he said was false.

They snaked through neighborhood streets that gradually steepened as they went. The fog had burned off and Roslyn began to sweat. The higher up the hill they got, the larger and more stately the homes. Rich people, she thought. Barton's people.

Here, his pace slowed. He stopped narrating. Was he nervous, now that they were close to his home? Roslyn had grown nervous herself. What would Barton do, once they arrived at his parents' house? She wished she could have come alone at first, to smooth the way.

Barton, as they walked, looked down alleyways, peered into open windows, craning his head back and up toward the sky.

"Is your family's home nearby?" Roslyn asked.

"Oh no. My family doesn't live here. I'm looking for the devil woman. She's from my memory. But it's not a real memory because it never happened. Anyway, I have some questions for her."

Of all the nonsensical things she'd heard Barton say in the past three days, this was by far the worst. It was crazy nonsense, she knew. Some delusion of a man who'd cracked open and could not be put back together. But still it chilled her, this talk of devils. She was tempted to pry him for details but didn't want to encourage him.

Instead, she said, "Do you know your parents' address? Perhaps I could help us find it if I knew what street we were looking for. We could stop and ask for directions."

To her surprise, Barton took the cue.

"No, that's not necessary," he said. "I can take us there. We can go now, if you really want."

"I would like that, yes," Roslyn said.

He turned and led them back down the hill, then up another hill, which was steep and covered with large homes just the same as the first.

Barton took Roslyn to a house that looked as if it had once been the envy of the neighborhood. It was a white colonial with a wide porch, big windows, and columns on either side of the door. Time had not been kind to the structure. The exterior paint was dull, more yellow-brown than white in many places. The windows were near black with dirt. The porch bowed and appeared in the process of being eaten whole by a tangle of ivy. Clearly, upkeep was no longer a primary concern of the homeowners.

Barton tried the knob on the front door and, finding it locked, seemed baffled. It occurred to Roslyn that his parents may have moved, or died, and the house was now occupied by someone else, or perhaps even abandoned. She stepped forward, took hold of the door's oversize knocker, and put it to use.

Then she and Barton waited. No sounds came from inside, nothing to indicate occupancy. Which was why it was all the more surprising to Roslyn when the door opened. Behind it stood the human equivalent of the house itself: a woman who looked as if she'd once been quite attractive but was now in the process of falling apart—hair thinning, clothes drab, eyes sunken. She was slim and stern and old. She stared at them, saying nothing. Roslyn felt a chill run through her and wondered if perhaps she was looking not at a real person at all, but at a ghost. She was dumbstruck, unsure what to say to break the icy moment's lock upon them.

So, once again, it was Barton who led the way. He sprang forward, pushing Roslyn to the side.

"Mommy!" he cried. "I've come home!" And he swept the specter into his arms.

6

B arton's father was already dead.

His mother shared this news once Barton and Roslyn were settled into the home's parlor with cool drinks in hand, finger sandwiches and cookies on the table. Hospitality to the point of absurdity, Roslyn thought. But then, how does one behave in the company of an adult son, more than a half decade estranged and clearly changed for the worse, and his unfamiliar female chaperone? Perhaps any course of action would have seemed absurd.

Mr. Heydale had passed away two years prior, the result of some heart-related troubles.

Roslyn looked to Barton, trying to read his reaction. She couldn't tell if he was sad, angry, or even disappointed. She couldn't tell if he cared at all.

"Why didn't you ever write to me?" Barton's mother asked him. "I had no idea where you went."

"I'm sorry," he said. "I shouldn't have done that. I never intended to hurt you."

When he said this Roslyn felt a weight lifted from her. She had been right to bring Barton home after all. Here was someone who loved him, and who could still evoke from him a real, human response.

They sat quiet for a moment. Then Mrs. Heydale's attention turned toward Roslyn.

"And how are you acquainted with my son, Miss Beck?"

It was a question Roslyn had anticipated. Still, she was not prepared to answer, at least not in Barton's presence. She found she did not have the words to explain her role there.

Barton, however, was at no such loss.

"My apologies, Mother! I should have explained sooner. Roslyn is my fiancée. We are in love, and engaged to be wed."

"Oh, how wonderful!" Mrs. Heydale said, and Roslyn thought the woman might stand to hug her, or bombard her with questions about wedding plans or how the pair had met. She braced herself for this onslaught.

But no further show of enthusiasm was forthcoming.

Since they were not yet married, Barton and Roslyn were forbidden to sleep in the same room. Mrs. Heydale explained this to them after dinner. She would have no impropriety under her roof, she said, in a tone that suggested an enthusiasm for scolding others about impropriety, and an excitement at being able to use said tone now. This arrangement came as a relief to Roslyn. Mrs. Heydale escorted her to the quarters that would be hers—a small bedroom and washroom at the top of the stairs, on the opposite end of the house from where Barton would be.

This was how she would make her exit, Roslyn thought. She would leave after Barton and Mrs. Heydale were asleep. She could walk right down the stairs and out the door without them hearing. She'd leave a note, something kind for Barton, and her job would be done. He was home safe, cared for and loved. He was not dead and he was no longer alone. It was better even than she'd hoped. Better than he deserved.

When it came time to retire for the evening, Roslyn went through the motions of getting ready for bed, so as not to arouse suspicion. Not that it mattered. Mrs. Heydale's attention was for Barton. Roslyn could hear her tending to him at the end of the hall. Did he have enough blankets? Did he want tea? Milk? What about sleeping clothes? A light snack of toast or a turkey leg? Barton as well seemed caught up in his mother's affections.

Roslyn lay in bed until after midnight, breathing the stuffy air of the guest room. She listened to the house, heard nothing, and was certain the other occupants were asleep. She dressed, gathered her things, and made her way down the darkened stairs.

She almost didn't believe it was him at first. He was sitting so still, she wanted to think he was a statue, or even a ghost—an apparition of one of this unsettling home's previous residents. The late Mr. Heydale himself. But then he spoke, and of course it was Barton, slumped in an armchair, waiting for her.

"You're leaving," he said, like he knew it to be fact.

"Yes," she said.

"Please, don't."

In the slats of moonlight that escaped that parlor's curtains, Roslyn

could see Barton was recently groomed—hair slicked and bushed—
and he was wearing pajamas a size too small. Had Mrs. Heydale
bathed him? Whatever the case, he'd never actually gotten into bed.

"Barton," she said, "you're home with your mother now. You
don't need me anymore."

"That's not true! Mother is expecting you and me to marry. It
will break her heart if we don't. I need you more than ever. If you
go, I'll kill myself. I was planning to kill myself before I fell in love
with you. You saved me. But without you I'm nothing. I'm already
dead. I'll do it right here and now."

In her vision, Barton's body was lying on the side of the road.
Because no one was with him when he died, his corpse remained
exposed, curled in an odd posture. The cause of his demise was
unclear, as was the location. Roslyn had assumed the street on which
he lay was in Spokane Falls. But what if it was Portland? By returning to Barton, she hadn't saved him. She'd put him on a path to
self-harm, creating within him the willingness to take his own life.

"It's okay, Barton," she said. "I wasn't leaving. I was only coming
down for a glass of water."

Then she went back up the stairs, where she returned to bed but
did not sleep.

In the morning, Roslyn was filled with self-loathing. She felt certain
Barton didn't really intend to commit suicide if she left. It was just
another one of his lies to keep her nearby and helpless. But she had
no way to be sure. She didn't know what to do. To go or to stay? And
if she stayed, for how long? How much of her own life did she need
to sacrifice in order to preserve Barton's? She wished for another

vision, for some direction outside herself. Nothing came. She thought of levitation. Wasn't this a worthy reason to break her promise? But there was no benefit in trailing Barton unseen. Everything there was to know of him now was already on full display to her. There was no influence she could exert that would change his course, whatever it was.

She lay in bed until she heard Mrs. Heydale stirring in the kitchen. She went to see if she could be of help.

Barton was still in the armchair, though now he was dressed for the day, this time in an outfit as poorly fitting as his pajamas had been. More of his father's clothes, Roslyn assumed.

"Doesn't he look sharp?" Mrs. Heydale asked, appearing from the kitchen.

Roslyn thought Barton looked like a sausage stuffed in too tight a casing.

"The fashion is changing so quickly for men these days," Mrs. Heydale continued. "Tell me, do you prefer sack coats or frock coats?"

"I'm sure both are fine," said Roslyn, having no idea as to the definition of either.

"See, that's just the thing," Mrs. Heydale said. "I've always liked the frocks myself, but I don't think the younger men care for them anymore. A shorter coat is all the rage now. Though, aren't they not as warm? That just seems impractical to me. A shorter coat and a longer beard—that's what the young men want and so they'll have them, I suppose."

"I do like a long beard sometimes," Roslyn said.

"Well, if you listen to the magazines, then there's plenty more where that came from. Beard-wise, I mean. And I do listen to the magazines, myself. I take several. But it gets lonesome without anyone to talk to about them."

"Are none of your friends very interested in fashion?" Roslyn asked, but then regretted the question, as she suspected she already knew the answer.

"No. No friends interested in fashion. Isn't it a pity?"

Roslyn agreed it was.

Meanwhile, Barton, who wore no coat or beard, had begun to hum slightly to himself. She knew the melody; it was a song her father had taught her, which she loved and had played on Barton's piano while in his home as a way of grounding herself, reminding herself who she was and where she had come from. She was gripped by the urge to slap it from Barton's mouth. How dare he take that song as his own. But of course she did no such thing.

The day dripped by. Mrs. Heydale doted on Barton, offering snacks, blankets, books, reading aloud to him from the paper, and enlisting Roslyn to help in his care. Roslyn wondered how the woman had been filling her days before their arrival. Anytime his mother was out of earshot, Barton hissed at Roslyn the most awful things. *Don't go. Don't go. I'll die if you go. I'll drink poison. I'll do it right now. Say you'll stay. I'll hang myself. I can't suffer this earth without you.* Desperate to calm him, she assured him over and over she wasn't going anywhere.

She remained true to this promise for four more days.

Mother and son slipped into an easy routine. Barton spent most of his waking hours reading, or simply sitting in the parlor, staring at nothing. He napped frequently. Roslyn couldn't tell if he had come to think of himself as someone very young or very old.

At first, Mrs. Heydale included Roslyn in her ministrations to

Barton, asking her to take him tea or seeking approval for a change of clothing. This didn't last. Roslyn was in the woman's way. Mrs. Heydale made it clear she would be happier, her life simpler, with-out Roslyn around. Barton, however, still clung to her, alternating threats and platitudes, though only when his mother was out of the room. It was as if he needed some woman doting on him at all times; it did not matter who.

And then, after a while, they were never alone. In the first days, Mrs. Heydale was a flurry of activity, in and out of the house on constant tasks. But her travels slowed, then ceased. Roslyn realized what she'd witnessed was a kind of laying-in. The older woman had been making preparations so she would not have to leave her son's side so often, or maybe not ever. The pantry was stocked. The linens were cleaned. New books had been purchased. All through this, Roslyn waited. She felt paralyzed by her desire to ensure Barton's safety, and also by her resentment of the very same desire. She found herself envying Barton. In spite of his failings, the man was never at a loss for action. Even when he was living in his lean-to, he had managed to justify his life circumstances to himself. In his own mind, he was never wrong, and so he was never lost. Roslyn longed for such certainty, such selfish clarity. She'd come into the Heydale house without an exit strategy and for that she'd been a fool. She was a captive of Barton's once more by her own acquies-cence.

On the fifth day after their arrival, Mrs. Heydale did not leave Barton's side in the parlor at all, except to prepare food for him, and neither of them spoke to Roslyn beyond passing pleasantries. At supper, Roslyn dragged herself from her room to the dining table to find only two places set, Barton and Mrs. Heydale already installed in them. They were talking animatedly, and though Mrs. Heydale gave her a sharp look from the corner of her eye, Barton did not seem to even register her presence.

"I'm going to pack my things and go now," she said, testing the waters. And when she got no response from either Heydale, she knew she ought to feel relief, but she found instead a shame so deep it nearly brought her to her knees.

7

Roslyn received her first vision when she was thirteen. As if the horrors of puberty weren't already enough. It was of a horse cart flipped over on the main street of Steilacoom, the driver's leg broken in a particularly grisly way. It upset her deeply, this waking dream that appeared without warning. She knew right away what it was—an image of something real from the future. She went to her dad and told him what she had seen.

"We have to warn him," she insisted.

Her dad laughed his good-natured laugh. He was unflappable in all circumstances; the news that his daughter was receiving premonitions did not mark an exception.

"Warn who? Warn him when?"

Roslyn took his point. The man in the vision was someone from out of town, a stranger. Nor could she say when the accident would occur.

"A thing like that, it's none of our business," her father said, when she pressed further.

The horse cart tipped two weeks later. Roslyn was at home and did not see it, but she heard accounts repeated many times over the coming days. It was the most exciting thing to happen in town in some time, and everyone was eager to share their "Where were you when . . . ?" story. Each one made her sick to her stomach.

The next vision came six months later. In this one, an elderly woman was leaving the Steilacoom post office when she tripped on a loose step and fell into the street, landing on her face and shattering her jaw. This situation seemed more straightforward, and Roslyn was grateful for that. She took a hammer and nails from her father's workshop and went to the post office. But when the postmaster caught her working on his steps, he shooed her away.

"Someone's going to get hurt if this isn't fixed," Roslyn insisted.

"Well, that's for me to worry about," was all he said.

So she went to warn the elderly woman, whom she knew vaguely. But the woman paid her no attention.

"What's it to you where I walk and how careful I am? Did your daddy put you up to this?"

She tripped the very next day.

Roslyn came to have a reputation in Steilacoom, as small-town children who are odd or precocious often do. There were some people who believed she could see the future, and they went to her for advice and predictions, only to be turned away disappointed.

Her father had suggested she might as well entertain these folks, a small fee charged. But she declined. That was his game, not hers.

Mostly, people dismissed her the way they might a boy a with a unicycle, or a girl who has memorized the Bible. The residents of

Steilacoom liked Roslyn, as they liked her father, and they tolerated her dire warnings just the same as they did his hapless grifting.

Roslyn, for her part, disliked herself. She could not stop the visions, which were always violent, never anything nice. She could not stop the real events from happening. She wanted a normal mind, one like everyone else's. When she complained about this to her father, he brushed her hair from her face with his fingers and tsked. "You're a special gal, Ros. I wish you could see yourself the way I see you."

"Did Ma get visions too, when she was alive?" Roslyn asked once.

Her father shook his head. "Your mother was a certain kind of woman, for sure. But visions? No. Not that she ever shared with me."

Though this brought her little comfort, at least Roslyn knew what to call herself after that. Not a witch, not a lunatic. A certain kind of woman.

It was a year after she began teaching at Steilacoom School that the visions became unbearable. She loved that job. And the parents and children of Steilacoom loved her equally. She'd grown, in their eyes, from an odd teen to a smart, patient, caring woman, a perfect fit for the one-room schoolhouse tasked with educating all the tiny city's youth who wished to attend. In the time she taught, more and more children came to school, spurred on by the enthusiasm of their peers. She was good at what she did and it brought her joy.

But then the visions. They began to tumble over her. A new one every few days, a frequency she had never experienced before. They were of things that would happen to her students. Sometimes, the visions were of events far in the future, which she knew because in them, the children were grown—before her eyes, they grew old, grew sick, died in accidents, died in childbirth, were beaten by spouses, were beaten in fights with strangers, were robbed at gunpoint, were cast out of their homes for unclear reasons. Worse yet, some visions were closer in time, the children still children. One, in which the house of an eleven-year-old boy named Jonah collapsed, pinning him under the rubble, was so vivid, she was convinced it had happened in that very moment. She ran to his home only to find the family enjoying dinner safe and sound, though very confused by her visit. "Would you like some soup, Miss Beck?" the boy offered.

She took to drinking in the hours she was alone. She started with bottles her father had hidden and forgotten in his workshop. He was dead five years by then. There was no one left to say uselessly reassuring things. Then she started frequenting the bar he'd liked best.

The parents of the schoolchildren were so kind. Many of them had known Roslyn her whole life. They let her stay a full year longer. They had hoped, perhaps, this was just a passing phase.

She'd been gone fourteen years. Alone in Portland, she let herself remember everything she could of those days. The moss on the schoolhouse roof. The fireplace that had made the room smoky in the mornings. The children's bad haircuts. The way they'd outgrown the schoolroom eventually and the little ones had to sit on the floor without desks but didn't complain. The way they'd looked up at her with patient eyes while she drew maps, held up pine cones, described the way to calculate the radius of a circle, and let them all share the compass her father had made for her when she was learning the same concepts herself. She wondered who taught at the school in Steilacoom now.

She thought if she could pick one mistake of her life to undo, it wouldn't actually be to act upon any visions she'd ignored, not even the fire. It would be to have kept that job.

When she left the Heydale home, she simply retraced her steps, back down the hill into downtown. She took a room at a clean but inauspicious hotel. She resumed her habits from Coeur d'Alene: walking, reading, sleeping late, and napping frequently. She felt she should get on with her life. The time had come to take action in some direction or another. But she could see no path. She was stuck, and her guilt poured in, washing over and over and over her.

8

One day, Roslyn walked north and then west to a pleasant, tree-lined neighborhood. She wandered its streets up and down in a slow zigzag. It wasn't like the neighborhood where the Heydales lived. This one was more modest—a place where any normal person could have a very fine life. She lingered into the evening and when she got hungry, she found a restaurant both casual enough for eating alone and nice enough that a woman by herself would not be harassed. She sat at a table near the back of the room, ate the evening's special—a hearty stew with fresh bread—and found it excellent.

It wasn't until the end of her meal that she became aware of a certain pull on her attention. There was something flitting at the edges of Roslyn's consciousness as she finished her last bites of food. It was as though she were having a vision. Though this vision was not of the future. It was of the present, right there in that very room with her.

It was a person. A man. He was somewhere behind her in the room. She could see his face without turning to look, and it was unfamiliar to her. They hadn't met before, but she knew him. His relevance to her, and to her current situation there in Portland, was clear. The more her mind was drawn to him, the more certain she felt of this. It seemed absurd for them to be in the same place at the same time. Absurd, or fated. He was not someone she ever would have thought to seek out. But now that he was here, she was excited.

She looked and found the man who had appeared in her mind, just where she knew he would be. He was tall, young, and serious in both his clothing and demeanor. He, like Roslyn, was dining alone, though his meal was more elaborate than the stew, his plate piled with meat and potatoes, along with a bottle of wine. She wondered if he was celebrating something.

Roslyn paid her bill and continued to watch him. She was certain he hadn't noticed her, or if he had, he'd taken no interest (and why would he?). For the first time since arriving in Portland, she felt emboldened, even powerful in a way. She rose and walked to his table.

"I know a man who wants to kill you," she said, hoping to startle him.

He looked up at her and smiled, calm and pleasant as if she were the waitress coming around to ask if he'd like another drink.

"Well," he said, "that's a lot of men. You're going to have to be more specific."

"Mr. Barton Heydale."

Hearing the name, the man gave a reaction, but not the one Roslyn had expected. He smiled and slapped his hand against the table.

"Heydale! Heydale's alive? And seeking vengeance? Sit," he said, kicking out the chair opposite him with a long leg. "Sit and tell me everything."

So she did. She sat down at the table with the con man Quake Auchenbaucher.

She'd been wrong about him not recognizing her. Though they'd never met, he knew her right away.

"You're Heydale's girl, from the hotel, right?" he asked, as soon as she took her seat.

Of course he would know, she realized. Anyone who'd spent time with Barton after she left would have heard about her. Though God knew what the man had said. Regardless, this Quake Auchenbaucher knew her name. He knew where she'd lived. He knew what she'd done for a living. There was a certain relief to this. It meant Roslyn did not have to explain things about her life in Spokane Falls.

"The police thought he started the fire because of you," he said.

Roslyn shook her head. "He didn't start the fire. Everyone knows that now. They let him go after they figured out who you really were."

"After everyone figured out who I really wasn't," Quake corrected.

"His house was burned in retaliation."

"A steep price to pay for not starting a fire."

"Indeed. Which is why he has vowed revenge," Roslyn said, leaving out the part about Barton also seeking revenge on his father and then seeming to forget Quake entirely.

"I'm certain he did. But the Barton Heydale I saw last could barely vow to buckle his own belt. I'm not worried."

"Maybe you should be. He's here in Portland."

A glint of uncertainty crossed the con man's face. "Is he, now?" he asked.

This pleased Roslyn. It was the response she'd hoped for in the first place, though she lacked the guile to keep up the ruse.

"Yes," she said. "But he's not really after you. He's convalescing with his mother. He's quite unwell."

"And you know this because you've been in touch with him?"

"I helped him get here," Roslyn said. "I traveled with him from Spokane Falls."

"Well, isn't that something." A statement, not a question. Wasn't it something indeed, what she had done? Even this man she'd only just met could see as much. They were both silent for a moment.

"Would you like a drink?" Quake asked, gesturing to the bottle on the table.

There was, suddenly and absolutely, nothing Roslyn wanted more in the world than to share a drink with an interesting stranger. She could already feel the warmth of it in her throat, washing away all her loneliness, her insecurity, her guilt.

"No, thank you," she said. "Maybe just some water."

Quake signaled to a waiter for a tumbler. He poured water from his own carafe. She thanked him again and took a sip, eyeing his wine.

"As I understand it, you stole a lot of money from the bank in Spokane Falls," she said.

"As I understand it, so did you," he replied. "Cheers to that." He raised his glass and knocked it against hers.

"But really it was Barton who stole the money from the bank," she said. "I stole it from him. That's much easier."

"Well, I suppose I did the same," Quake said. "But in reverse. So, cheers to Heydale—the bank robber's best helper!"

Another tapping of glasses.

"Isn't it bad luck to cheers with water?" Roslyn asked.

"Only if you're someone who's inherently thinking of bad luck." Roslyn felt he'd hit the nail on the head, though they'd known each other only a few moments. "Isn't a cheers by its very nature good luck? Let's just enjoy the good."

"What do you mean when you say 'in reverse'?"

"Heydale stole by giving out counterfeit notes of sorts, then pocketing the real money. So I stole by claiming that what was left in the bank after he'd been caught was counterfeit as well, and saying I needed to confiscate it for evidence of his crime."

Roslyn hadn't known this—about how Barton had been getting the money out of the bank. Only that the money from the bank hidden in the walls of his house represented an opportunity, which she had taken.

"Trusting of you to admit," she said. "What makes you think I'm not an undercover agent of the Spokane Falls police, come to extract a confession from you?"

"Because I've spent time with the Spokane Falls police and I happen to know you are far too smart to be one of them. And too good-looking."

It had been a long time since anyone besides Barton told Roslyn she was good-looking. She doubted Quake meant it, but she felt herself blush nonetheless.

"In fact, I think you're the first decent person from Spokane Falls I've ever met," he added. This, to Roslyn, felt more sincere. Though how would he know her to be decent? Perhaps he only wished it to be the case. Perhaps he was lonely, like she was, and wanting to trust.

He was still talking. Spokane Falls remained the topic.

"It really is an awful city," he said. "I've traveled quite a bit and I can't think of any place I've found more unpleasant."

"Well, it was just on fire," Roslyn said.

"Yes, but even before that."

The people he disdained, he said. But also the way the city was situated, with its downtown all scrunched up between the river and a hill. It gave the whole place a claustrophobic feel. Then there was the heat and the dust. The way the air sat stale in the valley. How he couldn't tell the liars from the honest men, and was therefore forced to assume everyone was always lying.

"I liked it," Roslyn said after a while. "I thought it was a fine place to live."

"To each their own." Quake gestured for another cheers, but his glass was empty. He called for another bottle of wine.

"Well, you surely love Portland indeed, to risk coming back here," Roslyn said.

"What risk?"

"Everyone in Spokane Falls knows you're here. Quake Auchenbaucher from Portland, Oregon."

"Right. So it's the one place they're certain I won't be."

"How's that?"

"Because I told them I lived and worked in Portland. And since I lied to them about everything else, I must have lied to them about that too."

Though she knew who he was and what he'd done, this was the first thing he'd said that really made her think him a criminal.

"There. You know all my secrets," Quake said with a wink. "So now I get to ask you a personal question. Why on earth would you go back to Heydale after you stole from him? Do you love him?"

Roslyn laughed. The fun of talking to Quake, and his bravado in the face of all things Barton, made her feel far removed from the man himself. As if her life with him had belonged to someone else entirely. No, she said. She didn't love him. She didn't even like him.

"I wanted to do something good," she said.

"Why?" Quake asked.

"I think I've always wanted to do something good. This seemed like it might be the thing, helping Barton."

"But it wasn't," Quake said.

No, Roslyn agreed. It wasn't.

9

M y apartment's just around the corner," Quake said. "Come up with me."

This was as they left the restaurant, Quake holding the door for her.

"Just for a quick minute. Nothing improper," he added.

She didn't believe him, but she said all right and followed him anyway. Quake had finished his second bottle of wine and Roslyn had watched his developing drunkenness with interest. She'd managed to keep her hand steadily clasped around her tumbler of water in his presence. But she feared if she was left alone, she wouldn't be able to stop herself from drinking. Just like on her last night in Spokane Falls. The impulse was so strong as to feel like someone pushing her from behind, or pulling at her feet by the buckles on her shoes. She'd buy a bottle of her own on the way back to the hotel and that would be it.

Going with Quake seemed the safer option. At least whatever

happened with him, she could tell herself it had not been entirely her fault.

They walked the short distance in silence, which made the arrangement seem all the more ominous. In the restaurant, there had hardly been a pause in the conversation, as if they had both been so eager to divulge the secrets they'd acquired in Spokane Falls. Though Roslyn hadn't told Quake everything. She'd left out the details of her time as a captive in Barton's home.

Maybe it's not just sex he wants, she worried. But still, her fear of the alternative—being alone—was greater.

The building he led her to was inauspicious, but inside, the apartment revealed itself to be quite large, taking up an entire floor. It was airy with big windows. Furniture and decoration were minimal, though clearly of good quality.

"Wait here," Quake said, gesturing to the expanse of his living room. He disappeared down the hall. Roslyn remained standing in the entryway and wondered what he would return with. More alcohol? A weapon? Or would he simply come back without any of his clothes on? Some men moved so quick.

He reemerged, and there was something in his hand.

"Here," he said, extending it toward her, and when she looked down, she saw it was money.

She laughed. She knew right away where it had come from: the First Bank of Spokane Falls. What had her life become that she so often dealt in stacks of cash from the First Bank of Spokane Falls?

"It's your cut," he said. "If it weren't for you, there'd have been nothing for me, after all."

"How do you mean?"

"You're the one who broke Heydale. Were he not so badly damaged, no one would have believed what I said about him."

"I didn't break Barton," Roslyn said, and she wanted to believe herself.

"Well, you did something," he said. "I want to thank you for that."

She pushed the money back toward him. "I can't accept it," she said.

He shrugged. "Okay then, back to the vault with this," he said, gesturing to the cash, and turned again toward the hallway.

In his absence, she wandered the living room, examining the few objects in it: a bookcase, a trunk that proved empty when she opened it, a long oak table with photographs in frames perched at one end. One was of Quake as a boy sitting astride a mule. She picked up the frame and undid the hooks. "Dan Kite—Black Hills" was written in faded script on the back of the picture. Of course Quake Auchenbaucher wouldn't have been the man's real name. Roslyn felt it gratifying to have gained this little bit of insight on him. And when he returned, his face displaying the stoic confidence he'd worn all through dinner, even when she'd first approached to say she knew him, she felt again the desire to shock him.

He started to say something, but she held up a hand, pretending to study him. She furrowed her brow and leaned close. Then she snapped her fingers. "Wait a minute, are you Dan Kite? I thought I recognized you! Oh, one of my old students from the Black Hills, after all this time."

Quake looked as if he might tip over. "No," he said. "I didn't go to school. I don't think I went to school."

Roslyn laughed. "Relax. I'm only fucking with you," she said.

"Then how do you know my old name?"

"I have mastered the ancient Eastern art of soul reading," she said, thinking of words Ernest might have used. "I can see into your innermost core. I can see little Dan Kite there in his short pants."

He looked ashen. Could it really be so easy to dupe a man who made conning others his life's work?

"You can see that?" he asked.

"No! I'm fucking with you again."

She picked up the small photo and told him she'd looked beneath the frame and seen the inscription on the back.

"It's the only picture ever taken of me," he said. "How did you know I was the boy?"

Roslyn studied him a moment and decided the question was genuine. The man had no idea how he looked, or that the look had always been with him, even when he was little Dan Kite.

It was in his eyes, mostly. Deep set and haunted. Like fear turned to rage turned to indifference. As an adult, he wore the look well. He was not unattractive. But it was an unsettling thing in the face of a ten-year-old child. She set the photo down.

"You were willing to believe I could peer into your soul?"

"Yes," he said without hesitation. "There's something a little mystical about you."

He was the first person to ever see it, this thing that pushed and pulled at Roslyn's life without discretion or direction. She thought of how she'd labored unsuccessfully to make the people of Steilacoom heed her dire adolescent warnings, and then the ill-conceived work it had taken to convince Ernest she could levitate. And how she'd kept those secrets ever since. Now here was Quake, a man she'd known just a few hours, who was not only willing to believe something extraordinary about her, but claimed to know it for himself.

She felt something should come after this. Sex or a fight or a long evening spent telling each other everything there was to know about themselves, things they wouldn't have dared admit in the restaurant. None of that happened. Instead, Quake offered to hail Roslyn a carriage back to her hotel, which she accepted. So that was it, she thought. Her single, strange evening in the company of the con man.

But then, three days later, she walked out of her hotel and found Quake leaning against the building near the front door. Waiting for her.

10

Quake was nervous in a way that made Roslyn think of how some of her older boy-students would approach her, back when she was a young and pretty teacher. There was that same bashfulness, but also the fact that in the light of day, Quake's youth was more apparent. He really could have been one of her schoolhouse charges back then. There were a dozen years between them, at least.

"I'd like you to accompany me," he said, his eyes jumping between her face and his own shoes. Nervous. Was there any man, in any station, not constantly mortified by the prospect of female rejection?

She shook her head. "I'm not in that line of work anymore," she said, though she knew that wasn't what he wanted.

"I just meant to the park," he said. "I'd like you to accompany me to the park. For a walk."

"All right, but what for?"

"Because I enjoyed talking with you the other evening and would like to do more of that. I thought you might feel the same."

She agreed and he extended his arm to her like such a proper gentleman, she almost laughed. She found his interest so unusual. It had been many years since she'd been on a real date.

Quake led her to a trolley stop and paid her fare. It was her first time on a Portland trolley, though she was too embarrassed to say so. She'd been walking everywhere, but why? Force of habit, fear of new things. This was better. Like a carriage, but more egalitarian. It pulled them in comfort through unfamiliar neighborhoods, until Quake gestured for her to stand and they left the car. They'd been let off at a stop across the street from the largest city park Roslyn had ever seen.

"Where are we?" she asked.

"This is City Park. Crown jewel of our fair city. It has gardens and a forest and a zoo. There's a fine bear pit. Would you like to see the bears?"

"I wasn't expecting bears today."

"Well, that's your mistake. You ought to always be expecting bears."

They went to the zoo. Quake told her the first animals had been donated by a Portland businessman. He'd rescued them from sailors who'd acquired the creatures on their travels to exotic locales and then, once arriving in port, realized they were in over their heads. He had kept the cubs in his yard, as playmates for his children, until they grew too large and he urged the city to build a sanctuary, which became the zoo.

"The great city of Portland is currently, here in the year of our Lord eighteen eighty-nine, home to fifty thousand souls. We are the largest metropolis in the region, exceeding even Seattle by almost ten thousand . . . though perhaps even more now, considering their unfortunate disaster of late. Ninety percent of the city has electricity. Even the streetcars are on their way to electrification. There's a five-year plan and then the horse-drawn ones will be obsolete."

Quake delivered this information as parody, with grand gestures and flourishes. But Roslyn could tell he liked to be the sharer of facts, and he was good at it. Such a stark contrast to the tour Barton had given her on her first day in Portland.

"That's a shame about the streetcars," she said. "I like the horses."

"Me too. Who doesn't? Such beautiful animals. Speaking of which, have you ever felt you had a connection with animals? That they understood you, in a certain way? And you them?"

Roslyn shook her head. She did not.

"Pity," Quake said. "You struck me as someone who might."

He continued his tour-guiding: the approximate number of ships traveling the Columbia River this time of year; the impact of the Chinese Exclusion Act on the city's growth (which he thought was a damn shame, to say who is and who is not welcome); the names for the trees they walked past.

"Have you ever killed anyone?" Roslyn asked, when Quake paused in his narration.

"Why? Have you?"

"Of course not," she said, and then felt a shudder pass through her at her lie. The man who'd died in the fire—she'd gone nearly all day without thinking of him. "I just thought in your line of work there might be killing."

"No, I'm not that sort of criminal. Never had the stomach for violence of any kind. Though bad things may have happened as a result of the information I've provided to others. I was going to let them hang Heydale. I thought they had until you told me otherwise."

"How does one become your sort of criminal? The kind that doesn't need to kill?"

"Luck."

"What does that mean?"

"It means I saw an opportunity and I took it. Then I figured out how to make the same opportunity happen over and over."

"Every time there's a disaster?"

"Not just disasters. Really anything people are afraid of. Or angry about. Or anything they hate. Hate is the best, actually. People are willing to part with a lot of money in the name of hate."

"I'd imagine. What about love?"

"No. There's no money in love as far as I'm aware. People tend not to pay out for things they like."

"There's something bleak in that."

"It's bleak that I can't exploit love?"

Roslyn laughed. "I suppose that's more my line of work. A whore can exploit love. Who else?"

"Is it love, though?"

"Well, lust. Intimacy."

"But not love, really."

She conceded he was right and thought it a nice sentiment.

"What did you do before you were a con man? Little Dan Kite wasn't born a shyster, was he?"

She could see Quake bristle at the use of his old name.

"Oh, I did lots of things. I was a bricklayer, a train robber, a cavalryman. All the usual sorts of vocations."

"You don't seem like the cavalry type."

"I wasn't. Too much of a coward. My gun didn't even work. I had a gun that worked, but I traded with a man whose didn't so I wouldn't ever have to fire it. He gave me fifty cents to trade and I thought I came out ahead."

It was a warm day and Quake stopped at a cart to buy ice cream. They sat in the grass to eat, surrounded by young couples and families. She wondered what those around them thought. Probably nothing. Probably took them for just another pair of lovers, not a set of thieves who'd found each other through supernatural means.

After that, she didn't see him for a few days. She went back to her usual routine—walking, meals, reading, sleeping—and wondered if he'd turn up again, or not, and how she might feel about either occurrence. She decided, ultimately, she would like to see Quake, but not so much so that she needed to seek him out. She felt no pull, psychic or otherwise, in his direction across town.

Then she found him leaning against the exterior wall of her hotel again one morning, same as the last time.

"I'm sorry I didn't come by sooner," he said when he saw her. "I didn't want to seem too eager."

This admission, of course, made him seem more eager than anything else he could have done. She went with him and had a fine time, just as before. From there on they saw each other most days. They were both, after all, people with plenty of free time and disposable income. They went for walks and ate in restaurants and talked in their flirty, bantery way. Fun, that's what Quake was. What a marvelous respite from Roslyn's solitary days of lurking through the city, weighed down by guilt and self-loathing. Even before she'd come to Portland, it had been a long while since she'd had very much fun. Quake, however, seemed the sort who had it all the time with whomever he liked. And so Roslyn felt grateful that, at least for the time being, he wanted to have fun with her.

"Why aren't you working now?" Roslyn asked him one afternoon. "Do con men take holidays?"

"Sure. Everyone needs a holiday now and then," he said.

"How long will yours last?"

They were sitting at a café, at a sidewalk table, drinking lemonade. The glasses were tall and cold, each with a single lemon slice floating at the top. Quake reached into his glass, plucked out the lemon, and set it on his tongue. He sucked on the lemon for a moment with the expression of someone enjoying a piece of candy.

"I don't know," he said. "Until I find my next job, I suppose."

"Isn't that as simple as finding the next fire? Or is fire season over for the year?"

"Oh, my sweet dear, it's always fire season if you know what to look for."

"All right. Then what's the holdup?"

"Are you trying to get rid of me?"

"Absolutely not."

"I'm waiting to see if your compatriots in Washington are going to gain statehood, for one thing. A sudden enthusiasm for government and rule of law is not exactly the kind of climate I want to be working in. And so I am considering other ventures in other locations."

"I was looking forward to statehood when I was there," Roslyn said. "It seems like a step in the right direction for us."

"Yes, that's exactly the trouble."

His time in Spokane Falls had unmoored him temporarily, Quake admitted. He'd felt anxious and unsafe in a way he was not accustomed to. There had been too much at stake—too many different parties with something to lose and something to gain. It had made him doubt not just that particular job, but his whole line of business.

"I've recovered from that bit of irrational thinking," he said. But the experience had left him with what he called a healthy appreciation for the growing risks of his occupation. So, he was taking some time to reassess.

"Are you also reassessing?" he asked. There was a note of caution to this question, like he was unsure if it was wise to ask it in the first place, but she said no. She was not reassessing. She was retired from her old profession.

"I don't know what I'll do with myself now," she said. "But not that anymore."

"And what about Washington? Will you be returning?"

She didn't have an answer to give. She took another sip of her lemonade. A trio of young women passed by on the street, all twirling parasols, though it was neither raining nor particularly sunny. Roslyn found herself wondering what Mrs. Heydale might think of such impractical fashion.

On another day soon after, Roslyn and Quake had sex in her hotel room. This too, just like their walking and talking, felt easy to her—

another way to have fun, as long as there was fun to be had. Sex, as a general rule, didn't mean much to Roslyn. She didn't believe this had anything to do with her former occupation. She'd felt the same about it before she became a prostitute. She'd had boyfriends on and off everywhere she lived and she'd had sex with them without compunction. Sometimes it was enjoyable and sometimes it wasn't, but it was never much more than that. She thought perhaps this was because she'd never been in love with any of the boyfriends. She'd met them all after she'd started drinking, when she didn't really love anything, aside from Mud Drink. Though she had made sacrifices for these men, shifted her life around to accommodate them.

It was thanks to a boyfriend that she'd ended up in Spokane Falls. After she lost her job teaching school in Steilacoom, her boyfriend at the time said he knew someone who owned a bar in Spokane Falls where they could work serving drinks. So they went. But the boyfriend had been a drunk too and eventually he got them both fired for some infraction Roslyn could no longer remember. So she'd taken up with another man at another bar who said he could get her work there, but the work at the new bar wasn't waitressing like at the old place. *Entertainment* was the word he'd used. Roslyn had laughed at the idea and said no, but then somehow ended up doing it anyway, and it wasn't as bad as she'd thought. Actually, it was fine. Just like the sex she had for free with the boyfriend. This boyfriend too had drifted off someplace eventually, and Roslyn, at the suggestion of another woman, left the bar and rented a room at Wolfe's Hotel, where she'd stayed for almost a decade. It hadn't felt like that long to her. In fact, there were whole years in that time to which she could attach no specific memories.

Now, with Quake, the sex felt special, but only because it was new. In a few days, it wouldn't be new. Just another thing they could do together to while away their Portland days. His long body was a puzzle of sorts. What to do with a man who was all limbs? He was gawky—awkward without his crisp, tailored suit. She liked that, the vulnerability of him. She maneuvered him in the ways she wanted, and when they were done, she looked up to see his face stuck in the same pleased shock as when she'd first suggested he come upstairs with her a half hour earlier. He hadn't done this very much before, she realized, and said it out loud: "You haven't done this much before."

"How could you tell? Was I awful at it?"

She pulled him to her again and reassured him, no, he was fine. "I can just tell. That's all. Nothing bad."

"Of course you can," he said. "You can tell about everything."

Then he closed his eyes and pushed his head into the crook of her arm, a position she knew to be a classic for comfort seekers. For men who wanted more.

She began to see she'd misread the situation entirely. She'd misread Quake entirely.

II

Quake: What's the thing you are most ashamed of in your life?

Roslyn: Goodness, why would you ask such a question?

Quake: Isn't that what people do after sex? Talk about intimate matters?

Roslyn: No. Usually they sleep. Or they make polite small talk.

Quake: I stand by my original question.

Roslyn: Oh, many things.

Quake: Pick your favorite.

Roslyn: I had my job as a schoolteacher taken away from me, years ago. I loved teaching. I thought it would be my life's work, but I was careless. I was a drunk for a long time. They didn't want me near the children when I was like that. It shames me terribly.

Quake: I see.

Roslyn: And you?

Quake: I'm a coward.

Roslyn: I don't know what that means.

Quake: Sure you do. It means what you think it means. I'm no good in a fight.

Roslyn: And when would you have wanted such a fight?

Quake: When I was in the cavalry, we forced Paiute families to march hundreds of miles. It was winter. I would like to have fought then.

Roslyn: You would like to have fought the Paiutes? Were they violent?

Quake: No, the other cavalrymen. I would like to have killed them, given the families their food and horses. They could have gone where they liked.

Roslyn: A nice idea. But it wouldn't have worked, would it? There's always more cavalry.

Quake: I suppose. I also don't know who my parents are.

Roslyn: That's nothing to be ashamed of. It isn't your fault.

Quake: I abandoned the woman who raised me. I left without telling her and sent no word after. I don't even know now if she's still alive.

Roslyn: This is beginning to feel like confession at church. Are you seeking absolution?

Quake: No. It just feels good to talk, that's all. It's been a while.

Roslyn: A while since what?

Quake: Since I talked to anyone. How about you?

Roslyn: I can't even remember.

12

It was the next day that they saw Barton. He was at a distance. They were out for a walk, crossing a footbridge, and he was down below, on a park bench. He was hunched, seemingly against a non-existent breeze. His mother sat beside him, facing straight ahead, still as a statue.

Roslyn was the one to spot them, and her first impulse was to say nothing, to keep walking and pretend they weren't there at all. But she was unnerved and did not want to be alone in that feeling.

"Look," she said, without pointing, just a quick gesture of her head. "There's Barton."

Quake peered over the edge of the bridge. He leaned against the railing so his feet left the ground a few inches, his torso tipping into nothingness.

"Well I'll be," he said. Then, "My God, he looks awful. Even worse than before."

"You aren't surprised to see him?" Roslyn asked.

"Of course not. Any big city becomes a small town if you stay long enough."

"How quaint."

"Isn't it?"

They walked on and Roslyn was flooded with disgust that she had chosen to remain in a small town with Barton Heydale.

She wanted to be like Quake, who seemed to have brushed the image of Barton off like water from a duck. But what did Quake have to linger on? He'd said he felt guilty for getting Barton hanged, but then Barton hadn't been hanged after all, and so Quake felt fine. He even hummed a little to himself, the whole scene either dismissed or forgotten entirely. Roslyn wished it could be so easy for her.

As they walked on, she found herself testing the waters.

"Perhaps I will leave Portland sooner rather than later," she said to Quake.

He didn't ask why, only nodded, and she took this to mean he understood her angst.

"I've been mulling over the same," he said. "I think some time elsewhere could be grand for us both. Very grand indeed."

Roslyn wasn't sure what Quake meant, but he wasn't talking about Barton after all. His tone was too light, his words suggesting something that had been bouncing around in his own brain well before they sighted Barton. It reminded her of the way Barton himself sometimes spoke, so caught up in his personal schemes that he could fold Roslyn's words into whatever he wanted, regardless of what she'd said. A trick of men in all states of mind, she thought, but she did not bother to correct him.

———

They saw Barton a second time a week later. They were at the Central Market in downtown Portland. The market was indoors, a sprawling warren of shops and stalls. Roslyn and Quake weren't there for anything in particular—just to wander and look. Something to do. Quake had bought her a flower, an orchid in a pot. The orchid was tall and as she walked, she struggled to find a way to hold it that did not obscure her vision in some way, but eventually she gave up and just let the thing bounce around in front of her eyes—a blur of color adding to the disorientation of the market. So, perhaps because her eyes were busy elsewhere, it was Quake who spotted Barton this time.

"Oh ho! Your buddy's back."

"He's not my buddy."

"Nor mine," Quake said, pulling her by the arm down a narrow aisle and into a bookseller's stall. They crouched between tables piled high with paperbacks.

"Do you think he saw us?" Roslyn asked.

"Absolutely not," he said. "We were far too cunning and crafty."

She watched from her awkward hiding place as Barton's slouched form shuffled by. He was, like in the previous week, wearing too many clothes—dressed for a season later than it really was. This time he was alone. No mother by his side. Maybe the old woman had died. That was Roslyn's first thought and it gave her the creeps: an image of Barton living in the company of a corpse. He seemed the sort of man who might do such a thing.

She was startled from her morbid reverie by footsteps so close as to be just behind her. Barton had seen them and was now upon them, with what intentions, she didn't know, but they couldn't be good. She closed her eyes tight, like a child who still believes not seeing is the same as not being seen.

"Buy a book or move along," a voice said. It belonged to the foot stepper. Not Barton at all; only the owner of the haphazard book-stall.

"Dammit, man! Can't you see we're in hiding here! This is serious business," Quake hissed. But when Roslyn looked, he was smiling.

"Come on," he said to Roslyn, taking her arm again, "let's follow him."

"Why?"

"To see what he's doing, obviously. Aren't you curious?"

She let herself be led. Always so much easier to follow than to say no.

They walked through the aisle, popping back into the market's main thoroughfare a few shops down. They were behind Barton now, but not far. Quake bobbed and weaved as they went, encouraging Roslyn to do the same, ducking behind stalls and shelves to exaggerated effect. None of it was necessary. Barton didn't look back. That didn't seem to matter to Quake. He was having fun, making a game of it.

When Barton went into a store, Quake tiptoed right up to the entryway and pressed himself against the outer wall. Roslyn did the same, thinking, if anything, they were making themselves more conspicuous with this behavior. Quake peered through the doorway.

"Look," he said.

She looked. The store was cramped, full of little decorative things arranged across shelves and in bins. Barton walked like a man on his way to someplace else. But every few feet, he'd pause just long enough to tip something from a shelf into one of the pockets of his unnecessary coat.

"Is he stealing?" Roslyn asked.

"Most certainly."

When he reached the end of the shop, Barton turned, facing back toward Roslyn and Quake. Roslyn felt a crush of fear press through her, but he wasn't looking at them. She and Quake stepped out of the doorway and he passed right by them. His eyes had a glazed look, as if he were so focused on his task, or so unfocused entirely, that he was incapable of seeing anything in particular at all.

Roslyn relaxed a little then, and they continued to follow him. Every so often, he would move near enough to a vendor's stall to pocket some small good or another. There was no theme to what he took, beyond objects little enough to swipe.

"We're onto his game now! Stay low," Quake said. "No, no, now go high."

Roslyn laughed and put her hand to her mouth to stifle the noise.

"You're getting the hang of it," he said.

"I learned from the best. A man of cunning and intrigue taught me everything he knew."

"Well, not everything. I've still got a few tricks up my sleeve. But stick with me and you'll be a master spy yet."

Roslyn laughed again, caught up in Quake's game. It felt good to let herself go along with this reality where Barton was a ridiculous plaything.

Barton entered another shop. This time Quake held up a hand and told her to wait for him. She did, and watched as he walked at normal speed—no more effort, real or fake, to stay hidden—to the storefront. For a moment, Roslyn thought he was going to go inside and confront Barton. But no. He stopped out front to talk to a man seated in a chair. The store's proprietor, she guessed. After a moment, the man in the chair nodded, stood to shake Quake's hand, then disappeared inside the shop.

Then he was back at Roslyn's side. "Let's go back the way we came."

"You don't want to see if he'll be caught?" she asked.

"No. It'll just get sad from here. We've had our fun."

It was exactly the kind of scenario Barton might have concocted in his own mind, Roslyn thought: Quake Auchenbaucher, not content to have ruined him in Spokane Falls, was now following unseen to make his life miserable in Portland. Too bizarre and paranoid to be true. Except that it was.

She found the feeling of Barton-as-a-game lingered even after they'd left. What if everything could be a game? That was how Quake lived, wasn't it? He had even made a game of the fire. Wouldn't it be lovely to turn all her guilt, all her remorse, all her visions that followed her like hungry dogs, into some sort of plaything? It seemed Quake had the power to make it so. This revelation made her now consider seriously an offer he'd presented two days prior, for which he was still awaiting her response.

13

Quake: What do you know about San Francisco?

Roslyn: It's a city in California on the coast.

Quake: It's on a bay.

Roslyn: All right. In California on a bay.

Quake: Do you want to go there with me?

Roslyn: Why?

Quake: I need you for my next venture.

Roslyn: You need a lady to help with your next con?

Quake: That's not what I said. I need you. No one else will do.

Roslyn: What's the gimmick?

Quake: No gimmick. No con at all, in fact. We'd be offering a service. That's all I can say right now.

Roslyn: You always think you're offering a service.

Quake: Not always. In Spokane Falls I was only serving myself. I'll more than readily admit to that.

Roslyn: And who would we be serving in San Francisco?

Quake: Whoever might benefit from the knowledge we acquire. And that's really all I can say right now. I mean it this time.

Roslyn: You always think you're offering knowledge.

Quake: San Francisco is very metropolitan. People come from all over the world. It's a city of hills. And fog. And the whole place smells like the sea.

Roslyn: Even though it's on a bay.

Quake: The whole place smells like a bay.

Roslyn: You've been there before?

Quake: No, but I've read about it in magazines and correspondence.

Roslyn: With whom in San Francisco do you correspond?

Quake: Other people's correspondence, I mean.

Roslyn: You are a very suspicious fellow, you know that.

Quake: I'm aware. Will you come with me? I'd like for you to come with me. I'd like your help. And your company.

This was the thing he'd been hinting at when Roslyn said she might like to leave Portland. She told him she would think on it. She hadn't said no.

He was in love with her. She'd realized it since the first time they'd had sex. The revelation came as a surprise. His bravado had thrown her off. She knew he liked spending time with her, as she did him. But she thought he saw her as a novelty—a souvenir of sorts from his Spokane Falls con. She hadn't known it was love. Perhaps the signs were there and she hadn't seen them because she didn't feel the same.

But so what? Why not just go? Quake was an intelligent, attractive man. He was kind to her. He was interesting and clever, with the capacity to help pull Roslyn from the depths of her own mind. And he wanted to be with her. How many chances did Roslyn—homeless wanderer, former whore, accidental arsonist—think she had at this kind of companionship?

But was the life of a con man's sidekick the life she wanted?

Again, why not? Who said she had to be good? Who said she had to make up for the fire, for Kate, for the dead man, for the Steilacoom schoolchildren, for all the times she'd levitated to steal, or the other visions she'd had and ignored? No one. She could live like Quake, get rich off other people's misfortune, and never feel bad. She could live *with* Quake and swap her own worries for his, which were almost nothing at all.

14

For their third Barton sighting, they were back in City Park. They were visiting the bears and eating ice cream, as they'd done often since their first date. It was a favorite of Roslyn's, this leisurely, sunny-day activity, a luxury in its wholesomeness and universality. There, they could be anyone. Who doesn't like a day at the park?

Who indeed. He was with his mother again. They were walking, slowly, arm in arm, as if one were supporting the other, though Roslyn could not tell who was playing which role. Maybe they were both, in equal parts, holding and being held.

They shambled past the entrance to the zoo just as Roslyn and Quake were leaving.

"He's everywhere," Quake said.

"You said it yourself—even a big city is small if you live there long enough."

"But how long have you and Barton been here? More than a month?"

"Yes. What are you suggesting?"

"That you're being followed."

She knew he was joking, always joking. But she didn't like the idea.

"I don't care to see him so often," Roslyn admitted. "He makes me uneasy."

"Can't have that."

"No. But what's to be done about it?" *Move to San Francisco*, she thought he would say.

"Should we kill him, do you think?"

"You mean now?" Roslyn asked. "Or another time?"

"Oh, certainly now."

Still joking. Though something in the way Quake said this chilled her. There was that thing about him, that haunted, hollowed look, which at times made the man himself seem like a weapon. She wondered if his oft-lamented pacifism could be a lie. Another Quake charade. It reminded her how little she truly knew of the man with whom she was considering traversing the West and embarking on schemes unknown.

"Let's just go," she said. She took him by the arm and led him out of the park and away from Barton, away from the prospect of violence, be it real or imagined.

They went back to his apartment, which was spacious and clean as always. It was early November now, but still warm. So unseasonable as to be almost alarming. An Indian summer, she'd heard people say. It was more than that, as if summer was so persistent, it had pushed fall out of the way entirely. Roslyn felt the coming of winter would be a shock, waking up to one frozen day all of a sudden. They kept the windows open while they made love. Practiced and routine already. When they were done, they lay side by side in Quake's large bed.

"Are you coming to San Francisco or not?" he asked.

"Not," Roslyn said.

"Are you coming to San Francisco or not?"

"Absolutely. I'm all packed and booked on the next steamer."

"Are you coming to San Francisco or not?"

"I don't know, Quake. Why don't you tell me what, exactly, we'd be doing there?"

"Okay, okay, that's reasonable. I've got my ducks in enough of a row now that I suppose it's safe to say. What do you know about shanghaiing?

"I'm not helping you do that."

"I'm not asking you to."

"Then, what?"

The shipping trade in San Francisco was experiencing a tremendous boom, Quake explained. Roslyn leaned back onto her pillow and closed her eyes. She assumed she was in for one of Professor Quake's scholarly lectures, as she called the instances when the man spoke at length and with joy on some subject or another.

He continued, saying the demand for sailors out of the harbors of San Francisco was so great that captains struggled to find enough men, particularly for undesirable routes or when they could not offer the highest wages. And so these captains had begun instead employing gangsters to trick, drug, and capture sailors bound for other ships. When they woke up, broke and naked, the sailors were already far at sea, with their previous employers having no knowledge of what had happened to them.

"It's occurring here in Portland as well," Roslyn said. "I've read it in the paper."

"Yes," Quake agreed. "But it's a small-time enterprise compared to San Francisco."

Quake's plan was to interrupt the kidnapped-sailor supply chain. "We'll place ourselves in the vicinity of where this is all happening. There are known brothels and boardinghouses these fellows are working out of; it's no secret. Get to know some of the key players involved. We'll find out where the victims are being kept once they've been abducted and then sell this information to their real employers—to the captains of the ships who stand to lose them."

"Why not take the information to their families, or the police?"

"Families, maybe. If we know they come from money."

"And where do I fit into this?" Roslyn asked.

"You're how we know where the captives are being taken. You would use your . . . ability."

She told him that was not how her ability, as he called it, worked.

"What makes you think I can do that sort of thing?"

Quake took his time with his answer. He stretched his arms up and yawned, then brought one hand down to scratch the back of his head. Miming comfort.

"It's what Heydale told me about you."

"Barton the lunatic shyster told you I could read minds, and you believed him?"

"Not at first. But there is magic to you. I'm right about that, aren't I?"

Roslyn didn't have an answer for this. It unnerved her to consider that Barton had observed this in her too, even if he'd gotten it wrong. "I just don't like to think of you getting ideas from Barton," she said finally.

"What did you ever see in him?"

"What do you mean?"

"You lived with Heydale," Quake said. "You were his girlfriend. What did you see in him?"

"I lived with him, but I wasn't his girlfriend," Roslyn answered.

"How's that?"

"After the fire, he offered me a place to stay and I accepted. Then he tried to convince me that I ought not leave because I was a suspect in the arson investigation—the original one, before they called you—and that I was only safe if I stayed hidden with him. I knew he was lying, but I stayed anyway." She hadn't told him this part before. Beside her, she felt Quake's body tense.

"And what did he get out of this arrangement?"

"He got me, I suppose."

"Sex, you mean."

"Yes."

"Why would you have sex with him if you knew he was lying? Why would you stay with him at all?"

She thought of how to formulate an answer. She didn't want to say any more about the fire. So she told him about Mud Drink. About the state she was in, her first few days with Barton. The haze and sickness and how it was easier just to be there, to let whatever was happening happen, to have a place and be safe in it for what it was, even if it was all wrong.

"I wish I could say it was a long con," she said. "I wish I could say that I always meant to rob him and that was the reason I stayed. But it was only happenstance."

"I should have really killed him," Quake said. "I will if I see him again."

"You will not."

"He's a monster. What he did to you." He was turned toward her now, his whole body leaning in, like he might pounce. "You understand that, don't you? When you talk about it, it doesn't sound like you get that."

"I know," she said.

"Do you really? Because you went back to him. You brought him here. You helped him. You helped a monster."

Roslyn stayed still and tried to force her breathing to slow.

"If I see him again, I'll kill him," Quake repeated.

"You will not," she said. "You abhor violence."

"In this case, I'll make an exception."

"I don't think you will. I don't think you're capable."

"Well now," he said. "Well now, there that is, and you can't take it back."

He removed himself from the bed, dressed, and without saying anything, left the apartment. Roslyn thought she too should leave in a huff, but stayed. She didn't want Quake to get the last word. How had a conversation where she'd admitted something so vulnerable and so repulsive turned into a tiff over Quake's bruised ego?

Twenty minutes later, he was back.

"He's close," he said. "Staying at a boardinghouse about ten blocks from here."

Though Roslyn knew whom he was speaking of, she felt disoriented by the information. Quake hadn't left because he was angry with her. He'd left to find Barton.

"No," she said. "That's not right. He lives on the other side of the city. I don't know the name of the neighborhood, but it's on one of the hills with the big houses. He lives with his mother."

"Guess she kicked him out."

"But he was with his mother in the park. We just saw them."

"Merely a social call on her part? He's taken a room here near us. To be near us, don't you think?"

"We were only joking about that, weren't we? He's not really following us. It's coincidence."

"We were joking until you told me the true nature of your relationship with him. Now I am absolutely convinced you're being stalked."

"How did you find this out?"

"I have eyes and ears everywhere in this city. All I had to do was ask.

"I'm going there now," he added.

"Is it because I called you a coward?"

"Yes and no."

"I'm coming too," she said.

15

Quake could move fast when he wanted. Roslyn struggled to keep up, taking little jumpy run-steps every few paces.

"What are you going to do?" she had asked as they left the apartment.

"I'm going to make it clear to Mr. Heydale that he's no longer welcome in your life."

"But I already did that."

"Needs doing again."

Seven blocks had passed and they hadn't spoken since. Quake gained further ground. There were now twenty yards at least between them. Roslyn didn't want to be near Barton. Why had she insisted on coming along? To stop Quake from what she feared he might try to do?

Or because she wanted him to do it, and she wanted to see it done? She felt ashamed of herself and was about to say as much to Quake, to try to turn them both back, when suddenly she felt a vision coming on.

Not now, she thought, more irritated than afraid.

But fear did come. In front of her eyes, a city block jolted by an explosion. An inferno tumbling from the bowels of tall buildings, rushing up brick facades and wooden staircases. Black smoke encasing the people inside, many of them children. Then it wasn't just one block, but the same scene over and over like dominoes. All up and down hilly, crowded streets. A vast city trembling and burning.

Roslyn felt her chest tighten and her throat ache, as if she too were inside this smoke. She stopped to catch her breath, dropped her hands to her knees, and found her eyes clouded as though she might pass out. She'd never had a vision like this before—so gruesome, so sweeping. There was no marker she could pin to it; she recognized no one and nothing. The street wasn't in Portland. It wasn't in Spokane Falls. It was *a city of hills.* But those weren't her words, they were Quake's. As quickly as the vision had appeared, it was gone, just like always. Roslyn felt herself wanting to hold this one, to piece it together. It was too terrible to be ignored.

But as her eyes cleared, she became aware of something perhaps also terrible taking place right in front her. Quake had stopped at a house up the street and was ringing the bell. She ran to catch him. By the time she got there, he was already speaking to someone inside, a housekeeper maybe, asking after Barton. His hands were jammed into his vest pocket like he was holding on to something.

"Quake!" Roslyn called to him as she jogged the path to the house. "Quake, let's just go. There's no need, really. Let's just—"

She was beside him then, her palm on his back, his muscles tense through his clothes, which were damp with sweat. The person he was speaking to was no housekeeper after all. It was Barton himself.

"Roslyn?" Barton said, his voice deep and cool like back when he was the banker, coming to her apartment twice a week to exchange money for sex. "What's the matter? Has this man done something to upset you?"

This man. Roslyn watched Barton's eyes track from her to Quake. He had no idea who Quake was, had not placed him as the person who'd ruined him once and for all in Spokane Falls, though he'd vowed vengeance less than two months prior. Maybe none of it had ever really happened, each man only a hallucination to the other. There was something unsteady in all this, the world tipped askew.

"It's okay, Ros," Quake said. "We're only talking. Having a nice chat about Mr. Heydale's behavior as of late. That's all."

"Quake, there's no need," Roslyn said. "Let's leave now."

"No. I believe there is a need. A great need. I feel I need very much to clarify something for all of us."

There was in Quake's voice a tremor. A quiver. It made her wish for him a different name, something that did not conjure the image of shifting and wobbling in times of uncertainty. Could this be the same person who had convinced Spokane Falls to give him thousands of dollars from their bank vault on the strength of his words alone? No wonder Barton didn't recognize him.

"We know what you're up to, Heydale," Quake continued. "Following us. You're scheming something. I'm here to put a stop to that."

"Roslyn," Barton said again. "I think you should get away from this fellow. He seems agitated. I am concerned for your safety."

"Jesus, man," Quake snapped. "Don't worry about her. Be concerned for your own safety. Don't you get what I'm saying to you?"

Now Barton's eyes seemed to narrow with recognition and Roslyn thought he was finally catching on. But when he spoke, it still wasn't to Quake.

"Roslyn," he said softly, "it was you the whole time, wasn't it? You are the devil woman from my dream. You're the devil, who came to my house and made me do bad things."

"What the fuck are you talking about?" Quake barked, still trembling.

"Yes, it was me," Roslyn said, and somewhere behind her she heard the roaring inferno of her most recent vision, the sound of fire pulled by oxygen to new strength.

"I knew it," Barton said. "You bitch."

"Hey now!" Quake said, and made as if to lunge for Barton, but Barton was faster. He reached with his hand and slapped Quake across the cheek. Then he stepped back into the house and closed the door.

Quake grabbed at his face and whined. It was such a pitiful little whimper that Roslyn couldn't help but laugh, even as Quake recovered himself and pounded on the door, shouting, "Open it, you sick fuck! We aren't done!"

The door did reopen, but it wasn't Barton behind it this time. Instead, it was a shrunken woman with gray hair who resembled Barton's mother so closely that Roslyn wondered if it was her they'd seen in the park with him.

"Quiet, please," she said, pressing a finger to her lips. "This is a home for convalescents. Mr. Heydale has retired to his room for a rest."

Then Roslyn and Quake were alone on the stoop.

"Please stop laughing," Quake said.

"I'm sorry," Roslyn said for the second time that day without meaning it.

"At least I said my piece. I made my point known."

"Did you?" Roslyn asked.

"What would you have had me do?"

"Nothing," she said. "That's what I was trying to tell you when I got to the door."

"Honestly? You wanted me to kill him. Admit it."

"Not kill, no."

"Well, I guess you were right about me, then. I'm not capable."

She could tell he wanted her to correct him. But the thought of having to coddle him in that moment was exhausting.

They walked back to Quake's apartment building. Roslyn intended to leave on her own, but instead he did what he always did, which was to hail her a carriage and ride with her to her hotel. He didn't speak as they rode; he kept his face turned toward the window, his shoulders slumped. But once they were downtown, he said he was hungry and asked if she'd like to get something to eat with him. He led her to a dim basement café. They ordered and ate in silence.

"If you're angry, just say so," Roslyn said finally. "What's the point of riding around with me and buying me dinner if you aren't going to talk?"

"I suppose the point is so you don't take up with another man in my absence simply because he's bold enough to lie to you."

"Don't be cruel," she said.

"I'm sorry. I'm just hurt."

"Well, that's not exactly an exclusive club tonight," she said. Then, "You never did *sense* anything magical about me, did you? You were just parroting what Barton had told you."

"Barton told me a lot of things, not all of them worth repeating.

I had the good judgment to know this was something he was right about."

"Speaking of men telling lies. You really are a liar to your core, aren't you?"

"I thought you liked that about me. I thought we were in agreement. Two peas in a pod."

"What, exactly, did Barton tell you about me?"

"That you put bad ideas in his head and made him do things."

"Nope."

"And that you were the devil. Which you strangely agreed to today."

To this, Roslyn said nothing.

"I'll help you out. Finish this sentence. *I worry I might be the actual, literal devil because . . .*"

"Guilt, I suppose. I sometimes have terrible visions of the future. I saw the fire in one of them. But I didn't do anything to stop it. Then I saw Barton's death in another and that's why I brought him to Portland, to try and save him, but I don't know if I have."

"Visions. That is quite the power," Quake said, softening now.

"It would be a power if I could stop them from coming true. But I never could."

"Maybe you aren't supposed to stop them. Maybe you are supposed to know they are going to happen so you can do something afterward."

It was an idea so simple Roslyn wondered why she hadn't thought of it in all her years of premonitions. What freedom it held, what possibility.

"And what should I do after Barton dies?" she asked.

"Throw a fucking party." He was smiling when he said this, but then he turned his face to his food and did not look back up. Still sore.

"Portland is also a city of hills," Roslyn said. "What's the difference between Portland's hills and San Francisco's?"

Now he did return her gaze.

"Steeper," he said. "And the buildings are all close together like teeth in a mouth. It's a bigger city in a smaller space. They've got to be economical."

Then he added, "You'll like it. It's nice."

"Is it?" she asked.

"No. But it's our kind of place, I think. Plenty of work to be done."

16

Alone in her hotel room, Roslyn wondered what was wrong with her that she could not keep a simple promise to herself. It had been little more than three months since she vowed to stop drinking Mud Drink and to stop levitating. And though she had been tempted toward Mud Drink, she had stayed true. Levitating was different. Had she ever really believed she was done with it for good? Or was there always somewhere in her mind that knew she'd return to it? And if so, did that matter?

The morning after her argument with Quake, she followed her old routine. She found it an easy action to slip back into. Just like riding a bike, as the saying went. Although Roslyn had never learned to ride a bike herself.

She sat on her bed. She breathed and thought of nothing until she felt her mind begin to peel away from her body. Once she was free of herself, she went outside, through the morning streets—busy as always—toward Quake's apartment. He'd admitted to lying to her, hadn't even been ashamed of it. And maybe, like he'd said, she'd known all along. Wasn't that part of the appeal of Quake? A liar who could make lies come true? She wanted to see who he was when there was no one around to lie to. Then she would decide if the lies mattered or not.

It was early, and when she arrived, he was not yet awake. She lingered in his room, watching him sleep. He slept like a child, curled into himself, one arm thrust over his head. When he finally woke, he lay in bed for some time, as if considering a problem, so deep in concentration he could not be bothered to move his body in the slightest. Roslyn wondered if the problem was her—the things she'd said the previous night.

Finally, whatever spell was over him broke and he rose from his bed. Roslyn watched as he went about readying himself for his day—shaving, combing his hair, selecting his clothes. He left the apartment for his breakfast, eating at a small café nearby. He lingered, moved slow. She didn't know what Quake did on his days away from her, but she suspected that, like her, he was largely idle, simply passing time. Indeed, after breakfast, she followed as he took a leisurely, loping walk around the neighborhood. From time to time, he would stop to chat with someone. He knew his neighbors and seemed well liked.

The conversations Quake had on the street were dull. There was none of the cleverness he employed with Roslyn. Just small talk, being polite. He bought a paper from a news stall and then continued to a very small park—a house-size plot of land that was nothing more than grass, a tree, and a bench. He sat on the bench and read his newspaper. Though there was nothing, really, to be learned from this, Roslyn stayed nearby. On the way back to his apartment,

Quake stopped to buy a sandwich. He ate at the table in his living room while hunched over a map with no label. Roslyn wondered if it was San Francisco. She too studied the document, though she gleaned nothing concrete from it.

In all this, Quake was remarkably quiet. Not the kind of man to talk to himself while alone. Even his breathing was slow. It would be easy to take the apartment for empty.

After some time, he left again, and Roslyn followed him back to the market where he'd bought his sandwich. This time, he purchased sacks of flour and sugar, a pound of butter, and some other pantry staples, and from the butcher next door, some sort of meat. This surprised Roslyn. To her knowledge, Quake didn't cook and hardly ever had food of any kind in his house. When he returned to his building, instead of going back to the top floor, he knocked on a door on the first. A thin woman with gray hair answered, and Quake held out the box of groceries to her. She shook her head. "There's no need—" she started, but Quake cut her off. "I hope Marcus is feeling better. Please let me know if there's anything else I can do."

Then back to his own apartment, where he began tidying the already tidy space. Books in stacks moved to shelves. Windowsills dusted. Coats on hangers straightened.

None of this revealed anything to Roslyn about the mystery of Quake, except perhaps that there was less mystery than expected. It made her like him more, the gentle quietness of his days. But it didn't make her trust him.

Above all else, she found herself jealous of him.

Here was Quake, living for himself and no one else. He did not question himself in the day-to-day. He did whatever he liked in the moment. He slept late. He was kind to his neighbors. He stole money and hid it in his home, spending it how he wished.

It was in his study that Roslyn got an idea of what she might like to see. This was the smallest of Quake's rooms and a space she had never been invited into. She knew it was where he'd emerged from that first night with his fist full of Spokane Falls bank cash. She felt she ought to see more of that room. After all, whatever tools of his trade Quake did keep here in his home, Roslyn assumed they were in the study. If there was a gun, it would be here. That would tell her something, she felt. One way or another.

He was hunched over the desk, using a rag to clean an ink stain from its surface.

Open the drawer, she thought. *Open all the drawers.*

He did. And more. He set the rag to the side and pulled his key ring from his pocket. He opened the drawers, revealing a collection of gray-green metal lockboxes. He removed one, lifted the lid, and took out a tidy pile of money, which he spread on the top of the desk.

Quake stepped back, extending his hands.

"There," he said. "Is that what you want? You've been following me all day, for Christ's sake. Is that what you want, or isn't it?"

She thought she might vomit. Was it possible to vomit while separate from one's corporeal self?

I'm sorry, she thought. *I only wanted to know you better!* It sounded so childish when she put it like that. She didn't know if he could hear her words or sense them. As with Kate the day of the fire, she was unmoored. Suddenly vulnerable and exposed, she fled the scene. But this time no cities burned. Just the small town she and Quake had built between them.

———

She didn't want things with Quake to end like that. In the morning, she returned to his apartment in her normal, non-levitating form. She knocked on his door, thinking he might not even open it for her, would just tell her to go. But the door did open and there he was with his haunted, hollow eyes finally seeming like they had a reason to be so sad.

He stepped aside and Roslyn entered the room. "I've come to apologize," she said.

"Because you made a mistake. You got caught."

Not sad at all. Mad. His voice was cool with it, the way men can be when they feel anger gives them advantage.

"Never pull the same scheme twice," he said.

Roslyn shook her head. "It wasn't my intention."

"I'm not the fool Heydale is. My money isn't here. All that's in the desk is pocket change. You want it?" He strode out of the room and returned a moment later with one of the gray-green lockboxes. He lifted out a stack of bills and thrust it toward her. "You want this? Take it."

She waved the money away, just as she had their first night together. There had been a playfulness to it then—both his giving and her refusing. It made Roslyn sad to think how quickly things had changed.

"That doesn't give you the moral high ground. You broke into my house," Quake said.

"I didn't think you'd be able to see me. Normally people can't see me." Except for Ernest. And then Kate. And now Quake. Why? The answer came easily this time: *Because she'd wanted them to.*

She'd wanted Ernest to see her so she could prove her ability to him. Then Kate, whom she'd been equal parts jealous of and guilt-ridden for—which of those emotions had overflowed the day of the fire? Now Quake, with whom conflict had been gathering like storm clouds. Perhaps she'd wanted to be the clap of thunder that got his attention.

Still, she repeated her earlier excuse. "I meant no harm."

"Of course not. You know, you didn't mention any of this when you told me about your terrible visions. You pretend to be a victim of yourself? Maybe keep your mind-control trick under wraps."

She wasn't sure what to say after that. She let Quake fill the silence.

"Did you ever put ideas into *my* head? I mean, aside from making me open drawers so you could take my money?"

"No. I swear it."

"What about before I knew you? Ideas like daydreams? I had one where we were in a forest, but then you wanted me to feel guilty for how I live. You called me a wildfire grown too wild."

It seemed to her that his anger had turned to delirium. Like Barton with his devil woman. It shook her in a way that felt personal, even though it had nothing to do with her. But this time, she had no intention of agreeing with him. She wondered if there was someone else pulling strings in these men's heads. Probably not, she decided. He was simply casting about for somewhere to place blame. If you've got a certain kind of woman on your hands, well, you can blame her for anything. Even things that happened before you knew her, and who's to say you're wrong?

"I'm not sure what you're saying. A daydream in a forest? I can't do that," she said. "I wouldn't even if I could."

"How do I know that? How do I know what's real here?"

"I'm sorry. I can't answer that," was all she could offer.

"Right. Nothing more to say? Then I think you should go."

So she did.

Later, though, alone again in her room, it did come to her what she would like to have said. She thought she might want to tell Quake that following him had shown her something of value after all, and so it was not a crime, nor a waste of a broken promise. It was an idea about the difference between a burden and power. Why did people like Quake and Barton get power, while Roslyn had only burdens? Being a certain kind of woman, that was a burden. But if Barton or Quake had magic like hers, they would not be *certain kinds of men*. Not because men are never afflicted in such ways, but because they are allowed to use their afflictions without scrutiny. So theirs are not afflictions at all. For her whole life, Roslyn had been hunching her shoulders, hiding so as not to be seen, running from her visions, levitating just to pay rent. What if she acted like the men she knew instead? Took what she wanted, lived the way she liked? Quake was right that she need not be a victim of herself. All she had to do was act more like him.

She wanted to say this. But she decided, in the end, that it had little to do with Quake himself, and so it was best kept for her after all.

17

Three days later, on November 11, 1889, President Benjamin Harrison issued a proclamation granting Washington Territory statehood, and Roslyn knew that she would see Quake. He arrived at her hotel just before noon, holding a newspaper.

"You and your kind are real Americans now," he said.

"We were always Americans."

"How would you like to celebrate?"

So it was that simple.

The weather still hadn't cooled. They walked without coats. "What if there is no winter at all this year?" Roslyn asked.

"Then good riddance. Winter is a burden. We're better off without it."

"Doesn't the earth need winter? Plants and animals, their whole way of being is based around the seasons. How will they live?"

"Splendidly. They'll adapt. They'll thrive in this new pleasant sameness."

That was what Quake wanted for himself too, Roslyn thought.

He'd been mad three days ago, but now he'd pushed it off in the name of pleasant sameness.

"There will be more fires," she said.

"A natural hazard of warmth, yes."

"It's upsetting to think about."

"The cities will rebuild. And the forests will survive. They're meant to burn and regrow and burn and so on and so forth."

"How do you know that?"

"I worked with an ecologist on a job in Port Gamble once. He told me."

"You mean you swindled an ecologist in Port Gamble."

"No, an ecologist helped me swindle other people in Port Gamble."

"But surely there is a point at which it becomes too much. Too much destruction, not enough time for repair. What then?"

Quake only shrugged. She took this to mean it was not his problem, and if it was not his problem he couldn't see why anyone else should care either.

They spent the afternoon wandering the streets of downtown, stopping for food periodically, browsing in shops. Quake carried on his breezy banter and it seemed little effort was required from Roslyn for him to keep going. Entertaining himself, as always. He said he was planning a trip up to the new Washington state the following week to pick up something he'd left (money, Roslyn assumed), but after that, he would be done with his work there.

"It's not the Wild West anymore," he said. "People aren't going to keep falling for my shit."

Roslyn smiled.

"What? I am capable of being honest about myself occasionally," he said. Then he winked, a gesture guaranteed to undermine all claims of honesty.

"The place was already changing," he said. "But when government comes in and works, when little towns get connected, get less isolated . . . people aren't so willing to go along with just anyone who can string sentences together and tell them what they want to hear."

"Oh, don't be so hard on yourself," Roslyn said. "People always want someone to come along and tell them what they want to hear."

"Well, it'll be a different game in San Francisco."

"They've had statehood nearly a half century."

"And become complacent in it. A system already well worn and failed. People don't believe their officials truly protect them anymore."

"Does all that really matter?"

"No," he said. "Not in the slightest. But you'll come with me, won't you?"

She said she was still thinking about it, and for the first time all day he grew silent, as if finally remembering the complexity between them. Like a switch flicked. Why was Quake the one who got to control the mood of any conversation? Roslyn could no longer bear it. She announced she was tired, and though she allowed him to walk her back to her hotel, she did not invite him up.

She didn't want to be with Quake. She'd decided that much. She didn't want his body, or his company, or his cloying boyish needs, or his banter, or his big plans for his next con. The only thing about him that interested her anymore was San Francisco.

She'd seen the vision of the new fire twice more since the day they'd knocked on Barton's door. She now felt certain it was San Francisco. Was this a coincidence? Or something predestined? She decided it didn't matter. Each time, there was the burning city. People everywhere, the streets choked with human activity. The visceral sensations were overwhelming and would, in the past, have driven Roslyn to Mud Drink. Now she welcomed them. She wanted all the information she could get. The flames crowded in. She was fearful of this, for herself and for the people who lived there. But it wasn't her job to stop the fire or to save those people. Quake had given her that freedom when he'd said maybe the visions were really about preparing her for what came after, and now she knew. What might have been different if she'd gone to the man in the horse cart after his accident? The woman with the shattered jaw? Her school-children? Following them all their lives to pick up the pieces? She could not go back, could not help the people she'd known in Steilacoom or Spokane Falls; she could not help Kate. But she could move forward. There was more to do.

With the vision of this new fire, she could see it—the after part, her part. Not in the same way she could see the destruction, in all its consuming horror. This was a quieter sort of vision, couched at the edges of her sight, but she trusted in its truth.

In this city she'd never seen and knew nothing about, there was a place for her. A chance to do something right and good.

And so when Quake asked her, "Are you coming to San Francisco?" her heart raced.

She would go, she'd decided. But not with Quake.

18

Roslyn wasn't sure how to end things with Quake. She had come to resent him. This made her sad. They'd had fun together, and he'd helped her pull herself from her guilt-ridden stagnation—the days when she could do nothing but walk and regret. He'd given her, one way or another, the power to move on. What to do with a man like that? She argued with herself.

Quake, he's just like Barton, she thought.

Then, *No, Quake is my friend. He abhors Barton. He would never do what Barton did.*

No, not in such a way.

But in some other ways.

He wants you in his life on his terms. Only his terms.

I don't want that.

Well then, make it your terms. There's some use for him yet.

This voice was her voice, but she pretended it was her father's. Sometimes when she tried to make decisions, she imagined what her father would say. Not that she ever actually wanted the man's advice; he'd made such a mess of his own affairs, what use could he be to hers? It was just an exercise in loneliness. The same thing everyone is always doing with the dead people in their lives. Holding on in some way.

Were he alive, her father would have had much kinder words about Quake. He would have been charmed by him. Though Roslyn wished her father would have wanted better for her than dating a con man, she knew that wasn't the case. He rarely drew lines between honest and dishonest. Only likable and not, fun and not. It was part of what had made him a terrible criminal himself. He'd never bothered to see anyone for who they were. He would have liked to show Quake his magic tricks, taught him the words to his dirty song.

Roslyn had long thought that if her father had been a better blacksmith, he would not have been compelled toward grifting. And if he'd not been a drunk, he would have been a better blacksmith. But probably none of these things were related in the slightest. Her wish for him now, she realized, was only that he could have been a better con man.

Money can't buy happiness, but it can get you pretty damn close is what his actual voice would have said.

And *This is the westernmost city in the world. There's nothing past us but the edge.*

And *You're more than the apple of my eye, Ros. You're the peach of it.*

And *Never pull the same scheme twice.* Except this last one wasn't her father. That was Quake.

Her father, lazy happy sweet grifter that he was, would absolutely have pulled the same scheme twice. Perhaps, Roslyn thought, this was what she ought to do after all: stay true to her roots. It was what her own voice meant when it said there was use for Quake yet.

Though Roslyn had not traveled widely, she believed every city had a Trent Alley. This was because every city had drunks and gamblers and people living on the edge of society who needed one another in such a way, who could not survive alone in the wider well-lit streets, and so instead cloistered themselves and preyed on the vices of those who came from other neighborhoods seeking things they didn't want to find close to home even if they could.

She asked at the front desk of the hotel first, as though she were inquiring about a recommendation for a restaurant, and was treated to a look of such shock from the clerk that she almost laughed in the poor fellow's face. Imagine, being a grown man and so easily scandalized, she thought.

So she walked in the direction of the harbor, and when she spotted a sailor who looked like he knew where he was going, she stopped him and asked, "Excuse me, where can I go to buy opium?"

"Oh no," the young man said, "you don't want nothing to do with that trouble, ma'am. It'll kill you."

"I'm not going to smoke it. I just want to know where it's sold."

The sailor gave her directions. They led her to an alley, not far from the harbor, with little shops tucked into the facades of larger buildings, the sun on that bright day nearly blocked from view. She hummed as she walked—a funny little ditty about a woman on the Mississippi River.

Where there was opium, there was Mud Drink. They were cousins in indulgence, substances that could separate you from the world. Mud Drink in Portland looked just like it did in Spokane Falls—gray in mason jars on a shelf. Though when she asked the store's proprietor what he called the substance, he said, "Angel Piss," which Roslyn found crude. She preferred the name Mud Drink and would always refer to it as such.

She took the streetcar to Quake's neighborhood and visited a grocer and then a butcher shop. It was dark by the time she got to his apartment, the days getting shorter, but still warm. The leaves had not yet changed color. Would birds migrate? Roslyn wondered. Would squirrels be caught unprepared with no winter nuts when the cold finally did come? What about the bears? Would they hibernate, or stay up all winter?

She knocked on Quake's door. When he answered, he was smiling.

"It's good to see you," he said, and it seemed so earnest, Roslyn felt the whole of herself waver. What if she just gave in and said *Yes I'll be with you I'll go with you I love you too okay?*

Instead, she said, "I brought food. I thought I would cook for us."

"I didn't know you could cook."

"Well, maybe there's a lot you don't know about me."

He chuckled like he thought she was being coy. But then he said, "Yes, I'm aware."

She prepared the meal—a whole trout with carrots and potatoes. They ate at Quake's grand dining table, sitting at opposite ends like rich people, like how Barton and his mother had.

"I've brought something else for us as well," Roslyn said.

"Wonderful," Quake said. "Keep the delights coming."

She went to retrieve the Mud Drink from her bag and when she showed it to him, she watched his face, but could not parse the reaction.

"I thought we could drink this together," she said.

"You told me you didn't do that anymore," he said. "You used to, and then you stopped, and it meant a lot to you—to have stopped."

"Yes."

"Then I don't understand."

"I want you to know what it was like for me. This was a big part of my life for so long. The biggest part, actually. If you want to know me, I think you have to know this drink. That's all. To know me better. Who I used to be, at least."

His damned inscrutable face with those eyes so deep in their sockets.

"Okay. If it's important to you. Gladly."

He went to the kitchen but returned with only one glass.

"How about if I just drink it? You don't have to. I'll tell you what I'm experiencing and we can talk about if it's like what you used to feel."

"That's a kind thing to do," Roslyn said, and meant it.

He opened the jar, poured a little into his glass, and sipped. "It's not as bad as it looks," he said. "Sort of piney."

Roslyn picked the glass from his hand and set it on the table. She took Quake by the arm and led him to his bedroom.

"I didn't know if we were still doing that," he said after, when he was still naked and pressed up against her like a caterpillar too long for its log.

"You were going to buy me a ticket to San Francisco even if I wasn't sleeping with you anymore?"

"I don't know. I guess I figured we'd sort ourselves out eventually."

She stood up and went to get the Mud Drink and his glass, which she handed to him. She repositioned herself by his side. He drank dutifully.

She wasn't going to let him drink the whole jar. She'd been planning to split it with him. And even once he said he'd drink without her, she had still thought, *Half's enough.* But she wasn't paying attention and when she realized what he'd been up to, the Mud Drink was nearly gone.

"How do you feel?" she asked, pointing to the jar.

"Amazing. I see the appeal."

"It's strong."

"Very. I feel just like you. I know your whole being now, inside and out. This experience has been very illuminating."

"I don't believe you."

He laughed. "I don't believe myself. I wish there was something from my life I could give you to let you see inside of me too."

"I tried to do that on my own," she reminded him.

"Yes. Did it work?"

"I suppose not. What should I have done instead?"

"I don't know. What lets you turn into a lonely boy with a pet mule? What turns you into a cowardly man who can't protect anyone, not even the woman he loves?"

Roslyn shook her head. "You think you're not brave. You think that's your problem. But you're wrong."

"Thank you. That's worth a lot, to hear you say it."

"No, what I mean is, you've got other, bigger problems instead."

"See now there, I can't tell if you're joking or not."

"Do you have to stand up for any reason?" Roslyn asked.

"Not as such right now, no."

"Good. Probably best not to for a while."

Quake licked the last of the Mud Drink out of the jar. "I see what you mean. I will heed this advice."

He closed his eyes, his head tipping back to meet the pillow. Roslyn counted to one hundred, listening to him breathe. Then she counted again. He was snoring, but lightly. His face looked very, very young. She hoped he wouldn't let this experience make him bitter, or keep him from pursuing love again in another place and time.

He didn't move when she stood from the bed. She picked up one of her shoes and dropped it, just to be sure. She had lost so much of her adult life to Mud Drink. Half days at a time gone to dead sleep. Quake now, a mirror of the worst of her. She didn't envy him.

The key was in the top drawer of the desk. She opened the lockboxes one by one and put the money in her bag, then put the boxes back and the key back and closed all the drawers. Not that it mattered. Not that he wouldn't know immediately what she'd done when he woke and found her gone.

In the morning, she would book passage on the next steamer to San Francisco, any ship and any room available. She doubted Quake would follow. He didn't need the money she'd taken and, really, he didn't need her either. His plan for San Francisco was no good, never had been. He'd realize it once she was gone and figure out something else.

The streetcars were still running when she left Quake's apartment; she didn't have to wait long. She was the only one in the car.

She wished at first for company. She wanted the presence of others who would think nothing of her—the purifying anonymity of a crowd. Instead, there was only the sound of the machine wobbling on its tracks and the sight of Roslyn's reflection grinning back at her in the darkened window.

Quake had asked her once, on one of their sunny-day park walks, how she had felt when she stole Barton's money. She made some answer of saying she'd felt justified and brave, having gotten the better of a crooked man. Quake smiled at this and asked if it really mattered that Barton was unscrupulous.

"Remove Heydale from the equation," he'd pressed her. "You didn't take the money because you should. You took it because you could. How did it feel?"

Finally she'd acquiesced. "It was the first thing I think I've ever really done for myself. For me and no one else."

She had thought it might be different this time. She didn't need every remaining cent from the First Bank of Spokane Falls all for herself. This was for others, whom she had not yet met, and who she was trusting—hoping—could benefit from it. But she felt the same, regardless.

Inside the empty streetcar on that November night, she was shrewd, powerful, and rich. Just like the men Quake and Barton and her father had all wanted to be.

Before she left Portland, she levitated again. First, she went to visit Mrs. Heydale. Was Barton dead yet? Roslyn didn't know. She wondered if she could help the older woman, even in some small way.

She had thought of her often, living in the decaying house, kept company only by her deceased husband's vast wardrobe. She levitated to the Heydale home and found Mrs. Heydale alone and sad, unoccupied. *Find your sewing machine,* Roslyn said enough times until the woman went to exhume the apparatus from under a pile of bric-a-brac. *Get your magazines. Get one of his jackets.* When Mrs. Heydale had all her supplies laid out in front of her, Roslyn left. She'd thought maybe the woman could remake herself as a seamstress, refashioning old clothes and selling them. Or she could just fix up Mr. Heydale's suits and donate them to younger men in need. More likely, she'd make some repairs and put them right back in the closet. But it would give her something to do, and wasn't that a good thing? Roslyn acknowledged she could not control the outcomes of her power. She would have to learn to be okay with that if she was going to continue to use it, as was her intention.

Then she went to see Quake. He too was easily found, alone in his apartment. She took no pains to hide her levitating form. If he saw her, fine; if not, also fine. She had not come to say she was sorry, or to say goodbye. Just to look. But almost as soon as she entered the room, he locked onto her and she had to say something. *Peeka-boo, Dan Kite, I see you.* She watched his dark eyes flare with anger, which then turned quickly to delight. So the man could still take a joke. She left before anything else could transpire between them.

Then she went to see the bears in the bear pit. *Climb the walls and leave,* she said. She did not know if her power extended to animals. But Quake had given her the idea and she felt it was worth a try.

An Event from the
Unknowable Future

Seventeen years had passed. Roslyn was in San Francisco. She was a teacher again. She was the proprietor and sole employee of a grade school at the edge of the city's Mission District, a neighborhood that was so many things at once, Roslyn had come to think of it as a city all its own. There were apartment buildings in tight bunches that housed new immigrants, mostly Germans and Italians. Then, just blocks away, the spacious Victorian homes of the rich. There were factories and warehouses and a baseball stadium. There were people everywhere all the time. At first, it seemed to Roslyn they all wanted something from her—to sell her something, or garner her attention in some way.

A few days after her arrival, a tall man with a smug look thrust a pamphlet into her hand. Would she like to see the last known California grizzly bear? he asked. It was on display, but for a limited time only. Surely, she would not want to miss this once-in-a-lifetime opportunity, he said, and she thought this must be a scam of some sort. A year later, she did visit the zoo and see the famed bear (and suggest that it too *Climb the walls and leave*). But still, whenever she caught sight of the barker who had given her the pamphlet, she felt compelled to look closely at his face, to make sure he wasn't Quake. And he never was.

Roslyn's school was a single room in her house, purchased and maintained with the money she'd taken from Barton and Quake, which they had taken from the First Bank of Spokane Falls. The money was enough for what she needed. And for what she'd always thought she would need in the future. Though she never knew quite when that future might come. She charged no tuition. She taught all subjects, cleaned the classroom at the end of the day, and then in the morning woke early to make breakfast for her students so there was no risk of anyone trying to learn on an empty stomach. She was a comfortable fixture in the Mission. Everyone seemed to know her. She'd been at it so long, some of the students from her first classes had returned with kindergarteners of their own for her to educate. Roslyn tsked at these girls, too young to be mothers, but she happily took this second generation under her wing. They were, secretly, her favorites. The brightest and the kindest, she thought. Roslyn still had visions about her students. Whenever possible, she would seek them out to see if anything could be done in the aftermath. Sometimes she appeared as herself on these errands. Other times, if she felt it best to stay hidden, she levitated. Occasionally, she was able to see what good came of her interventions, though usually not. But she tried her best, and her burden did not feel so great anymore.

On April 18, 1906, there was an earthquake and then there was a fire. The earthquake shook gas lines apart and from this seepage, an inferno. Roslyn had taught the children: *In an earthquake, get out of the way of anything that can fall on you, or better yet, go outdoors; in a fire, stay low to the ground.* They practiced, year after year, which the children always thought great fun. When the fire finally came, she watched from her kitchen window. It was everywhere and she thought she could easily die that way, but she knew she wouldn't. The fire ate the city from the center out. But thanks to the winds, shifting west at the last minute, the Mission was largely spared.

Three days later, when the fire subsided, her students came to school rubbing ash like sleep from their eyes. "Go get your friends," Roslyn told them. "Anyone who needs breakfast or a place to stay." They did as they were told and children of all ages filled her small school. Some had lost their houses. Some had lost their parents. Roslyn purchased tents and set them in the school's yard. When she'd first bought the house, she'd hired contractors to build an addition. "Bedrooms," she said. "Just make me bedrooms," which then sat vacant. After the fire, she told homeless families they could stay in the tents as long as they needed. The orphans got the rooms. She continued making breakfast and teaching anyone who wanted to come to classes in her schoolroom. The kids all did. They wanted their normal routine. Some of the parents came too. They stood in the back and out of the way. They counted on their fingers and mouthed the answers to questions but did not speak out loud.

Refugees from other parts of the city poured into the Mission. They camped in the parks and on the sidewalks. And with them came the police, more than Roslyn had ever seen in the neighborhood before. As if by virtue of being made destitute, the city's new homeless were now criminals. The children shared a rumor that the police were shooting looters on sight. Roslyn was horrified and kept her students indoors, though her rooms were crowded and the air thick with smoke and human anxiety. Then the police gave way to men from the city government. They were interviewing everyone, trying to determine who belonged, an excuse to oust the new immigrants. "What do you mean by this?" Roslyn asked the man in an ill-fitting suit who appeared in the doorway of her school one afternoon, inquiring after her charges, both the children and the adults. But he wouldn't answer. "It doesn't impact you personally, so don't worry about it," is what he said. Roslyn saw him and others like him around for a while, holding maps, pointing and scowling. Each time she looked at his face to make sure he wasn't Barton. And he never was. *Get away from here*, she instructed, secretly following him whenever she was able. Eventually, he stopped coming, all his question-asking having been for naught. San Francisco rebuilt around the Mission. The families in the tents moved on, to new apartments and jobs. This was good, Roslyn thought. She was content to have been their port in the storm. With the orphans, it was harder. Some of them left and got new families and new homes. It broke Roslyn's heart, though she didn't show it. Others stayed and she became their family and their home.

The fire was long over, but the children without parents continued to arrive, sent by word of mouth. They came from other tragedies. Or they were runaways. Or who knows what; Roslyn did not ask if they didn't want to say. She added onto the house again. She cooked, she taught, she cleaned, she listened, she smiled, she nudged, she held. The storm in the Mission never stopped. She was always a safe harbor.

She lived a long time like this and was happy with the work she had done.

Epilogue

In the years between 1915 and 1920, the city of Portland found itself in the grips of a fad that captured the attention of people from nearly all walks of life. It was not a fashion of clothing or art, but rather a fashion of mind, so to speak. It was the metaphysical that had so enraptured citizens of Stumptown, a passion for the occult. Specifically, a desire to communicate with the dead, and to see into the future. This was a veritable boom time for the city's mediums, tarotists, and palm readers.

But of course in any cultural moment, there are always the naysayers.

The psychiatrist Anthony Galbraith was one such skeptic. In the winter of 1919 he set out to write an article for a prominent medical journal exploring what he called "the exploitation of Portland's collectively weakened psyche by a new class of opportunists and charlatans."

Unsurprisingly, he was having trouble finding subjects to interview, both among the exploited psyches and the opportunists and charlatans.

Eventually, though, he did find three spiritualists willing to entertain his questions, insulting though they were. Esme Aberdeen, Elizabeth Crossroads, and Maisy Van Vannen shared a storefront that was frequented by neighbors and crosstowners alike. Their readings and séances were worth traveling for, was the general consensus among those in the know. It goes without saying that the monikers they worked under were not their real names.

These women were confident in their work and their business. They felt they had the luxury to be generous with Galbraith. He was no threat to them. Better he come to their door, they felt, than go bothering any of their less established peers.

Galbraith opened the conversation with a question about Ouija. Were the boards purely devices for tricksters to con the vulnerable and unsuspecting? Or was a built-in deceit part of the product's very design?

"Deceit? Dr. Galbraith, have you been hearing bad voices from your Ouija game?" Maisy Van Vannen asked.

"It's an amusement," Esme Aberdeen offered. "Something for the parlor, and a little scare for the kids."

"Does yours grow legs in the night and make off with your silver? I am unclear of your question." This was Maisy again.

Galbraith cleared his throat, intending to clarify. He felt he was being misunderstood, though he could not tell if it was a willful misunderstanding or the fault of the poor-quality minds whose company he was in. But Elizabeth Crossroads cut him off.

"Doctor, perhaps it would help if we told you a little about how we approach our work. Do you know what it means to be a medium,

I am wondering? It is not what the sensationalists in the news and in church might have you believe."

Galbraith rolled his eyes. He gestured for her to continue.

"Spiritualism is belief—any belief," Esme said. "It's whatever you're seeking, and to which you wish to gain access. A medium just helps you get there—she's the person in between, the bridge. That's all. Nothing of substance is there which you haven't supplied yourself."

"I see my role more as realigning the living with those who they have lost," Elizabeth said. "A connection to the afterlife, and those who have moved on. The spirit world is a mystery to us, and always will be. This is true. I work in allegory, abstraction. I acknowledge that freely."

"Not me," Maisy said. "I see ghosts. I see literal fucking ghosts. I can see the ghost of your mom right now. She hates your hair. If you want to make her ghost happy, get it cut."

Galbraith laughed, but he was unsettled. Not just by the remarks about his deceased mother, but by all three women. They were not what he had expected. He was unsure how to square them with the article he wanted to write. He asked a few more questions, all of which were met with answers he found strange at best, if not wholly inscrutable. At the end, he thanked the women for their time, though he clearly didn't mean it, then scurried from their presence.

The women, for their part, were torn on how to proceed. Esme and Elizabeth felt they had said their piece and needn't have any further involvement with the small irritant that was Dr. Galbraith. Maisy, the youngest and most impetuous of the three, did not agree.

—

The next morning, Galbraith woke with an itch he could not scratch. Or rather, he could scratch it, but it would not stay scratched. It was on the tip of his nose and would not leave him. He scratched until it was a raw sore, an ugly blemish that drew the eyes of everyone he came in contact with, which caused him great embarrassment. But he was powerless to stop scratching.

Then came the figures in the mirrors. Wisps of human faces that appeared above his left shoulder each time he looked at himself. They were never the same. They were never his mother. They refused to make eye contact.

Then a high-pitched ringing sound, but only while he was seated at the dinner table. Then a smell of smoke or peppermint candy at times when there was no fire or candy nearby. He became fearful for his health and went to his personal physician, but when the doctor told him there was nothing wrong with him except a budding infection of the skin on his nose, he was forced to seek guidance from a fellow psychiatrist. This man too proved unhelpful, suggesting Galbraith's symptoms were a manifestation of repressed childhood trauma.

"Your mother was cruel to you. Admit it and your problem will cease."

"My mother was an angel in life, as she is in death, you fucking cretin."

He spent the rest of the day looking over his shoulder. He got a haircut but second-guessed the style and went back for another.

Then he returned to the spiritualists' storefront, where he found Esme manning the shop.

"I need help," he said, his eyes on the floor. "I believe I am having troubles with my dear departed mother."

Esme led him to a small table and took his hands lightly in her own, turning them palms up. She talked for a while on the nature of his discomfort, a push-and-pull from the world beyond the here and now, and the ramifications of the loss he'd suffered. But the gist of it all was simply: *Your mother is proud of you and she knows you love her. Your difficult times won't last forever.*

Galbraith found comfort in this, more than he had expected. He thanked Esme effusively. Not long after, he would abandon his article writing as well as his public denouncements of spiritualism in general. He asked Esme her fee, but she waved him away.

Later, when Maisy came in, Esme said, "Let's leave Dr. Galbraith alone now, hmmm? Seems you've had your fun."

Maisy rolled her eyes at her business partner, but agreed. They had known each other (and Elizabeth as well) almost their whole lives, since they were children in San Francisco, attending the same neighborhood school. Their teacher had been an eccentric, and a woman of many and varied powers. It was from her that they'd learned their trade. Not the specifics of tarot and palm reading, et cetera, but to harness the natural gifts that allowed them to be persuasive in these undertakings. She was a mentor to girls of uncommon talents, girls of a certain kind—a profile Esme, Elizabeth, and Maisy all fit. The teacher would gather them early in the mornings, before classes started. There were no lessons to speak of, but there was encouragement. She'd ask the girls to speak about what they could do, and what they thought they could do if they tried. "Show me a trick," she might say, and she'd delight in whatever was demonstrated. Then, another morning, she might say, "No tricks.

That's not all you are. Close your eyes and think slow instead. Think about the girl next to you." Esme had not known what this meant at first and it frustrated her, as she had many, many tricks to show. But over time she figured it out and was grateful.

Esme was the oldest of the three, and she remembered when the teacher had approached only girls whose gifts were clearly visible, nearly pulsing from them, for such mentorship. But as the years went by, the barrier for entry to this club had fallen away. By the time Esme was in her teens, the teacher would take on any girl who expressed interest in her craft. They could all be made into a certain kind, it turned out.

Acknowledgments

First, I'd like to say a tremendous thank-you to the friends who were kind enough to read and provide feedback on this novel in its early and awkward stages: Jon Frey, Matt Furst, Lauren Hohle, Melissa Huggins, Aileen Keown Vaux, Elizabeth Moore, Aaron Passman, Marianne Salina, Sharma Shields, Cathie Wigert, and Maya Zeller.

Thank you to Sarah Bedingfield, my brilliant agent, whose vision and insight propelled this story forward in ways I never would have considered.

Thank you to my wonderful and talented editor, Allison Lorentzen, and to the entire team at Viking. I am so grateful for all your hard work, and for the care and enthusiasm you have shown this project.

Thank you to my parents for your love, support, and babysitting.

Thank you to Bixby and Walden for being hilarious and beautiful and perfect.

Thank you most of all to Scott for bringing me breakfast burritos while I write, and for never ever wavering in the belief that *Fire Season* would someday be a book, even when I doubted it myself. I love you so freaking much.